Here's what some bestselling authors are saying about Diana Whitney:

"Diana Whitney is that rare talent who can blend irrepressible humor with heart-tugging pathos for a joyous, emotional roller coaster of a read! If you want to laugh and cry and be fabulously entertained, you'll love Diana Whitney."

—Bestselling author Suzanne Forster

"Diana Whitney brings you characters you can laugh and cry with in a story you will never forget. A book by Diana Whitney will steal your heart and leave you chuckling in delight."

—Bestselling author Christine Rimmer

"A unique and gifted writer, Diana Whitney knows how to wring emotion from the first scene to the last."

—Bestselling author Pat Warren

Dear Reader,

March is a month of surprises and a time when we wait breathlessly for the first hints of spring. A young man's fancy is beginning to turn to love...but then, in each Special Edition novel, thoughts of love are everywhere! And March has a whole bouquet of love stories for you!

I'm so pleased to announce that *Waiting for Nick* by Nora Roberts is coming your way this month. This heartwarming story features Freddie finally getting her man...the man she's been waiting for all of her life. Revisit the Stanislaskis in this wonderful addition to Nora Roberts's bestselling series, THOSE WILD UKRAINIANS.

If handsome rogues quicken your pulse, then don't miss *Ashley's Rebel* by Sherryl Woods. This irresistible new tale is the second installment of her new series, THE BRIDAL PATH. And Diana Whitney concludes her PARENTHOOD series this month—with *A Hero's Child*, an emotionally stirring story of lovers reunited in a most surprising way.

Three veteran authors return this month with wonderful new romances. Celeste Hamilton's *Marry Me in Amarillo* will warm your heart, and Carole Halston dazzles her readers once again with *The Wrong Man...The Right Time*. Kaitlyn Gorton's newest, *Separated Sisters,* showcases this talented writer's gift of portraying deep emotion with the joy of lasting love.

I hope that you enjoy this book, and each and every story to come!

Sincerely,

Tara Gavin,

Senior Editor

Please address questions and book requests to:
Silhouette Reader Service
U.S.: 3010 Walden Ave., P.O. Box 1325, Buffalo, NY 14269
Canadian: P.O. Box 609, Fort Erie, Ont. L2A 5X3

DIANA WHITNEY

A HERO'S CHILD

Published by Silhouette Books
America's Publisher of Contemporary Romance

To my mother, Gloria Dalton, from whom I inherited
my love of books

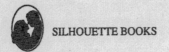 SILHOUETTE BOOKS

ISBN 0-373-24090-2

A HERO'S CHILD

Copyright © 1997 by Diana Hinz

Printed in U.S.A.

DIANA WHITNEY

says she loves "fat babies and warm puppies, mountain streams and California sunshine, camping, hiking and gold prospecting. Not to mention strong romantic heroes!" She married her own real-life hero over twenty years ago. With his encouragement, she left her long-time career as a municipal finance director and pursued the dream that had haunted her since childhood: writing. To Diana, writing is a joy, the ultimate satisfaction. Reading, too, is her passion—from spine-chilling thrillers to sweeping sagas, but nothing can compare to the magic and wonder of romance.

Dear Diary,

Today is my birthday. I am 9. You are my mommy's present to me. She said I could tell you stuff and feel better, but I feel okay. Mom and Gramps take good care of me. I just wish my daddy was here but he died before I was even born. He was the bravest soldier in the whole world. Mom says he was a hero. I wish he had not been so brave. Then I would have my daddy back.

But I am glad I have you, diary. Mom was right. I do feel better.

Love,

Marti Hooper

Chapter One

The hitchhiker dropped his duffel, then leaned against one of the telephone poles beside the quiet rural road. He adjusted his sunglasses, squinting at a sign faded by decades of weather and neglect. Gold River, 6 Miles. The sign pointed the way to times forgotten and unremembered yesterdays, to ghosts of those who'd never left and those who'd never returned. He had only to follow the rutted road, if he dared.

Behind him, the clack of a diesel engine grew closer. A dented old pickup rattled to a stop. The driver, a grizzled old guy in a plaid work shirt, leaned out the window. "Where you headed?"

He nodded toward the worn sign.

The driver frowned. "You sure?"

He hesitated. The sign beckoned. The road called. A whisper echoed from beyond the golden hills. "Yes, I'm sure." Hoisting his duffel, he climbed into the truck cab. One journey had finally ended. Another had just begun.

* * *

"Madeline, please, if the residents don't all work together on this project, we'll never finish the renovations before summer." Clamping the receiver between her chin and shoulder, Rae Hooper shifted in the diner's vinyl booth, stretching the cord from the public wall phone around the corner. "Even worse, if the town can't keep its part of the bargain, the state could yank the block grant money and then where would we be?"

A high-pitched snort filtered over the line. "It would serve them right for bargaining with the devil."

"Oh, c'mon, Madeline," Rae murmured, riffling through the documents spread across the table. "You know as well as I do that with the highway rerouted to the other side of the river, the only way any of us will survive is by pulling tourists off the interstate with an attraction that makes their trip worthwhile. The alternative is to sit back and watch the town die."

"Everything dies," Madeline snapped. "Animals, people, towns. Nothing lives forever. It's God's will."

Rae slumped forward, raking a messy spiral of tangled curls out of her eyes. She took a deep breath, fingering her thick hair for the loosened barrette. Finding it, she tucked a reddish blond hunk behind her ear and clamped it so tightly that her eyes watered. Madeline Rochester was a withered prune of a woman who found biblical fault with anyone or anything that displeased her. And she was a woman easily displeased.

At the moment, her primary irritation was Gold River's massive renovation project, the last gasp of a dying town. But it wasn't just any old town. It was the only home Rae Hooper had ever known, and she wasn't about to sit back and watch it expire just so an eccentric recluse could bask in isolation.

Rae moistened her lips and spoke in a firm voice that shook only a little. "When my grandmother opened this diner, talking pictures were considered a fad, flappers raised eyebrows with bare knees and bobbed hair, and back room speakeasies got rich on bathtub booze. My mother was born in Gold River. So was I, and so was my daughter. You've only been here a few years, Madeline. You don't understand how much this town means to those of us who've lived our entire lives here. Gold River is special.''

"And how special is it going to be all phonied up like a Hollywood sound stage? Tourists clogging the sidewalks, snapping pictures of fake saloons and a silly museum filled with junk out of Annie MacPherson's attic. It's heresy," the woman insisted. "Like painting a clown face on a corpse."

Rae winced. "Oh, really, Madeline."

"I may not have been born here, Rae Hooper, but I love this town, too. It pains me, what you all are doing. Places are like people, you know? If they live with dignity, they got a right to die with dignity. You're turning a sweet piece of history into a circus, you and that young man of yours, and you should be ashamed of yourselves."

A twinge of regret caught in Rae's throat, although she couldn't be sure if the unpleasant sensation was caused by Madeline's genuine dismay or by the reference to Steve Ruskin as Rae's "young man." The implied intimacy made her cringe.

Despite an enigmatic uneasiness, she felt compelled to defend poor Steve, who despite notable lack of commitment on Rae's part had doggedly courted her for nearly a year. "Steve simply handled the grant application," she told Madeline, without mentioning that he'd also used his influence in Sacramento to push a politically motivated appropriations bill through the state legislature.

All of which was nonetheless morally justifiable, Rae reasoned, considering the nobility of their cause. After

all, what could be more important than rescuing the life-
style and livelihood of an entire town?

Convincing the intractable Ms. Rochester, however,
seemed a fruitless task, although Rae was committed to
try. "Besides, you have to admit that the plans to renovate Gold River into a tourist attraction are exciting.
Imagine Main Street looking exactly as it did a hundred
years ago, right down to the wooden sidewalks."

A scornful snort filtered down the line. "Humph, that
ought to look right smart running by a row of gas
pumps."

Rae sighed. "Naturally, we'll have to make a few con-
cessions to modern convenience. The point is, we're
making an effort, and the mad bustle of activity is actually kind of invigorating, with all the sanding—"

"Sawdust makes me sneeze."

"And painting—"

"Fumes give me a sick headache."

Tossing a pencil across the table, Rae flopped back in
the booth, completely frustrated. There was no sense arguing with a woman who wasn't happy unless she was
miserable.

In the distance the thrum of a noisy engine caught her
attention. A bus, perhaps, filled with hungry passengers?
She straightened, listening.

Against her ear the receiver vibrated with a wheedling
whine. "It's easy for you," Madeline was saying.
"You've got yourself a big, strong man to do all the
fixing."

Blinking, Rae pulled away from the phone, staring stupidly at the receiver as she realized that Madeline was
referring to her scrawny, bowlegged father. Hobie
Hooper was an amiable old coot, devious as the devil
and just as lazy. Everyone in town was painfully aware
of Hobie's faults; most liked him anyway. Madeline was
particularly taken with Hobie, and had made no bones

about her interest in him. Over the past few months she'd been particularly brazen about trying to intrigue Hobie in one or another of her unique holistic healing hobbies, which ran the gamut from herbal medicine to transforming pinecones into curative amulets.

Just as Rae was beginning to wonder if there was an underlying method to Madeline's maddening complaints, the woman blurted, "How do you think it's going to look with every place on the street all gussied up, and my poor little house all patched 'n peeling?"

Rae's compassion was tempered with caution. "You won't be left behind, Madeline. I promise that by the time this project is finished, your home will be an absolute showplace. As a matter of fact, Steve has arranged for a volunteer crew from the high school to work weekends here as part of a senior project—"

"Teenagers!" Madeline spit the word out like a bad taste. "I'll not have a gaggle of big-footed boys tromping my prized nasturtiums."

"But—"

"Of course, a mature man would know how to help an old widow woman without squashing her posies."

Rae rubbed her eyes, smiling to herself. "A man like, say, my father?"

"Why, what a fine idea! I'll expect him first thing tomorrow."

Rae's smile faded. "Hobie has his hands full scraping and painting the diner. It'll be at least a week or two before he can even consider your request—"

"Tomorrow," she said cheerfully.

"Wait a minute, Madeline.... Madeline?"

The line was dead. Puffing her cheeks, Rae blew out a breath and wondered how on earth she'd gotten her poor father into this mess. Even more crucial, how could she get him out of it?

There were few things in this world Hobie hated more

than physical labor, with the exception of whatever effort was reasonably required in his all-consuming pursuit of gold. The search for that precious yellow metal was the driving force of her father's life and the bane of Rae's. Hobie spent every free moment on the river, digging and panning and, for the most part, coming up with empty hands and an ever-hopeful heart.

Rae usually indulged her father's whim just as her late mother had done, but on those occasions when it was absolutely necessary to commandeer him for other projects, she again followed her mother's lead by resorting to threats and coercion. Padlocking the beer supply was usually effective.

It would take a heck of a lot more than that to get him over to Madeline Rochester's place, although Rae would have to worry about that later. Right now, the continued idle of a vehicle engine in the diner parking lot had visions of a jingling cash register dancing in her head.

Scooting out of the booth, she hastily cradled the wall phone receiver, then tidied her apron and rushed behind the counter. A glance out the front window proved disappointing. There was no busload of tourists. There wasn't even a station wagon filled with hungry kids. Instead, there was only a battered diesel pickup, pausing only long enough to deposit a shaggy stranger with a bulging duffel before hanging a sloppy U-turn and roaring back toward the main highway.

Terrific, Rae thought, tucking the useless order pad back into her pocket. A hitchhiker with holes in his jeans was hardly a thrill. Transients passed by occasionally. They never had any money, but Rae couldn't stand to see anyone go hungry, so she fed them anyway.

From her vantage point, this mustached, long-haired hippie-type looked no different than others of that adventurous breed. Windblown hair brushing his shoulders. A worn cap turned backward so the bill shaded his neck.

A graying T-shirt beneath a denim jacket with frayed holes where the sleeves used to be. And the real give-away, scuffed hiking boots instead of fashionable sneakers worn by wanna-be road warriors.

This, Rae judged, was the real McCoy, a dusty asphalt soldier at war with conventional society and, if intuition was any clue, at war with himself, as well.

After hoisting the duffel he stood there a moment with lean legs splayed, gazing around the tiny town with what could have been a wistful expression. Of course, it could have been one of disdain as well, since his eyes were concealed by reflective aviator-style sunglasses. There was something nostalgic about his body language, though, a subtle tension, the slight slump of his shoulders that made his stance, and the man himself, seem oddly vulnerable.

When he turned toward the diner, that stance stiffened with apparent apprehension. The poor fellow must be half-starved, Rae thought sadly, but was probably too proud to ask for a handout. For a split second she feared he would turn away. He didn't. Instead, his chest vibrated as he sucked in a breath, then he flexed his fingers around the duffel strap and strode toward the diner.

Rae ducked down to retrieve a tumbler from the neat pyramid of sparkling glassware stacked beneath the counter. As the front door cowbell jingled, she was filling the water glass, and she offered a cheery greeting without looking up from her task. "Hi, there. Nice day out, isn't it? The rain always makes everything so fresh and tidy. Kind of like nature's Laundromat."

Flipping off the spigot, she pasted a welcoming grin on her face and spun around, still chattering. "Of course, there's always the mud to deal with, but..."

The words dissipated like so much steam.

She swayed as if struck by an invisible hand, clutching the frigid glass so tightly her knuckles went white. The stranger stood there, stiff as death. He didn't move. Didn't speak. Just stood in the doorway, staring at Rae as if seeing a ghost.

At least, she thought he was staring at her. All she knew for certain was that the metallic lenses of those atrocious shades were aimed in her direction, casting back dual reflections of her own stuporous expression. Her mouth was open. She closed it, sucking her clamped lips between her teeth so her nervous tongue could moisten them. Rae had no idea what was happening here. She'd never seen this person before, and yet there was an immediacy to his presence that stunned her to her toes.

Suddenly her deflated lungs refilled. "Just have a seat anywhere," she heard herself say, and was horrified to notice her free hand gesture toward the interior of the deserted diner. "Reservations are strongly recommended, of course, but under the current circumstance I think we can squeeze you in."

Other than the subtle vibration of his jaw, the stranger gave no evidence of having heard her.

"If you're looking for privacy, I'd suggest booth number two, but if you'd prefer a view, booth six provides an unobstructed prospect of the old post office building across the street. Sadly, it closed last summer. Now we have to drive all the way into Auburn to mail a package. At Christmastime, that can be a real bummer."

A booth with a view. Had she really said that?

Rae licked her lips, feeling profoundly stupid. Stretching her stiff cheeks in what must certainly look more like a grimace than a smile, she placed the water glass on the counter. "I'll, ah, just leave this here until you make up your mind about where to sit. No need to rush, of course. After all, mealtime ambience can set the tone for a person's entire day."

Mealtime ambience? Oh, good grief.

Cringing inside, Rae wondered what on earth could

have possessed her to spout such inane pap. She'd always been a talker—Hobie said it was part of her charm—but there was a major difference between making customers feel welcome and babbling on like a bubble-brained simpleton. She felt helpless, as if some mischievous word gremlin had taken control of her tongue.

At the thought, she clamped the offender between her teeth, biting down hard enough to sting. The sensation cleared her head. Sucking in a deep breath, she turned away to busy herself rearranging condiments. From the corner of her eye she saw the stranger cross the narrow room, drop his duffel beneath the counter and straddle the stool closest to the water glass.

"A counter man, eh? Good choice." Calmer now, Rae automatically slid a menu across the polished laminate.

He ignored it, but continued to follow her movements from behind his concealing sunglasses.

After a moment she retrieved the order pad from her pocket and sauntered over, smiling. "Today's special is tuna salad on white, wheat or a French roll."

For the first time since he'd walked in the door, the guy lowered his gaze, turning his face away from her as he ducked his head, fingering his lush, dark mustache. He mumbled something.

"Pardon me?"

Clearing his throat, he continued to study the counter as if mystical secrets were etched in speckled Formica. "Coffee."

A surge of compassion pushed away the final shred of peculiar wariness. "Did I mention that the tuna sandwich comes with a bag of chips and a pickle?"

He didn't look up. "Just coffee."

Sighing, Rae tucked the pad in her pocket. The lack of a food order wasn't unexpected, of course, but she was still saddened by it. He was obviously hungry. Judging by the man's gaunt features, she guessed that the poor fellow hadn't had a decent meal in weeks. She'd have liked to provide him with a meat-and-potatoes supper, but since the diner's current finances only allowed her to hire a professional cook only for the dinner shift, this luckless drifter would have to make do with a cold lunch.

After presenting him with a mug of steaming black coffee, Rae moved to the preparation counter and heaped a French roll with mounds of fresh tuna salad. A moment later she slid the luncheon plate in front of her startled customer. He looked up, his forehead furrowed.

"It's on the house," she said airily. "The thing is, I got carried away making tuna salad this morning, and ended up with enough to feed a small army. It would be a real shame to toss it out. Of course, if you hate tuna, I also have a generous supply of ham and cheese—"

He held up a hand, indicating that tuna was fine.

"I, ah, hope you like onions. There's a ton of them chopped up with the tuna."

His mustache tilted, so she assumed he was smiling. "I love onions. Thanks."

A peculiar tingling sensation slid down her spine. The terse statement, which she suspected was a major speech for this particular fellow, was issued in a voice that was soft and deep, but with a slight gravelly tone that was oddly alluring.

She wiped her palms on her apron. "Well, let me know if you need anything else. Our pies are baked fresh daily."

"You're very kind."

After a long moment Rae spun on her sensible sneakers and hurried back to the rear booth, where a pile of unpaid bills and a depleted checkbook awaited the monthly juggling act at which she'd become painfully proficient. Over the past year diminishing cash flow had caused an alarming shift in the paid-versus-delayed ratio, which had in turn resulted in a humiliating surge of

C.O.D. shipments from the diner's most important suppliers.

Right now her primary problem was a past-due notice from the electric company. She placed the invoice in the hock-the-silverware-to-pay pile. A second notice demanding payment for the used dishwasher that broke down every other week found a home in the when-hell-freezes stack, as did a half-dozen repair bills for the diner's continually malfunctioning refrigeration unit.

For some odd reason Rae had a love-hate relationship with appliances. She loved them. They hated her. Perhaps it was karma, retribution for having kicked a broken air-conditioning unit when she'd been a sweaty six-year-old.

Muttering to herself, she snatched up the checkbook and was soon engrossed in the grueling process of paying bills she couldn't afford with money that she didn't have. She worked methodically, oblivious to time until alerted by the familiar rumble of the school bus.

She blinked, glancing first at her watch and then at her lone customer, who was still seated at the counter twirling a presumably empty coffee mug. Rae hurried over, grabbing the coffee carafe on her way. "I'm so sorry," she murmured, refilling the mug. "The service here isn't usually this lousy. You should have whistled or something."

The man rested a pair of muscled forearms on the edge of the counter. "It's okay."

"How was your lunch?"

"Good. Thanks again." At that, he leaned back and reached into his jeans pocket.

"That's not necessary," Rae said quickly, using a rag to wipe up a dribble of sloshed coffee. "Just tell your friends about us."

He laid a five-dollar bill on the counter. "I don't have any friends."

Although the message was delivered in a flat monotone, there was an underlying sadness that didn't escape Rae's notice. She would have commented, except the diner door flew open and the room was suddenly alight with childish exuberance.

"Mom, Mom, I got a B on my math test, and James invited me to his birthday party, and I was first pick for recess kickball only we couldn't play because Jimmy got punched in the stomach and threw up, so teacher made us sit in a circle and talk about stuff." The final word was punctuated by a thud as the excited nine-year-old flopped a stuffed book bag on the counter and swept a curious glance around the diner. "Where's Gramps?"

"Isn't he outside sanding the clapboards?"

"Uh-uh, but there's a whole bunch of cans and junk piled up by the ladder."

Clamping her lips together, Rae flung down the rag and stalked out of the diner. A cold breeze slapped her face, fueling her anger. As she rounded the building she saw the abandoned ladder propped against the south wall. A quick glance at the peeling surface confirmed that there had been absolutely no progress since Rae had brought Hobie his lunch hours ago.

Rae reached down to unplug the sander from the extension cord, then balanced the unused tool in her palm, wishing she could blame the hapless little machine for her father's irresponsible behavior. She was about to fling it across the yard when she realized that her daughter was standing there, watching with wary eyes.

"Don't be mad at Gramps, Mom. He mighta just went to the house, you know, to go to the bathroom or something."

Swallowing hard, Rae laid the sander on a makeshift shelf of plywood propped between a pair of sawhorses, and slipped a comforting arm around Martina's thin shoulders. The girl's limpid green eyes offered a silent plea that struck a poignant chord from Rae's own past.

She remembered her own mama trying to explain that Daddy really did love his little girl, even though he wasn't around very much. Rae had wanted to believe that about Hobie then as much as Marti did now.

In fact, looking into her daughter's somber little face was like transporting herself twenty years back in time and staring at her own young reflection. Marti was the spitting image of Rae at that age, from the porcelain-pale complexion dusted by amber freckles to the unruly frizz of strawberry blond hair sprouting from her scalp like an electrified field of red straw. Rae loved the child so much that it hurt.

"I'm not mad at your grampa," she finally said. "I'm just disappointed that he broke his promise."

"But he did do some stuff," Marti observed, eyeing a minuscule patch of sanded wood. "And he never really promised to do the whole thing in one day, did he?"

It was that kind of skewed rationale to which Rae had been subjected since childhood. Now, however, it was a double-edged siege as Marti became more and more adept at defending her beloved grampa by emulating him.

Admittedly Rae adored her father, but she also adored her child, and had no intention of allowing Marti to pick up Hobie's bad habits. The trick here was to draw a behavioral line without criticizing Hobie outright, or forcing her daughter to take sides in the dispute.

As she considered how that could be done, Marti's gaze slipped to a point somewhere behind her mother. "Hi."

Turning, Rae stared into the reflective lenses of the customer she'd just abandoned. But those lenses weren't focused on Rae. They were aimed directly at Marti.

The stranger's mouth was clamped into a grim line. His entire body was on alert, reminding Rae of a soldier on reconnaissance in unfriendly territory.

After a brief moment he acknowledged the girl's greeting with a stiff smile, then, with some effort, looked away from the child and turned his attention to Rae. "I didn't mean to intrude."

"You didn't," she replied, trying to ignore the odd shiver of excitement that his husky voice evoked. "We're in the process of renovating the diner and I was, ah, checking the progress."

The man rubbed his chin, presumably scanning the work from behind his concealing shades. "There doesn't seem to be much. Progress, that is."

A lackadaisical shrug didn't quite come off. "Not yet, but we've just started."

His smile loosened with a knowing nod. Ignoring the glossy mane of hair blowing around his face, he reached out to finger the unused sander. Lifting the tool, he studied it with peculiar concentration, and would have spoken again had his attention not been distracted by the crunch of tires on gravel. A glance over his shoulder coincided with the slam of a car door. "It sounds like you have another customer."

"I wish," Rae murmured. Although the parking lot was out of view, she'd recognized the distinctive manner in which the driver had repeatedly revved the engine before switching off the ignition.

Marti, too, had recognized the sound of Steve Ruskin's vehicle, and screwed up her face accordingly. "I bet Gramps went to see Sadie," she blurted, referring to the euphemism Hobie used to describe working his claim. "I'll go get him."

"Oh, no, you don't." Rae snagged the girl's colorful T-shirt as she spun to sprint toward the creek where her grandfather's mine was located. "Hobie will come home when he's ready. You, on the other hand, have homework."

"Aw, Mom." Smoothing the eclectic collage of rock stars emblazoned on her flat little chest, Marti clicked her tongue, rolled her eyes and heaved a heartbroken sigh. "I got lotsa time. I'll do it right after dinner, honest I will."

"You'll do it now." The pronouncement was empha- sized with an affectionate pat on the seat of her daugh- ter's fashionably faded jeans. "You know the rules."

"Okay," the child muttered, feigning defeat as she si- dled toward the back of the building. "But first I'm going to tell my diary that my mother is a slave driver."

As the child turned to flounce away, Rae called out, "Marti, wait."

The sander slipped from the stranger's grasp, landing on the plywood with a startling thump. Rae noted the incident, but gave it no importance, assuming that he'd simply lost his grip. Besides, she knew her daughter well enough to understand that a moment's distraction was all it would take for the sneaky kid to slip into the shadows and head for her grandfather's mine.

It wasn't that Marti was deliberately disobedient; it was just that she'd learned Hobie's manipulative lessons much too well. The only way Rae could deal with either of them was to make her expectations absolutely excuse- proof. "Your books are in the diner. Leaving them there will not be considered legitimate cause to postpone your homework."

Her thin shoulders slumped. "Right."

With a dramatic pirouette Marti trudged toward the parking lot just as Steve Ruskin rounded the corner look- ing anxious and annoyed. Then again, Steve usually looked anxious, since the sharp arch of his brows gave him a perennially startled expression, and being a certi- fied anal-retentive personality type, it didn't take a heck of a lot to annoy him. He'd once spent a month brooding over laundered shirts that had been boxed instead of hung.

Now as Steve stepped to block Marti's rapid exit, his

tight little brows hiked high enough to pull his eyelids halfway up his forehead. "Good Lord, you didn't actually go to school dressed like that."

Marti tossed a frustrated glance over her shoulder, to which Rae replied with a shrug.

Ignoring both gestures, Steve continued to eye the girl's casual attire without bothering to conceal his displeasure. "Fortunately, I learned that your school photographs are scheduled for tomorrow and I took the liberty of purchasing something appropriate to the occasion. Now, now, don't look at me like that. You'll love it. It's very feminine, and quite chic. Ruffles are all the rage in Europe."

"*Ruffles?* Mom, help!"

Choking back a laugh, Rae simply waved as Steve grasped the girl's hand and hustled her away. Rae was still smiling when a gruff cough reminded her that she wasn't alone.

With his thumbs hooked in his pockets, the stranger pushed a rock with the toe of his boot and nodded toward the spot where Steve had been standing. "Your husband?"

"A...friend."

Although the man nodded, his expression remained unchanged. He turned his attention toward the empty ladder. "I could help, if you want."

"That's very kind of you, but my father will take care of it." A warm flush crawled up her throat as the shadow of a brow hiked from behind the chrome rims. She cleared her throat. "Eventually."

"I'm sure he will," the man replied, appearing to fight an amused twitch at the corner of his mouth. "Refinishing weathered wood can be tricky. The paint needs extra linseed oil or it'll bubble up and split when the sun hits it. Sanding's important, too. Like here—" He pointed to the small area Hobie had already done. "See those scratches in the wood? Paint will float over them, leaving air pockets underneath where water can condense and freeze. Cracks the finish.''

"Oh, my." Frowning, Rae studied the area in question, skimming a covert glance at the impressive presence beside her. "You, ah, seem to know quite a lot about this sort of thing."

"I spent some time working for a painting contractor in Atlanta."

"I see." She straightened, realizing that she was actually considering the man's offer, and wondering why. "Are you from Atlanta, Mr.....?"

"Flynn. Hank Flynn."

"I'm Rae Hooper. The smaller version with the smart mouth is my daughter, Martina."

Something flickered across his face at that moment. Rae wished he'd take off those horrible sunglasses. Instead, he shifted his weight, crossed his arms and returned his attention to the peeling diner wall. "I'd be more than happy to do the job for you."

"Frankly, I'd be more than happy to let you. As you've no doubt noticed, my father is less than enthused about the project. Unfortunately, I really can't afford to issue another paycheck right now, so—"

"I don't want money."

"Excuse me?"

"I'll do it for meals, and the use of a bungalow while I'm here."

The bungalows in question, one of her mother's few failed business ventures, were secreted in the thick woods beside the diner. Mama had thought seclusion would make the cottages more appealing, but since they were barely visible from the street, sleepy tourists searching for accommodations had passed them by. When a blizzard had finally flattened the tiny Motel sign, Mama hadn't bothered to replace it. If the town's renovation project was successful, Rae planned to tear down the bungalows and sell the bare lot to an entrepreneurial type with big ideas and a fat pocketbook. In the meantime, the little cottages were just sitting idle.

So was the ladder.

"You've got a deal, Mr. Flynn."

They shook on it, and Rae floated back to work. If she hadn't been so relieved to have resolved at least one of her problems, she might have wondered why the enigmatic stranger had avoided the question of where he'd come from. She might also have wondered how he'd known that the boarded-up bungalows belonged to her.

Long after Rae Hooper had retreated to the diner, Hank Flynn stared at the place where she'd been standing. Her scent still clung to the air. Alluring. Intoxicating. Dangerous.

He never should have come to Gold River. If he had a lick of sense he'd grab his duffel, stick out his thumb and head back the way he'd come.

But now that he'd seen Rae Hooper and her beautiful child, Hank knew that he couldn't leave. Not now. Perhaps not ever.

Chapter Two

"I'm sorry about that." Rae leaned against the counter, patting Steve's arm. "Sometimes Marti's mouth shifts into gear before her brain is fully engaged, but I'm sure she appreciates the thought behind your, ah, lovely gift."

"She said she'd rather have rats chew out her eyeballs than wear it," Steve reminded her. "If there was a shred of appreciation in that comment, I certainly missed it." Slumped on his stool, he cast a glum glance at the ruffled mustard-and-violet-print pinafore draped over the cash register. "I don't understand. The salesclerk said it was the newest fashion, all the rage for young girls of Martina's age group."

"Marti isn't much on style, I'm afraid."

"Well, she can't go through life wearing faded jeans and raggedy T-shirts. It isn't proper."

"She's only nine, Steve. Give her time."

"It's not just her poor choice of clothing," he insisted, his lips pursed with disapproval. "Martina continually behaves in a most unladylike manner. Climbing trees, for example. And I can't believe you actually allow her to play football.''

"She has the best rushing record on the team.''

"That's beside the point.'' Steve's eyes narrowed. "The child keeps a can of worms in her bedroom.''

"Technically, they're night crawlers. Excellent fish bait. Marti digs them herself.''

"Girls should not be digging worms.''

"Says who?''

"It's grubby and unfeminine,'' he muttered. "So is hanging out with ruffians.''

"Now, wait just a darn minute. Marti's friends are not ruffians.''

"They're boys.''

"So what? Didn't you have any female friends when you were that age?''

"No, as a matter of fact, I didn't. It wasn't—''

"I know, I know. It wasn't proper.'' Turning away, Rae swallowed a sigh and busied herself wiping down the already spotless counter. She hated these discussions about her daughter's so-called shortcomings, and resented issuing repeated explanations about the futility of trying to convert a scrappy tomboy into a genteel debutante.

It wasn't that Steve disliked Marti. On the contrary, he cared enough to fret about the child's future success, which he considered to be inexorably linked with conformation to societal standards.

Steve meant well. He simply didn't understand or appreciate Marti's, well, uniqueness.

The thought dissipated as Rae glanced out the front window to see her newest employee reluctantly hovering just outside the front door. Fearing he must have changed his mind about tackling an obviously odious chore, her heart sank. She would have left her post to confront him then and there, except that Steve's voice continued to drone through the diner like the hum of a pesky insect.

"So I took the liberty of requesting literature on the more promising ones."

Rae forced her attention back to the somber man who was rooting through the pocket of his neatly pressed blazer. "I'm sorry, my mind wandered for a moment. What is it that you were talking about?"

"Why, finishing schools for Martina." An annoyed frown puckered his pinched brows as the jingling cowbell announced Hank Flynn's entrance. Steve tossed the man a sour look, then pulled a leaflet from his pocket and continued his speech with increased enthusiasm. "There's a boarding academy outside Boston with impeccable credentials—"

"Boston!" Dropping the rag, Rae leaned across the counter until her nose was a scant inch away from the man's startled face. "You want me to send *my daughter* to the other side of the country to live in some kind of institution for the socially inept? Are you out of your mind?"

Clearly taken aback, Steve laid the brochure on the counter. "Finishing school is a privilege, not a punishment."

"I doubt Marti would see it that way."

"I'm merely offering an option. Nothing has been settled—"

"Oh, yes it has." Rae snatched the rag and flung it under the counter. "My child is not, I repeat *not,* going anywhere."

"But—"

"End of discussion." Rae ripped the brochure in half and hurled the pieces into the trash.

"I see." Steve stood, nodding as he smoothed his crisp white cuffs. "You need time to think about it. I understand."

Propping stiff arms on the counter, Rae simply stared at him. She was frustrated, she was furious, but there was simply no sense in arguing with a man who heard only what he wanted to hear and discarded everything else as extraneous noise.

Across the room, Hank Flynn cleared his throat.

Rae, feeling uncharacteristically snappish, skewered him with a hard stare. "I hope you haven't had second thoughts about our agreement."

The question seemed to startle him. "No, ma'am."

"Good," she murmured, feeling her stiff cheeks relax even as Steve's questioning gaze burned into her temple. "So, Mr. Flynn, what can I do for you?"

Hank shifted his weight, tilting his head so that it was impossible to tell if his shaded gaze was focused on her or on Steve Ruskin. Judging by the tight brackets at the corners of his mouth, her money was on Steve. Men, she'd noted, had a peculiar affinity for sizing each other up, although she'd never figured out why. Her fiancé used to do it all the time.

Not that Martin Manning had been the jealous type; he simply hadn't been able to stop himself from eyeing other men the way a prizefighter studies potential opponents. When she would question him, he'd just flash that endearing, little-boy grin and mumble something about finely honed male instinct. Then he'd sweep her into his arms with a passionate kiss that turned her knees to putty, initiating a considerably more intimate form of communication.

"I need a scraper."

"Hmm?" With some effort Rae refocused her attention on the shaggy stranger, who was as different from her clean-cut, military lover as night was from day. "What kind of scraper?"

"Nothing fancy. An old putty knife would be fine."

Steve, clearly chagrined that he'd not been acknowledged, now stepped forward. "Excuse me, I don't believe we've met."

After perfunctory introductions, Rae added, "Hank is repainting the building for us."

"Oh?" Steve's skeptical expression spoke volumes. "I thought Hobie was taking care of that."

"Yes, well, so did I." Moving behind the counter, Rae opened a drawer beneath the cash register, extracted two keys and offered them to Hank Flynn, who sauntered toward her, parting the air with his presence.

There was a majesty about him that captured her imagination, evoking provocative images of slick skin and flexing muscles that stirred a secret part of her soul. Her gaze remained riveted to the sexy roll of slim hips gloved by worn denim until the man had moved so close that the counter obstructed her view.

Swallowing hard, Rae dropped both keys into his extended palm. "The little one with the blue head fits a padlocked shed behind the diner," she murmured, dabbing her moist forehead. "You should find what you need in there. The larger key is for bungalow number six. It may be a couple of hours before I have a chance to hose the place out and bring in fresh linens, so if you want to put your things inside before then, you'll have to pry a few boards off the door."

"No problem."

Licking her lips, she avoided looking directly at his face, afraid of what she might see reflected in those sunglasses. If Steve's horrified expression was any clue, a sudden rash of hives must have welted the words *hot to trot* across her forehead. "There's, ah, no set time for meals. Just come into the diner whenever you're hungry."

"Thanks." Hank bounced the keys on his palm. "I'll check out the shed."

Rae would have returned his smile if she hadn't feared

her face would crack. She stood there, immobilized, until his tight, denim-clad tush had drawled on out the door.

A long-suffering sigh drew her attention. "Honestly, Rae, you must learn to control this compulsion you have for taking in strays."

"I hired a painter, Steve. Don't make more of it than it is."

"He's a drifter, a bum. For all you know, he could be a serial killer. You have a child to consider, Rae. For the life of me, I don't know what you were thinking."

Steve had a point, although it pained her to admit it. So she didn't. "The only thing I was thinking about was my immediate problem, and how Hank Flynn could solve it."

"But to actually allow the man to move in—"

"Oh, for heaven's sake. He needs a place to sleep, so I'm letting him use one of the cottages. Get a grip, Steve."

Shaking his head, Steve glanced at his watch with a disgusted snort. "I'm due in Sacramento for a meeting with the appropriations committee. We'll discuss this later."

Before Rae could do more than issue a weary sigh, he'd tossed her a reproachful look, hoisted his briefcase and marched out the door like the drum major of a pin-striped executive drill team.

Sagging against the counter, Rae cooled her face with her palms and tried to reason with herself. In point of fact, Steve had every right in the world to be concerned. She *had* acted hastily. That wasn't like her.

True, she did have a soft spot for people who were down on their luck. There was a haunted quality about them that touched and humbled her. She'd always done what she could to help, although thus far she'd managed to maintain a cautious distance, and had never, ever invited a stranger into her life.

Until today.

She told herself it was merely a matter of circumstance. Hank Flynn had appeared at a point when her resolve had been weakened by worry, and although her reaction may have been a bit imprudent, it was nonetheless understandable.

As was Steve's, she supposed. Despite her irritation with his constant interference, she had no doubt that the poor man's heart was in the right place. Too bad he didn't have the fashion sense to match his good intentions.

Rae's gaze was drawn to the gaudy pinafore, which was without a doubt the ugliest garment she'd ever seen in her life. She tucked it back into the bag, saddened that once again Steve's effort to please Marti had backfired. It seemed that the harder he tried, the less likely he was to succeed. Rae felt badly for him, because she understood his desire to provide her daughter with strong, parental-type guidance that he firmly believed a child of her age required.

On the other hand, Rae also understood her daughter's frustration. All Marti saw was an irritating busybody who was constantly in her face and took up too much of her mom's time. Marti was also displeased by the knowledge that if Steve had his way, he'd take up a lot more of Rae's time. It was no secret that he wanted to marry her.

What Marti didn't know was that Rae was seriously considering his proposal. Steve Ruskin represented everything she considered important in a husband and father. Unlike Hobie, who was a charming rogue at best, Steve was stable, reliable, financially astute and staid as bedrock. He understood that she wasn't in love with him, but insisted that it made no difference. From his perspective, Rae needed a husband and Marti needed a father. Love, he'd argued, would come later.

But Rae knew that it wouldn't. She'd already found the only man she'd ever love. And she'd lost him forever.

* * *

Hank was descending the ladder when a scrawny old geezer emerged from the woods wearing wet-to-the-thighs dungarees and lugging a medium-sized gasoline engine. The fellow hesitated, shifting his burden from one hand to the other, then lumbered into the clearing, whistling. He jerked to a stop just as Hank stepped off the ladder. "Who'n hell are you?"

"That depends." Hank wiped the putty knife on his pants. "If you're Hobie Hooper, I'm your replacement. If you're anyone else, I'm none of your business."

Hooper's sagging eyelids narrowed into droopy little slits, although he seemed more curious than angry. With a quick head turn, he spit on the ground. "I'm Hooper," he said, swiping a bony hand across his mouth. "Your turn."

Hank shoved the knife into his back pocket. "Hank Flynn. Your daughter hired me to finish up here."

"She did, huh?" A hint of amusement sparked his pale eyes as he hoisted the engine onto the makeshift plywood table. "Impatient gal, my Rae. Just like her mama, God rest her soul." Turning, he squinted up at the freshly scraped clapboards. "Been working long?"

"A couple of hours."

"That all?" Hobie let out a low whistle. "It'd take me the best part of a week to do that much."

"So I hear."

"Life's short," Hobie said, chuckling. "No sense rushing through it. Say, you know anything 'bout engines?"

"Some." Hank eyed the item in question, an antiquated five-horsepower stand-alone with an attached dredge pump. "What's the problem?"

"It don't run is the problem. Just started coughing and such, then rolled over and died without so much as a thank-you kindly." Heaving a morose sigh, Hobie gave the greasy engine a comforting pat. "Poor old girl is plumb tuckered. Can you fix her up?"

"Maybe." Shifting sideways, Hank examined the exposed fuel lines, then extended the choke and gave the start wire a hefty yank. The engine shuddered once, then fell silent. A second and third pull yielded similar results. Hank straightened. "I need a Phillips screwdriver and a paper clip."

"A paper clip?"

"Umm." Hank blew into the cooling fins to eject loose dirt. "I could use some pliers, too, and something sharp. A needle, safety pin…even an old fishhook would do."

Hobie shrugged, then wandered off, scratching his thatch of stick-straight gray hair and muttering to himself.

A few moments later, having returned with the requested items, Hobie clamped a dried weed stalk between his teeth and settled back to watch Hank work.

"Y'know," he said wistfully, "this kinda reminds me of the time me and Two-Toes Malone was high-banking off the Russian River. We was seeing good color in the riffles, and man alive, ol' Two-Toes was so het up about all them pretty flakes, you'd thought he'd died an' gone to heaven."

"Pliers."

Hobie slapped the requested item into Hank's outstretched palm. "Well, sir, we hadn't no more'n hit pay dirt when that old engine up and died. Two-Toes was so dadgummed mad, he done threw that useless pile of bolts in the river, then jumped in after it and no one's seen hide nor hair of him since. Some folks swear that every spring, when the river's rushing hard, they can hear the sound of a dredge engine and the ghost of ol' Two-Toes Malone, cussing at the moon. Whatcha doing to that paper clip?"

Instead of answering, Hank set the pliers aside and demonstrated by using the straightened clip to ream out clogged fuel lines and breather tubes. He blew them out, then turned his attention to the engine's miniature carburetor, using a flattened nail head to adjust the tiny idle screw. He also regapped the spark plug, tested the priming system and used some of the silicone caulk to reseat the pump gasket.

As Hank worked, Hobie Hooper hovered like a curious bee, abuzz with tidy tales of a dubiously colorful past. His latest yarn, from what Hank could tell, centered on having stumbled upon a cave of pirate booty that, oddly enough, was located in the Utah desert, hundreds of miles from the nearest stretch of ocean.

Such logic inconsistency, however, did little to dim the old man's enthusiasm. "Yessir, if that old mule hadn't tripped on a crevice, I'da passed by without a how-dee-do, and all them golden doodads woulda been lost forever."

Hank tried not to smile. In fact, he tried not to listen, but there was something compelling about the old coot's recitations. Compelling, not believable. Still, he had to admit that Hobie's tall tales were entertaining, fun and surprisingly well told.

Twisting a shop rag into a spiral cleaning probe, he slipped a sideways glance at Hooper. "So what happened to the loot?"

"Hmm?" A pair of rheumy eyes blinked up. "Damn government took it. Probably laid out under glass in some stuffy ol' museum. You gonna clean your ears with that thing?"

With a quiet chuckle, Hank inserted the cloth swab into a thin orifice below the carburetor to check for hidden leakage. The swab came out clean. Satisfied, Hank stuffed the rag in his back pocket, adjusted the engine choke and yanked the start line. The engine purred on the first pull.

"Well, I'll be a warty green hop-frog," Hobie mumbled, scratching his ruffled hair. "Danged if she ain't humming like a happy bride."

"Some of the parts are worn," Hank said, retrieving the rag to wipe his hands. "Screws are stripped, too. How long since it's been serviced?"

"'Bout two minutes."

"Before that."

"Well, lemme see," Hobie muttered, rubbing his whiskered chin. "I remember once in the spring of '62..."

Turning away, Hank tuned him out and concentrated on fastening a sheet of medium grit paper on the palm sander. He squinted up at the scraped area and was mentally noting chipped areas that would need a filler patch when Hobie suddenly snagged his arm.

"What say we grab a couple of cold ones?"

"I have work to do."

"It'll keep," Hobie insisted, plucking the sander out of Hank's hands. "Got something in the house that'll tweak your interest."

For some strange reason, Hank was sorely tempted. For all his ludicrous babbling, or perhaps because of it, Hooper was a likable cuss. Hank was enjoying his company. Still, his first obligation was to the woman who'd hired him, so in a last-ditch effort to soothe his conscience, he offered a feeble protest. "There's still daylight left."

"Oh, pish." Smelling victory, Hobie exhibited surprising strength to haul the larger man away. "A man's entitled to take hisself a break now'n again. Besides, I got me a piece of gold quartz back at the house that'll flat knock your eyes out. Ever seen gold quartz? Never mind. I guaran-damn-tee you've never seen nothing like this one. Fine as a sweet woman, it is. Sparkles better'n sunshine off a mountain lake."

While Hobie continued his colorful monologue, Hank

found himself being forcibly led through a stand of fragrant cedar toward a large old house about fifty yards behind the diner. They'd nearly reached the porch when Hobie suddenly fell mute. The old man laid a withered finger beside his mouth, then crouched down, sneaking past the porch to an entrance on the east side of the rambling Victorian house.

Once inside, Hobie made a production of closing the door without so much as a vibration, then grinned like a guilty schoolboy. "Got to keep it down a tad," he said. "Don't want Rae popping in, scolding and whatnot."

"I thought Rae was at the diner."

"Might be, but no sense taking chances. The cook came in at five, so Rae could turn up just about anywhere. I swear that gal's got antenna sprouting under that frizzy hair. Don't matter how quiet a man tries to be, she always figures a way to nose into a body's business. Just like her mama, God rest her soul." Rubbing his hands together, Hobie tiptoed toward another door at the far side of a massive bedroom cluttered with clothing and rusted tools. He'd just edged the door open when a horrific squawk spun him around.

"Dammit, Louie." Flattened against the jamb, Hobie glared at a cockeyed parrot perched in the far corner of the room. "Shut your noisy yap."

The bird twisted his green head. "Aww-rk. Lousy rotten claim jumper. Oughta be shot, oughta be shot."

Hank froze, staring at the parrot in utter shock.

Hobie, clearly frustrated, glared darkly at the creature. "This here is Louie-Louie, a dadgummed pain in the behind. I shoulda made a pillow outta him years ago."

"Shake your booty, you old cooty—awk!" Flapping his stubby wings, Louie ducked his head and let out a string of epithets explicit enough to make Hank wince.

Hobie, however, just fixed the bird with a narrowed stare. "That kinda talk is gonna land you in a stew pot."

"Up your nose," Louie squawked happily. "For itchy scalp and dandruff flakes—awk, Louie's a good bird—scrub your head with a garden rake!"

Rubbing his eyelids, Hobie shifted his weight, then tried another tactic. "Hey, Louie, are you thirsty?"

The parrot threw back his head and launched into a raspy rendition of "How Dry I Am."

"Whatcha want?"

"Gimme beer, dear."

"You gonna behave yourself?"

"Aww-rk. Louie's a good bird."

"That'll be the day," Hobie muttered. With a disgusted snort, the crusty codger opened the door a crack, pausing to toss a suspicious glance at his rowdy pet. Louie tilted his head but was silent, so Hobie slipped out of the room.

Hank remained motionless, half-hidden behind a rickety floor lamp. His breath came in short puffs, and he swallowed quietly to avoid drawing unwanted attention. Sweat beaded his forehead, chilling him to the marrow. Across the room, tiny claws shuffled along the wooden perch. Shifting his eyes, Hank tried to watch the animal without moving. To his horror, he saw that the bird was watching him, too.

Panic set in. Reaching behind him, Hank was fumbling for the doorknob when Hobie reappeared carrying two frosty cans.

"Rae ain't here," he announced, visibly pleased. "Marti's doing homework in the dining room, but I was real quiet. Not that she'd rat on her ol' gramps, but it ain't proper to coax a child to tell untruths, y'know?"

Ambling across the room, he slapped one can into Hank's limp hand, then popped the top on his own and hobbled over to the excited parrot. "I'm a-comin'. Don't get your feathers in a ruff," he said, dribbling a few drops of amber liquid into a jar lid. "And don't snort the foam, neither. A gassy bird is a right rotten roommate."

Fluttering madly, Louie hopped from his perch to the dresser and stuck his beak into the shallow lid.

Hobie chuckled. "The vet don't much approve, but ol' Louie's nigh onto twenty years old now, and he's been sipping brew since he weren't more than a hatchling. Even the bird doc figures it ain't hurt him none, so long as he don't drink more'n a few drops." The old man took a healthy swallow, then wiped his mouth, regarding Hank curiously. "What's wrong, boy, cat got your tongue?"

"Aww-rk, kill the cat, kill the cat."

"Cork it, Louie, I weren't talking to you." Turning back to Hank, he cocked his wizened head. "You've been a-staring at that bird like it was gonna peck your eyes out."

Hank licked his lips, aware that his gaze was darting frantically, but unable to control it.

Hobie nodded sagely. "Don't fret, son. I seen it before. Ain't nothing to be ashamed of."

Blinking, Hank silently questioned that statement with a quirked brow.

"Hell, lotsa people are scared of birds," Hobie replied. "Something about the fluttering and such, though I never could figure it myself. Me, I don't like bears. Why, I remember once when me and my hound, Dawg, got caught in a blizzard and ran smack-dab into a grizzly. Huge, it was. Big as a bus." Pausing for a quick swig, Hobie smacked his lips, continuing his tale with shiny eyes and palpable excitement. "Yessir, I thought we was gonna be that bear's dinner, but Old Dawg, he weren't ready to give it up without a fight."

With that, Hobie flopped into a beat-up easy chair, continuing to spew stories and gulp beer until Hank's defenses were worn to a nub and he relaxed, his fear momentarily forgotten.

After twenty minutes or so, Hobie ended the bear tale with a characteristic flourish. "And there ain't been a grizzly seen since the town made Old Dawg mayor. Whaddaya think of that?"

Grinning, Hank stretched out his legs, resting his forearms over the back of the wooden chair he was straddling. The story was outlandish enough to evoke his first utterance since entering the house. "I only have one question."

Hobie reared up, blinking. "What's that?"

"Bears hibernate in winter," he mused, crushing the empty beer can in his palm. "Why do you suppose that one was outside tromping through a blizzard?"

"Well, now, that's a puzzlement, ain't it? Only thing I can figure is that he weren't too bright as bears go, or maybe the missus kicked him outta the cave for snoring too loud."

Hank shook his head, laughing. "You've got an answer for everything, don't you, old man?"

"Hey, I ain't just a pretty face, y'know—" Interrupted by a frantic squawk, Hobie tossed an irritated glance at the corner perch.

Louie spread his wings, bobbing wildly. "Cheese puffs!"

Hank's blood went cold.

"Aww-rk!" Leaping from the perch, the parrot flapped his clipped wings to land on the unmade bed a few feet from Hank's chair. "Cheese puffs, cheese puffs!"

Hobie leaned forward, setting his beer can on the rickety TV tray that served as a table. "Well, ain't that something. Why, I can't hardly remember the last time—"

But Hank, who'd yanked the door open and shot outside, didn't hear the rest of Hobie's comment, nor did he want to hear it. The only thing in the world that mattered was how far away from that bird he could get and how fast he could get there.

Sprinting through the woods, he finally emerged behind the diner with his heart trying to pound its way out of his rib cage. Blood roared by his ears like a freight train. His lungs ached. His skull felt as if it would explode.

He stumbled toward the ladder, then sagged against the building, trying to catch his breath. Closing his eyes, he silently called himself three kinds of a fool. Coming to Gold River had been a bad idea in more ways than he'd ever have imagined. He should leave. Now. Right this very minute.

He *should* leave.

But he wouldn't. He couldn't, because as his pulse slowed and his breathing returned to normal, his gaze was drawn to the outline of rustic cottages visible through the woods. Faint light spilled from one of the units, a dim glow through the shadows of sunset. He realized that Rae must be inside the bungalow preparing it for occupancy, and couldn't keep his mind from wandering into forbidden territory.

He wondered if the linens would be saturated with her scent, and the thought made him shiver with anticipation. The light beckoned, inviting as a lover's smile. He could follow it and she would be there, a precious treasure at the rainbow's end.

Closing his eyes, Hank imagined how she would look with her hair slightly mussed, shiny tendrils curling against her damp skin. Her eyes, as green as winter moss, would smile a welcome. She'd twist her fingers together, embarrassed that she hadn't had time to whip the room into spotless elegance. Perhaps a giggle would escape her lush lips before she covered her mouth like a nervous schoolgirl.

The image made his pulse race.

God, how he wanted to follow that light, but he didn't dare. Instead, he reached under the sleeveless denim jacket to retrieve an object from his shirt pocket, an object that had given him the strength to survive the horror of war and isolation of prison, and carried him through lonely years of endless highways, nameless towns and faceless people.

The photograph had been his rock, his island of sanity in a world gone mad. It had been his life.

Hank slid down the diner wall to sit on his heels, gazing down at the picture with renewed awe and a sense of wonder. The face smiled up at him, as it had done for nearly a decade, but he saw it differently now. Older, gentler, softened by wisdom. And infinitely more beautiful.

Rae Hooper had been barely nineteen when the photograph was taken. Hank knew that because the date was scribbled on the back, along with a graceful inscription. "To Martin, my beloved. Keep well, keep safe, come home."

But Martin Manning would never come home. Hank Flynn had watched him die.

Chapter Three

"Madeline Rochester!" Sputtering, Hobie slammed down his coffee mug with enough force to splash a fair portion of its contents on the counter. "You gotta be joshing me."

Rae finished scribbling out her latest order without favoring her stunned father with a glance. "I would have told you last night if you'd bothered to show up for supper."

"I had a hankering to play a little pool," Hobie mumbled, scratching his ear.

"Really? Well, I'm glad to hear that. And here I thought you'd just sneaked your cowardly fanny out of town so you wouldn't have to explain breaking your promise to paint the diner."

"I didn't break no promise. I'da gotten around to it. Ain't my fault you got no patience."

"You're right, it isn't." Tucking the order pad back

in her apron, Rae flashed him a cheery smile. "Madeline expects you first thing this morning."

"Could be she expects the moon to fly outta the sky and land in her lap, too, but it ain't gonna happen."

Since initial sympathy over her father's dilemma had dissipated the moment Rae had seen the abandoned ladder, she wasn't in the mood to offer compassion. "Personally, I don't care one way or the other. Madeline wants you to paint her house. If you're not going to do it, just stroll on down the street and tell her so."

"Are you nuts, gal? That Rochester woman's tongue is so danged sharp, folks say she uses it to skin rabbits. I ain't gonna talk to her."

"Suit yourself. Of course, from what I've heard, Madeline doesn't take kindly to being ignored. She'll probably hunt you down and cut your heart out."

Hobie paled. "That ain't funny."

"It wasn't meant to be," Rae replied with a shrug. "When the worst happens, just remember that I tried to warn you. Good morning, Joe. How's Ida doing?"

The lanky man slipped onto a stool a few feet from Hobie. "She's better," he told Rae, nodding a thanks for the mug of coffee she set in front of him. "Doc says she's got to stay off her feet for a spell, but she should be right as rain in a couple weeks."

Rae continued to chat with the soft-spoken man, who'd been forced by economic circumstances to close the hardware store he'd owned for decades and find work at a nearby sawmill.

After a brief conversation, she snapped Joe's order sheet on a carousel at the kitchen pass-through counter and glanced at the clock, realizing that the cook's morning shift would end in less than an hour. It had been busier than usual this morning, which was a blessing, albeit a mixed one. During peak hours Rae couldn't handle both kitchen and serving duties, but extending the cook's hours meant extra payroll expense that wouldn't be offset by the price of a few extra meals. It put her in the unnerving position of losing money on customers that she couldn't afford to turn away.

"Uh…Rae, honey?"

She glanced over at her father. "Yes?"

"About this Madeline thing." Hobie hesitated, using his index finger to draw circles in the spilled coffee. "I thought mebbe you could find it in your heart to, y'know, take care of this for your ol' pa."

Rae fluttered her eyelashes, grinning broadly. "Not in this lifetime."

"Aw, that ain't fair, dadgummit. You was the one got me into this."

"Don't you dare lay this on me, Hobie Hooper. As long as you were repainting the diner, there was a perfectly legitimate reason to refuse Madeline's request, or at least postpone it. It's your own laziness that got you into this mess, and you can darn well get yourself out of it."

Rae saw her father flinch, and was satisfied that her argument had hit the mark. She would have added to her irritated commentary, except for the familiar rumbling outside the diner.

She glanced across the diner. "Marti, the school bus is here."

In the corner booth a fuzzy head vibrated. "Okay, Mom." A moment later Marti scooted from behind the table, snatched up her book bag and skipped toward the front door. "Hey, Joe, whaddaya know?"

The lanky customer smiled. "Hey, Marti. Study hard now, y'hear?"

"I will." The child paused by a rack filled with free advertising flyers, waiting for her mother to emerge from behind the counter.

"Did you remember your lunch?" Rae asked, smoothing her daughter's untidy hair. "I left it on the kitchen table."

"Got it."

"And your homework?"

"Geez, Mom, I'm not a baby."

"Yes, you are," Rae murmured, hugging her fiercely. "You're *my* baby, and you always will be."

Rolling her eyes, Marti heaved a martyred, prepubescent sigh and trudged out the front door with her fussing mother right on her heels.

"There's a cold front moving in this afternoon," Rae fretted. "I'm not sure that sweatshirt will be warm enough."

"It's fine, Mom."

"I could run get your jacket..."

The bus door folded open with a hydraulic hiss. "Gotta go," Marti announced with more than a hint of relief. She hit the steps running.

The door hissed shut, and the bus belched on down the road, leaving Rae standing on the curb, waving. It was barely seven and dawn had just begun to lighten the spring sky. Only after the vehicle's yellow rear had disappeared did she turn away, stuffing her hands into her sweater pocket as she plodded back toward the diner.

Every morning she saw her daughter off on the school bus. Every morning she remembered standing in that very spot, waving goodbye to a bus carrying the man she loved to a war from which he'd never returned. Every morning she relived that wrenching loss, along with a secret terror that someday her daughter's bus would come back empty, and the nightmare would begin again.

It was an irrational fear, she knew, comparing the fate of a soldier heading off to battle with a child going to school, although irrational fears were no less terrifying than those based on sound logic. Rae had learned to hide her feelings; she'd learned to cope with them. But she'd never learned how to abolish her secret terror, and doubted she ever would.

Lost in thought, Rae was crossing the gravel parking lot with her head bowed when a shadow loomed from the corner of the building. She spun around, startled, just as Hank Flynn emerged.

They nearly collided, and would have if he hadn't swerved. He reached out to steady her, seeming as surprised as she was by the unexpected encounter.

The moment he touched her, a soothing warmth radiated from Hank's hand to Rae's shoulder. Rocking slightly, she stared into the center of his chest, where a pair of sunglasses dangled from the neck of his T-shirt. Immediately she looked up, and was mesmerized by the intensity of his unshielded gaze. His eyes were dark, piercing. Relentless.

"Are you all right?"

She nodded dumbly.

His palm lingered at her collarbone, then withdrew slowly, brushing her upper arm with caressing softness. He said nothing.

"Did you sleep well?" Rae finally asked.

A brooding glint flicked through his unprotected eyes. "Yes."

"The mattress wasn't too firm?"

"No."

"So, ah, is there anything else you need? More towels, extra pillows, toilet paper?" *Oh, Lord, toilet paper?* Rae's smile stiffened into a grimace.

Hank seemed amused by the intemperate remark. "I'll let you know."

She cleared her throat. "Please do."

Behind her, the diner door opened. With some effort, Rae pulled her gaze from Hank long enough to see Hobie ambling toward his rattletrap pickup truck. "Are you on your way to Madeline's?" she inquired politely.

He tossed her a withering look. "No, I ain't on my way to Madeline's. I told you, I ain't gonna talk to that ol' shrew."

"In that case, does your will specify who gets Louie?"

Hobie spit on the ground, then tottered off to his truck, mumbling to himself.

Shaking her head, Rae returned her attention to Hank Flynn and was disappointed that his intriguing eyes were again concealed by the atrocious shades. "Most people wait until the sun is all the way up."

"Do they?"

"Yes, they do." She cocked her head, scrutinizing his freshly shaven jawline, and noting that the glossy hair that had blown wild yesterday was now tidily tied at his nape. "Then again, you're not like most people, are you?"

"No, ma'am, I guess not." He opened the door for her, then followed her inside the diner and took a seat at the counter.

Hank accepted a mug of coffee with polite thanks, then pretended to scrutinize the menu when in fact he was scrutinizing each move Rae made. Everything about her was fascinating, from the way she balanced an order tray to the ease with which she juggled two coffee carafes while carrying on cheerful conversation with customers.

The cowbell jingled with increased frequency over the next few minutes as more and more townsfolk filed in to enjoy their morning coffee habit and catch up on the latest gossip. Few ordered a full breakfast, although most did request a side order of toast or a bowl of cereal. Hank thought that strange. It didn't take astute business acumen to realize that a restaurant couldn't make much profit selling toast and coffee, but Rae still treated each customer like gold.

Hank glanced around the diner, noticing for the first time that the place was showing its age. The counter, although spotless, was scratched and worn. Gouges in the surface laminate hadn't been repaired, and the linoleum floor was positively ancient. Matching vinyl patches on the counter stool seats were brighter than the original fabric, which had faded with time. The deterioration was sad, Hank thought, and disturbing.

His contemplation was interrupted when Steve Ruskin, carrying a leather executive case and wearing a banker gray suit, rushed into the diner.

Rae, who'd just finished taking an order from an elderly couple in booth two, glanced up with a smile. "Good morning, Steve. I didn't expect to see you this early."

Ruskin pressed a proprietary palm at the small of her back as he brushed a kiss on her proffered cheek. Hank bristled inside, but couldn't tear his gaze away.

"I only have a moment," Ruskin told her, emphasizing the fact by glancing at his watch. "Are you free?"

She arched a harried glance around the bustling diner. "As a matter of fact—"

"Good." Cupping her elbow with his palm, Ruskin ushered her toward the cash register and hoisted his briefcase onto the counter. "While I was out and about yesterday afternoon, I happened upon this marvelous little shop that specializes in educational aids for the, ah, scholastically challenged."

Rae's pleasant expression faded into one of abject annoyance. "Marti is doing very well in school."

"Yes, yes, but you must admit that she's capable of more than simply average grades, and it occurred to me that the mastery of appropriate study habits would be immensely helpful."

"Helpful for whom?"

"Why, for Martina, of course. None of the truly fine universities accepts students with less than a 3.0 grade point average. Naturally, 3.5 would be better." Ruskin snapped open his briefcase, oblivious to the fact that

Rae's eyes were flashing green fire. "This," he said, laying a fat, soft-cover workbook on the counter, "is exactly what Martina needs."

Rae didn't spare the book a glance. Instead, she stared straight at Steve and spoke through clamped teeth. "How thoughtful of you."

Hank, who was openly eavesdropping, was bewildered not only by the conversation but also by his own mixed reaction to it. On one hand, he had to admire a man who cared enough to be concerned about a child's future. On the other hand, discussing college entrance credits in reference to a nine-year-old seemed a bit premature.

Childhood was a magical time, when kids were allowed to be impulsive and silly and most important of all, to have fun. At least, it was supposed to be, although Hank, who'd grown up without a father himself, had no such personal experience. Still, putting adult concerns on a little girl seemed, well, cruel.

Then again, childhood was also a period of intense learning, a time to sow seeds of responsibility that would mature into strong, adult values. Since Steve Ruskin clearly understood that, Hank viewed the man with new respect.

Rae, however, seemed to view him only with frustration. She slipped the book under the counter, offering a smile that could only be described as bleak. "Thank you, Steve. I'm sure Marti will be, um, surprised."

Ruskin beamed.

Rubbing her neck, Rae cast a quick glance around the diner. Seeing no customers in need of attention, she turned back to Steve. "Do you have time for a cup of coffee?"

He glanced at his watch. "Perhaps a quick one."

Hank watched as the man perched stiffly on the nearest stool, and couldn't help but notice how Ruskin's eyes also followed Rae's movements behind the counter. Unaware that his facial features were being furtively studied, Ruskin let his brusque expression soften, and his gaze took on a tender glow that stunned Hank to the marrow. It was obvious that the man was deeply in love with Rae. It was also obvious that his feelings weren't returned, at least not with the same measure of intensity.

Strangely, Hank found no pleasure in that. If his instinct was correct, and it usually was, Steve Ruskin was a good man who wanted nothing more than to make Rae happy. And Rae Hooper deserved to be happy. She deserved to be loved and cherished, to be cared for and cared about; she deserved a man like Steve Ruskin.

Hank found no pleasure in that, either.

By midafternoon Hank had the south wall completely scraped, sanded and ready for caulking, the final process before painting could actually begin. After spending half an hour rooting through a box of broken-down shed tools, he'd located an antiquated caulk gun that was close enough in size to be used with the silicone caulk tubes. Unfortunately, the trigger had been immobilized by rust. Hank had just finished oiling the thing into submission when he had the feeling that he was no longer alone.

He glanced over his shoulder.

A pair of curious green eyes was staring at him. "Hi," Marti said, holding out a paper bag and a can of soda. "Mom thought you might be kinda hungry. She said you never came in for lunch."

Hank's heart felt as if it had been squeezed. The girl was the spitting image of her mother, right down to that funny little dimple on her chin. "Thanks," he murmured, laying down the rusted tool. He put the bag on the plywood table and opened the soda. "Thank your mom for me, too."

"Sure." Clasping her hands behind her back, the child

tilted forward, eyeing the clutter of rags and tools strewn across the plywood. "What's that?"

"It's a caulk gun," he said, following her gaze.

Her nose wrinkled adorably. "Where do you put the bullets?"

"It's not that kind of gun."

"So what does it do?"

"Here, I'll show you." Putting down the soda, Hank bent to retrieve a tube of silicone from a nearby box. "See the way the tube is shaped like an empty paper towel roll, with a pointy plastic tip on one end and a flat metal bottom on the other?"

"Uh-huh."

"First, we slice a quarter inch off the tip." Hank demonstrated with his pocketknife. "Then we slide the tube into the gun, like this."

Marti hoisted herself on tiptoes for a better look.

"Each time the trigger is pulled, this spring-loaded plate ratchets one notch, which pushes the metal bottom up into the tube and squeezes a bead of caulk out the tip."

"Wow," she whispered, her eyes huge. "Just like toothpaste. Can I try it?"

"Sure, why not?"

Marti's eyes lit like neon as Hank handed her the tool, then stood behind her, clasping her small hands between his large ones to steady her grip. "Use steady, even pressure," he said when she squeezed so hard that her knuckles turned white. "It takes a little practice."

"Oh! Oh, look!" she squeaked as a gluey white glob emerged from the plastic tip. "I did it, I did it, I really did it!"

Hank grinned. "Good job."

She spun around, fried with excitement, her sneakered feet prancing in place. "I wanna caulk something!"

"I don't know about that," Hank said, laughing.

"Most of the vents and windows are too high for you to reach."

"But we've got a ladder."

"Uh-uh, no way."

"Please?"

Squatting down to the disappointed child's level, Hank laid a comforting hand on her shoulder. "Ladders are dangerous."

"I'd be really, really careful." On cue, a sheen of moisture brightened her eyes, and damn near broke Hank's heart. "Ple-e-ease?"

He took a deep breath and exhaled very slowly. "Tell you what. You can do the bottom of the windowsills and those lower exhaust vents, and I'll do what you can't reach. Deal?"

A ray of sunshine broke through the clouds with her crafty smile. Hank had just been snookered by an expert. And he knew it.

Sagging against the diner wall, Rae propped a slumping shoulder against the pay phone while a quiet voice on the line laid waste to her financial future.

"I'm sorry," he was saying. "It's bank policy. You understand, of course."

"Of course," Rae lied, clutching the receiver. She didn't understand at all, but would rather have chewed glass than admit that.

The voice droned on for a few moments, then the conversation ended. Rae hung up, sucked in a breath and headed toward the cash register, where a man and his two children hovered impatiently. Pasting on a cheery smile, Rae rang up the sale, gave each child a wrapped piece of peppermint candy and bid them a pleasant day.

As soon as they left, she squeezed her eyes shut to hold back tears. "I'm sorry, Mama," she whispered to the air. "I'm not as strong as you were."

She was torn by a sensation of total despair, a feeling of hopelessness beyond anything she'd experienced since Martin died. Then Rae had been devastated by his loss, and had thrown herself into the business to keep from going mad. The diner had been her salvation; that, and the precious legacy Martin had left, the daughter Rae loved more than life itself.

Martin had never seen his beautiful child. Even sadder, he'd never even known about her. Rae's exuberant letter announcing her pregnancy came back unopened, a week after the military chaplain—a personal family friend— had appeared on her porch with the shattering news of her fiancé's fate.

Little Marti would never know her father. And that was the saddest fate of all.

Shuddering violently, Rae wiped her moist eyelids, squared her shoulders and took a deep, cleansing breath. Wallowing in the past wouldn't do her any good, and it certainly wouldn't help Marti.

Marti.

Rae's gaze settled on the familiar navy book bag, which had been dropped beside the register before Marti had taken Hank Flynn's lunch out to him nearly an hour ago. A frisson of fear slid down her spine.

Ignoring the cardinal rule of never leaving customers alone with the cash register, Rae hurried past the elderly woman having pie and coffee in booth four, and rushed out the front door. Pivoting around the corner with her heart in her throat, she jerked to a stop, stunned.

Marti, her hands and face blotched by gloppy goo, was joyfully smearing gummy white caulk around the exposed base of the oven exhaust vent while Hank Flynn bent over her shoulder, scrutinizing her work.

"Smooth it out," Hank was saying. "We need a nice, even surface, or the paint won't adhere."

Concentrating so hard that the tip of her tongue peeked

from a tight corner of her mouth, Marti completed the chore, then looked up at Hank, grinning. "How's that?"

"Outstanding," Hank replied, ruffling her tousled curls. "We'll make a painter out of you yet."

"Aw'right!" She yanked down a victorious fistful of air, simultaneously spotting her dazed mother. "Look, Mom, Hank's teaching me how to do stuff."

"So I see," Rae murmured, eyeing the hardened chunks of caulk clinging to her daughter's designer jeans. "I wish you'd changed clothes first."

Hank, wearing a paisley handkerchief tied into a headband, stepped forward like a protective shield. "It's my fault," he told Rae. "I should have known better. It won't happen again."

Marti's jaw drooped. "But you promised!"

"I shouldn't have," he murmured, pulling off the headband and using it to dab at the child's caulk-encrusted face. "I had no right to promise anything without asking your mother. Geez, this stuff isn't coming off." He looked up, clearly horrified.

"Don't worry about it," Rae said, eyeing the two grubby creatures with exasperated amusement. "She's washable."

"It wasn't Hank's fault, Mom. I talked him into it. Honest."

"I'm sure you did."

"Next time I'll change clothes, okay?"

Rae quirked a brow. "Next time?"

"Uh-huh." The girl's face glowed with excitement. "Hank said I could help him every day. He said he'd show me how to patch and paint and do all kinds of super neat stuff."

"Did he, now?" Cocking her head, she fixed the chagrined man with a cool stare. "How very kind."

Hank puffed his cheeks, tried for a grin that didn't quite come off, then tossed the handkerchief aside with a sheepish shrug. "You're right, I blew it big time. Would you, ah, like me to go to bed without supper?"

Rae managed to rein in a smile. "Around here, Mr. Flynn, we don't use hunger as punishment. As a matter of fact, I'm going to give Marti permission to work with you, so long as her chores are done and her homework is completed. That, I suspect, will be punishment enough for allowing yourself to be so thoroughly manipulated."

"Yay!" Marti jumped up and down, clapping. "Thank you, Mommy! This is gonna be so fun."

"The operative words are *chores* and *homework,*" Rae reminded her. "Both of which are waiting for your attention."

Marti mumbled something, but Rae was suddenly distracted by the rumble of a lumber truck rolling down Main Street, toward the site where reconstruction of wooden sidewalks would soon begin. The activity was a grim reminder of how desperate the town was to survive—and of her own desperation, as well.

She wondered if she'd be here a year from now, still standing on the property that had been passed down for three generations. And if Rae failed, if she lost all that her mother and her grandmother had struggled to build, what heritage would her daughter have?

The question brought a massive lump to her throat.

"Mom?"

"Hmm?" Rae glanced down at her suddenly somber child.

"Your eyes are all red."

Turning away, she absently wiped her face. "I'm tired, that's all."

Marti considered that, but apparently didn't buy it. She cocked her head, regarding her mother with wise little eyes. "The bank man always makes you cry."

"I'm not crying, honey." Rae clamped her quivering lip between her teeth, angling a covert glance over her shoulder. Hank Flynn had removed his sunglasses and was staring at her with an intensity that left her breathless. She was immobilized by his gaze, pinned in place by a power so unyielding, so forceful that it seemed to penetrate her very soul.

He was reading her.

Rae felt exposed, vulnerable. And for the first time in more years than she could remember, she felt as if someone truly understood her.

The moon was bright enough to read by. Rae leaned over the porch rail, lulled by the distant croak of pond frogs and the occasional hoot of a lonesome owl. It was after midnight, the time when suppressed fears bubbled to the surface, spilling into sleep. Into dreams.

Shivering, she wrapped her jacket more tightly around her chest then descended the porch steps to follow a familiar path through the forest. Moonlight illuminated her way, casting silver shadows between stands of stately ponderosa pine and fragrant cedar. She walked briskly, with purpose, toward an ancient pine that breached a jutting mass of moss-covered bedrock.

The tree, scarred by carved initials, had once been their tree, hers and Martin's. Now it was hers alone. She traced the chiseled letters with her fingertip, as she always did when visiting this special place. It was a comforting ritual, offering a sense of peace and a closeness with the man she'd never stopped loving.

"Couldn't sleep?"

Rae spun around, gasping, her back pressed against the rough bark. Her heart raced as a figure stepped from the shadows.

"I didn't mean to startle you," Hank said.

"What...are you doing here?"

He leaned against the rock, careful to maintain a respectful distance. "Taking a walk."

"In the middle of the night?"

Moonlight skipped across the sharp planes of his face, illuminating an amused twitch at the corner of his mouth. "Apparently I'm not the only insomniac in Gold River."

She relaxed, but only a little. "The night air helps me relax."

He nodded, as if that made perfect sense. "So, are you?"

"Am I what?"

"Relaxed."

"Yes, or at least I will be when my heart stops trying to pry my ribs apart." She pressed a palm to her chest. "I hope you realize that you just took ten years off my life."

Although made in jest, the comment clearly upset him. His jaw tightened. His shoulders tensed. He raked his hair in frustration. "I should have known better than to leap out at you like that."

"Well, you didn't exactly leap."

"It was stupid of me."

"Please, I'm fine. Just forget about it, okay?"

He looked as if he wanted to say more, but instead he turned his attention to the carved trunk. His features softened. "I assume this tree has a special meaning for you."

She smiled, again reaching out to finger the roughly hewn initials. "My fiancé carved this the night he proposed. Kind of clichéd, I suppose, but at the time I thought it quite romantic."

Since the fiancé in question was quite clearly no longer in the picture, Rae steeled herself for the expected inquiry. It never came. Instead, Hank turned away, gazing into the distance as if staring at stars. "Marti's concerned about you."

That was not what she'd expected to hear. "What do you mean?"

He faced her then, with shadowed eyes and a brooding

stance. "She seems to think you received some bad news today, and is upset that you won't share it with her."

"She's just a little girl," Rae murmured, chilled by her inability to conceal her feelings even from her own daughter. "I don't want her worrying about anything except experiencing a wonderful childhood."

Shifting, he propped his hip against the rock and folded his arms, regarding Rae thoughtfully. "Did you?"

"Did I what, get bad news?" After he'd confirmed the question with a curt nod, Rae heaved a quiet sigh. "Yes, I suppose I did, although it wasn't unexpected."

"I'm sorry to hear that."

They stood silently for a few moments, not looking at each other, yet intensely aware.

"Can I help?" Hank asked.

"I'm afraid not, but thank you for asking."

Silence stretched between them, comfortable and unhurried. They spoke sparsely—mundanely satisfying conversation about nothing of consequence. Hank commented on a distant chirping. Rae noted the silhouette of a thrush nest in the bough of a gnarled branch. They agreed that the moon was spectacular, that it was cooler than usual for this time of year, and that the soothing babble of a creek was one of nature's sweetest sounds.

And then Rae heard her deepest fears expressed aloud in her own voice.

She didn't know how it happened. They'd simply been chatting amiably when Hank had asked a benign question, which had led to another benign question and before she realized what she was saying, her entire life history had gushed off her traitorous tongue.

She told him everything, from her grief at having lost Martin, to her current financial woes. "I offered the bungalow property as collateral," she heard herself say. "But today I learned that the bank won't extend my line of credit unless I include everything I own."

"The diner and the house, too?"

"Everything except Hobie's claim." She angled a rueful glance. "They don't consider that as having any legitimate value."

"I imagine Hobie would disagree."

"Yes," she murmured, struck by how the moonlight enhanced Hank's classic profile. "I imagine he would."

They were strolling back toward the house at a leisurely pace, and Rae paused as Hank pulled a droopy bough out of her way. She acknowledged the gesture, discomfited by having revealed so much of herself.

"Forgive my whining," she said suddenly. "I'm hardly the only one in town with problems. It's been a tough time for everyone around here."

To her surprise, Hank responded with a knowing nod. "A year or so ago I read something about a record number of small towns declaring bankruptcy for one reason or another."

"Gold River was one of them. It would probably be a ghost town by now if Steve Ruskin hadn't cajoled the state legislature into supporting our renovation project." Because Rae was watching Hank closely, she saw the subtle tensing of his jaw, and wondered about it.

"Ruskin must be a bright guy."

"I think so."

They walked a few feet in silence before he spoke again. "Are you going to marry him?"

Rae jerked to a stop, staring up in disbelief.

Hank looked away. "Sorry. It's none of my business. Marti just mentioned that you might be thinking about it."

"Marti said that?" Moistening her lips, Rae shook her head. "I didn't realize she knew."

"I suspect there isn't much going on around here that Marti doesn't know about." Hank plucked a small cedar twig, smiling almost proudly. "She's a clever kid."

"Yes," Rae murmured, unnerved by the unexpected twist in their conversation. "Clever and snoopy."

"Curiosity is the first rule of genius."

"In that case, my daughter is a budding Einstein." Rae ducked under a dipping branch, slipping a covert glance at the man beside her. A familiar tingle slid along her nape. She looked away, perplexed and unnerved by the effect he had on her. "When Marti was talking about, um, Steve and I, did she seem, well, upset?"

He considered that. "A little, but I wouldn't let that worry me if I were you. It's only natural that she isn't thrilled about sharing your attention."

That made sense, of course. "Marti and I have been very close," she acknowledged. "No matter what happens in the future, my daughter will always be the highest priority in my life. I thought she understood that."

"I'm sure that she does." Then, to Rae's complete shock, Hank took hold of her shoulders, turning her around. "Your daughter loves you. She'll accept Steve Ruskin or anyone else who can give you the happiness and security that you deserve." His fingers tightened into a desperate grip. "Just be happy, Rae. Be happy."

With that poignant plea, Hank Flynn instantly released her and disappeared into the night.

Chapter Four

At 5:30 a.m. Rae yawned her way along the darkened path from house to diner as she'd done every morning for the past twelve years. Usually she enjoyed the pre-opening ritual of perking coffee, polishing tables and indulging in an occasional chat with the pastry-shop delivery-man. On this particular morning, however, she felt as if she'd spent the night performing nocturnal calisthenics. Every bone in her body ached, and her head was throbbing like an erratic drum.

She'd been plagued by bizarre dreams, and recalled waking frequently, feeling disoriented; but when the alarm had finally jarred her unwilling spirit into greeting a new day, she hadn't been able to remember any of the dreams. All that remained were physical soreness and mental fatigue, both of which would serve as an unpleasant reminder of what had clearly been a miserable and less than restful night.

After unlocking the diner door, she flipped the wall

switch and crossed the room before the overhead fluorescents had completely flickered to life. As she moved behind the counter, she heard a soft splash. She froze, horrified, as the overhead lights burst into full brilliance, revealing that she'd stepped into a thin pool of water spreading across the worn linoleum.

Uttering a gasp of dismay, she stared at the steady stream lapping at her soles while her sleep-deprived mind struggled to comprehend the cause of the flood. "Water," she mumbled stupidly, blinking at the sink.

She yanked open the sink cupboards and stared at a jumble of perfectly dry pipes. Perplexed, she glanced toward the only other source of water in the area, which was an antiquated under-counter ice maker that was piped directly into the plumbing.

Sure enough, a thin dribble was bubbling from the plastic feeder tube. Muttering to herself, Rae rushed to the storeroom for a pair of pliers and a roll of waterproof tape.

Ten minutes later, with the leaky tube bandaged, Rae attacked the flooded floor with a rag mop.

Behind her, the front door swung open. "Morning, Rae."

She glanced up as Chad the deliveryman wheeled in a dolly of pies and sweet rolls freshly baked by Hilda Gardener, who ran a wonderful little bed-and-breakfast just outside Auburn. "Morning," she replied without much enthusiasm.

Chad pulled up short of the counter, eyeing the soggy mess. "Looks like you got a bit of a problem. Anything I can do to help?"

She leaned on the mop handle. "Want to buy a diner?"

"Nah. Too much work."

"Smart man." Stepping back, Rae waited until Chad had wheeled his goody cart into the kitchen.

A moment later he returned, dragging the empty dolly behind him. He cast a questioning glance at the half-mopped puddle. She pointed to the ice maker's taped-up water tube. He issued a knowing nod. "That thing's old as dirt. Might be time for a new one."

"Might be," Rae murmured as Chad wheeled on out the door. She leaned against the counter, feeling suddenly nostalgic.

Over the years nearly every appliance in the place had either been replaced or repeatedly repaired. Everything except the antiquated little workhorse that until this morning had never given her so much as a moment's grief.

She remembered the first time she'd seen it, cradled in Martin's arms. Even then the ice maker had been worn-out and nearly obsolete, having been discarded by a local restaurant undergoing reconstruction. It had been rescued by Martin, who'd routinely perused junk heaps with the adolescent excitement of a teenaged mall rat.

At the time, Rae had been less than enthused about the pitiful piece of machinery, but Martin had been so proud. She still remembered how he'd hoisted the ice maker into position, assuring her that all the worn-out appliance needed was a minor overhaul and a bit of tweaking.

"The chiller motor is good-to-go," Martin had explained with a grin bright enough to grow corn. "I'll just replace a couple of belts, oil her up and *voilà!* Instant ice."

She'd been skeptical. "I don't know, Martin. You'll have to saw out a big chunk of counter to install it, and besides, if it worked properly, it wouldn't have been thrown out in the first place."

"Ah, but that's the beauty of it," Martin replied, rubbing a fond hand around the stainless steel ice tub. "Machines are like people. Each one has a different personality, a unique style. They all want to please, they all want the satisfaction of a job well done, but they have to understand what's expected of them.''

"You make them sound like pets.''

"In a sense, they are. You just have to know how to talk to them.'' Martin squinted under the formed basin at the collage of colorful wires sprouting from the motor housing. "Ah, *mon petit*,'' he crooned in a comically exaggerated French accent. "You are so love-lee, so exciting. The smoothness of your silky steel belly, the delicate curve of your gearbox—'' Encouraged by Rae's amused giggle, Martin pressed both hands over his heart, feigning a swoon of ecstasy. "How I long to stroke your sweet connections, to feel the erotic hum of your purring chiller, to run my unworthy fingers through your flowing wires—''

"Oh, Martin, you are the silliest man!''

He threw his arms around the dented steel basin. "Run away with me, my love! We'll make such beautiful ice cubes together!''

Rae, who was laughing so hard her vision blurred, yanked a white paper napkin from the holder and waved it over her head. "Enough! You win.''

He straightened, eyes wide and hopeful. "You mean I can install it?''

"Yes, yes, install the darn thing,'' Rae murmured, using the napkin to wipe her moist eyelids. "But if you do anything else with it, our relationship is over. I won't tolerate a cheating man.''

"I swear, we're just good friends,'' he insisted solemnly, then leaned toward the ice maker with a whispered aside. "She's on to us. We must be discreet.''

Rae turned away, shaking her head and wondering how it was possible to be so very happy without positively exploding. In six short weeks her life had been transformed from one of boring drudgery to joyful anticipation. Martin Manning had done that, and so much more.

He made her feel beautiful. He made her feel cherished. He made her feel special, unique, unconditionally loved.

Then again, he made the ice maker feel that way, too.

She stepped out from behind the counter, giving Martin room to work, and found a spot where she could watch—and listen—in utter amazement. He carefully measured the countertop, discussing the dimensions with a small skill saw he'd named Luther, then Martin dropped the basin into the cutout and positioned himself under the counter with his ever-ready box of tools.

"Relax," he murmured, positioning a screwdriver to the motor housing. "This won't hurt a bit. Hmm? What's that?" He cocked his head. "It's cold? Oh, sorry." He blew on the tip of the screwdriver, then went back to work. "Better? Good. Oh, my. How long has it been since anyone's given you a good lube job? Tsk. Well, we'll take care of that, sweetheart."

As Rae leaned over the counter for a closer look, the memory faded. She blinked, disoriented, as she stared at the taped water tube. A lump lodged in her throat.

Flashbacks of Martin came less often now, but they were still as vivid as if she'd been transported back in time to relive the moment. Every detail was etched in her mind.

Martin had been so very young. Just a boy, really, but he'd been filled with sparkle and enthusiasm for a life that had been just beginning. Rae remembered everything about him—the way his eyes were always wide and round, viewing the world with open acceptance, and a guileless excitement that was contagious. He'd been twenty-three then, but he'd looked more like a teenager, with skinny arms, peach-fuzzy cheeks and a military buzz cut that made him look like a schoolboy playing soldier.

In his heart and soul Martin Manning was tender, generous, loving, honest, courageous, cheerful and outgoing.

He was also an adventurous risk-taker, as lovable and as irresponsible as her own father. Rae, having watched her poor mother struggle through life with a fanciful dreamer, had been determined that she, at least, would marry a banker or an accountant or a nice, dependable insurance salesman.

When she'd fallen in love with Martin, the sense that history was repeating itself had confirmed Rae's deepest fear while bestowing her greatest joy. His sense of humor had made her laugh. His passion had taken her breath away. And his creative ingenuity had left her speechless, because Martin's talent hadn't been limited to installing ice makers. Rae had discovered, much to her shock, that her talented, baby-faced fiancé could fix just about anything, from a reluctant refrigeration unit to a recalcitrant car engine. He'd once repaired an air conditioner with a rubber strip cut from an old pair of galoshes, soldered a circuit board with a flame-heated ice pick and rewired one of the guest cottages, all in a single weekend.

And as was his habit, every chore had been accomplished while conversing with his tools, making puppets out of parts and drumming a jazz beat with screwdrivers to make his mechanical patients feel more comfortable.

Martin Manning had been a most remarkable young man, and Rae hadn't been the only one who adored him.

Even Hobie, who'd previously found fault with every man Rae had ever dated, had believed that the moon rose on Martin Manning's skinny shoulders. When Rae and Martin had announced their engagement, Hobie was positively ecstatic. When Martin was ordered overseas a month before the wedding, Hobie had threatened to sue the army. When the telegram announcing Martin's death had arrived, Hobie had collapsed with grief.

And when his beautiful grandchild was born, Hobie Hooper had raised red eyes to heaven, thanking God for having left a bit of Martin behind.

The memories brought tears to Rae's eyes. Martin Manning had been special to everyone, but he'd been Rae's entire life, her one true love. She had cherished him above all others, offered him her heart, her love, her life. And he'd accepted her gift. For a while.

That's the secret Rae carried deep in her soul. Nobody, not even Hobie, understood the real reason behind Martin's abrupt departure from Gold River. Only Rae knew the truth. And that truth was shattering.

"So the vein was a-running through a granite shelf beside the creek bed, like this...see here?"

"Hmm?" Hank tore his gaze from Rae, who was serving a stack of flapjacks to a flannel-shirted lumberjack, and forced himself to focus on the irritable codger seated beside him. "Sorry. What were you saying?"

"Old Sadie, my gold mine," Hobie growled, poking a bony thumb at the map scrawled on a napkin spread out on the counter. "Yessir, that were the prettiest vein of quartz I ever did see."

From the corner of his eye Hank saw Rae straighten, laughing as she tucked the order pad in her pocket.

"'Course, that old rock hadn't seen the light of day in about a million years, so I didn't figure there'd be much gold in it." Hobie laid down his pencil, scowling at Hank. "On account of all them diny-sores eating the damn stuff and pooping nuggets in the creek."

"Uh-huh." Hank was raptly following Rae's progress back toward the counter when a disgruntled snort caught his attention.

"Might as well talk to my bird," Hobie grumbled. "At least the ornery cuss listens."

"I was lis—" Hank paused as Rae bent to retrieve a dropped menu "—tening."

As Hobie wadded up the napkin-map, muttering, Rae slipped behind the counter, snatching the coffee carafe.

She stopped in front of Hank, who felt the telltale bob of his Adam's apple, and hoped she wouldn't notice.

"More coffee?" she asked, smiling like the sunrise.

Since Hank had been dawdling over his breakfast for nearly an hour, he reluctantly refused. "No, thanks. I'd better get to work."

Rae nodded, but made no move to leave. "You've done a wonderful job so far."

"Thanks. Marti's been a big help."

"I'll bet."

"No, really. She's quite a little trouper." They smiled at each other for a moment, and Hank could almost feel Hobie's wizened gaze burning into his neck. Hank cleared his throat, pushing his empty plate back. Rae hovered there, seeming hesitant to leave. When she finally turned away, Hank stopped her. "You don't happen to have another caulk gun stashed somewhere, do you?"

"I don't know." She glanced at Hobie. "Do we?"

The old man shrugged, rubbing his chin as his shrewd gaze shifted between his daughter and Hank. "Don't rightly recall. Haven't had much use for such stuff for a spell."

"Unfortunately, that's all too true," Rae replied, frowning prettily. "Which is why the project is now so enormous." The frown melted as she turned to Hank. "If you tell me what you need, I'll call the supply house and have it delivered."

"No need. We'll make do."

Hobie chuckled. "Looks like ol' Hank here is a two-fisted caulker."

"That would speed the job along," Hank agreed, slipping on a ratty baseball cap. "But it's not what I had in mind. Marti's having trouble with the old gun. The trigger's too stiff. Gives her blisters."

Clearly surprised, Rae set the carafe down. "Blisters? She never said anything about that."

Hank suspected that Marti hadn't mentioned the subject because she'd been afraid her mother wouldn't allow her to continue working. If that was the case, he'd just blown it big time. "It's nothing serious," he assured Rae, hoping to mitigate the damage. "I cut down a pair of gloves for her. That'll help protect her hands."

Before she could respond, her attention was drawn to the jingle of the front-door cowbell. Her eyes widened.

A grating female voice boomed through the diner. "There you are!"

Hobie sprayed a fresh mouthful of coffee on the counter, dropped his cup and leapt from the stool as if his rump was alight. He spun around, horrified, edging along the counter until his shoulder blades bit the wall.

Perplexed, Hank glanced over his shoulder to see a squat block of a woman wearing a wild straw sun hat, a baggy print dress and army boots stalking straight toward the cowering old man. "Hobie Hooper," the woman railed, waving her fist like a sword. "I've been a-looking for you."

Hobie cringed like snared prey. "Now, Madeline, it ain't what you think…"

The woman, who was the same height as Hobie and twice as wide, trapped him in the corner. "You oughta be ashamed of yourself, making a poor old widow woman heave her arthritic bones all over town."

"I, uh—" Hobie's eyes darted wildly. "I been meaning to call."

Madeline cocked a mean eye. "Your dialing finger broke, is it?"

"Well, no, it's, uh…" He swallowed hard. "It's my back, don'tcha know."

The woman tottered a step. "Your back?"

Instantly Hobie twisted his upper body, bending his torso to the side with an agonized grimace. "Sprain. Bad one, too. Can't hardly move."

"You don't say?" Madeline's furrowed face softened. "Why, you poor, brave man. The pain must be right awful."

"Hardly tolerable," Hobie agreed, peeking up from beneath his droopy lids. "Ain't suppose to climb ladders and such for quite a spell."

"I should think not," came the indignant reply.

A triumphant flicker lit Hobie's crafty eyes. It was a brief victory.

"I got just the thing to fix you right up," Madeline purred. "Got me a book about acupuncture. Been dying to try it."

Hobie's eyelids shot up as if spring-loaded. "Needles?"

"Fix you right up, it will." Before the horrified man could do more than sputter a weak protest, Madeline Rochester snagged his skinny arm and hauled him out the front door.

Hank, who'd been watching the scene over his shoulder, now turned around. He glanced at Rae, hitching a brow to silently question whether or not the old coot was in serious trouble.

She shook her head.

Hank pursed his lips, glanced back out the front window and saw no one, indicating that the tank of a woman had managed to drag her captive out of the parking lot. No way, he decided, was Hobie going to get out of this.

Grinning, he plopped a dollar on the counter.

Rae cocked her head, eyes sparkling, then laid a matching bill beside Hank's and folded her arms, gazing through the front window with smug confidence.

Five seconds later Hobie Hooper charged through the parking lot, arms flailing, knees churning, his mouth open in a silent scream. Every head in the diner followed his progress from right to left, then swiveled back to watch

Madeline Rochester chug past, hanging on to her sun hat with one hand while furiously waving the other.

A moment later Hobie's old pickup truck roared out of the driveway, leaving the frustrated woman standing on the curb, shaking her fist.

Rae gave Hank a knowing wink, then scooped up her winnings and went back to work.

The rear wall of the oblong diner, which was half the size of the sides, was finished by midafternoon. After moving his equipment to the north side of the building, Hank glanced toward the parking lot, which had been out of his view while he'd been working around back. Hobie's parking space was still empty.

No one had seen hide nor hair of the old codger since he'd hightailed it out of town early this morning. The incident had, however, caused plenty of amused speculation among residents, most of whom were wagering that he'd holed up on his claim, and probably wouldn't be seen again until next winter.

The only person who didn't seem interested in or even concerned about Hobie's whereabouts was his daughter. When asked, she'd reply with a nonchalant shrug, saying only that he'd be back when he was ready. Everyone agreed that he probably wouldn't be ready until Madeline found a new hobby. One that didn't use needles.

A raucous squawk drew Hank's attention to a pair of jays hopping nearby. He hefted the plywood shelf between the sawhorses, then wiped a forearm across his brow and reached for his lunch bag. "You're late," he told the birds.

They hopped forward, cocking their blue heads as Hank dug a stale crust out of the bag. He broke up the bread, and was scattering the pieces on the ground when the familiar hiss of the school bus drew his attention. It was later than he'd thought.

Brushing crumbs off his palms, he eyed the north wall, realizing that there wouldn't be time to prepare even part of it for caulking before Marti would be here, bright eyed and filled with enthusiasm. Since Hank would rather walk barefoot on lava than disappoint her, he anxiously scrutinized the project, hoping to find something for her to do.

In front of the diner, the school bus rumbled away.

Hank eyed the sander, wondering if Marti could handle the power tool, but quickly discarded the idea. It was too heavy, and maintaining even pressure would be too difficult for a little girl. He picked up the flat-bladed putty knife, which looked like a narrow spatula. It wasn't particularly sharp. Maybe—

"Marti!"

Hank looked up. Was that Rae's voice?

"Marti! *Marti!*" The final cry was issued in abject panic.

Hank dropped the putty knife and ran to the parking lot, where Rae had just grabbed a shocked youngster by the collar. "Where's my daughter?" she hollered at the hapless boy. "Why wasn't she on the bus?"

"I dunno," he mumbled, struggling against the taloned grip on his shirt. "Maybe she got a ride or something."

"A ride?" Rae released the youngster so quickly he staggered, then she spun around, wringing her hands. "My God. Oh, my God—"

Hank touched her shoulder. "What is it?"

"Marti," she sobbed. "She didn't come home."

A coil of pure terror tightened around Hank's chest. He swallowed, forcing a calm voice. "She was probably fooling around and missed the bus. We'll find her."

"How?" Rae pressed her hands against her mouth. They were trembling.

"We'll take your car," Hank said, referring to the old

sedan parked beside the rambling Victorian house. "We'll just drive down to the school and—"

"It doesn't run," Rae blurted, her eyes growing wilder by the moment. "The water pump went out. I couldn't afford a new one. Oh, God, my baby is lost!"

"No, no." Hank gathered her in his arms with whispered assurance and as much warm strength as he could muster. Inside, he was dying. And he was terrified. Gripping Rae's shoulders, he took a step backward. "I'm going to find Marti," he said when he had her attention. "You stay here in case she calls."

"How can you possibly find her? You have no car—"

"I'll walk."

"The school is twenty miles away."

"I'll walk fast."

Setting his jaw, he released Rae and had taken two steps toward the street when a familiar pickup truck shuddered into view.

Rae saw it at the same time that Hank did. She dashed across the parking lot just as Hobie pulled in to his parking space.

Marti hopped out clutching a paper bag and grinning madly. "Hi, Mom! Guess what Gramps bought me—"

The question died in midair as Rae clutched her child to her breast, hugging her fiercely. Releasing her grip only long enough to frame her daughter's face with quaking hands, Rae emitted a choked sob and renewed the embrace with increased fervor.

Hobie stepped from the truck cab to cast a wary eye on the scene. He appeared to be considering a judicious retreat when Hank came up from behind, cutting him off.

The old man's gaze shifted downward. He thumped his heel on the ground as if knocking dirt off his sole, and made a production of studying the bottom of his mud-caked boot while his furious daughter confronted him.

"What were you thinking?" she snapped. "I've been half out of my mind with worry."

Hobie scratched his earlobe without looking up. "Didn't mean to fret you none. It's just that the tavern weren't more'n a mile from the school, so I figured Marti'n me could just take us a quick scoot to the hardware store to pick up a new caulk gun and such." He angled a glance up the street, where the yellow bus was unloading another group of children. "Guess we dawdled too long, huh?"

Marti, who'd pulled away when her mother's grip loosened, looked up with huge sorry eyes. "It's my fault, Mom. I asked Gramps to take me."

Hobie shook his head. "No, now, it weren't the child's doing. I shoulda knowed better."

Rae took a deep breath, exhaling slowly. "You both should have known better. Next time, pick up a telephone."

Two contrite heads bobbed in unison, then Rae shot her father a final killing glance before ushering Marti into the diner.

Puffing his cheeks, Hobie hooked a thumb in his pocket and rocked back on his heels. "I'm in a heap of it now."

"I'd say so," Hank agreed.

Hobie fell into step beside him. "'Course, I never woulda got into this mess if you hadn't been yapping on about that danged caulk gun."

Hank didn't bother to reply. Despite having deferred to his angry daughter, Hobie Hooper wasn't one to accept responsibility if he could find a suitable pair of shoulders on which to shift the burden. The way Hank figured it, his shoulders were as good as any, and he didn't mind being a scapegoat. God knows, it wouldn't have been the first time.

"Rae told me that the water pump in her car went out," Hank said, heaving the ladder up against the wall.

"Yep, last month. Heated up an' started spewing steam."

"Why haven't you fixed it for her?"

"Hell, I don't know squat about such things."

"That's why they have repair shops."

"Gyp joints." With a disgusted snort Hobie spit in the dirt, then ambled over to where the hungry jays were pecking up the last of Hank's bread crumbs. He eyed the birds curiously. "Seem mighty friendly."

"Hmm?" Hank glanced over his shoulder. "They're mooches. So what are you going to do about Rae's car?"

"Got a junkyard pump last week." Hobie's gaze slipped from the bread-pecking birds to Hank's wadded-up lunch bag and back again. "Been asking around for someone to trade a look-see for a couple of nuggets."

After testing the ladder's stability, Hank turned around in time to notice Hobie cast a final glance at the jays before laying a curious finger on the once-rusted caulk gun that Hank had buffed and oiled into near-new condition. Something in the old man's expression sent a sudden chill down Hank's spine. "Rae needs a reliable car," he said warily. "I could take a look at it."

Pursing his lips, Hobie fixed him with a look that was unreadable, but nonetheless unnerving. "You do that, son. You just do that." Then he stuffed his hands into his pockets and ambled away, talking to himself.

Chapter Five

"Go deep."

Marti scurried backward, swiveling through a stand of pines to a clearing beside the diner parking lot. "Throw me a bomb," she hollered, dancing sideways.

"You asked for it." Winding up, Hank looped a long pass so well aimed that it would have plopped at her feet. Marti, however, reached out to snag the football, tucking it under her arm and pirouetting a perfect roll to the right. "Nice catch," Hank called. "Now let's see what kind of an arm you have."

She rotated the ball between her palms, grinning madly. "This'll take the skin off your hands."

"I'll risk it."

"Don't say I didn't warn you." Scuttling backward, Marti raised her arm high, faking left, then right, then shooting a straight pass that was beautifully executed, but far enough off the mark that Hank had to dive for it.

He rolled over, laid the ball in the dirt and hoisted

himself on one knee. "Good style," he told the happy child who was loping toward him. "Bad aim."

Her grin faded. "But you caught it."

"Never make your receivers eat dirt. It ticks them off, and they can't sprint for the end zone when their noses are buried in AstroTurf." Hank stood, brushing the dirt off his knees as he eyed the unhappy girl. "Even so, that would have been a solid first down. Good distance, sharp snap. You've got a great arm."

"Yeah?" She scooped up the ball, clearly buoyed by the praise. "Coach mostly makes me take handoffs and run. I've got a thirty-yard average."

"You must be fast."

"Not really." She slanted him a mischievous glance. "The boys on the other teams are afraid to, you know, grab me and stuff, on account of they don't want to accidentally touch something they're not supposed to."

That surprising announcement, not to mention the spunky sparkle in her prepubescent little eyes, caught Hank off guard. He pulled off his paisley headband, choosing his words carefully. "Somehow, that doesn't seem quite fair."

She nodded happily. "Yeah, I know. Coach figures we can go for the championship when my boobs start growing."

Hank stared at her, not knowing whether to laugh or scold. "How old did you say you were?"

"Nine, but I'll be ten next fall. Mom says that's too young to worry about boobs and stuff, but there's this girl in grade six who looks like Dolly Parton, so I figure mine could start popping out any day now."

"And this is a good thing?"

"Sure. I mean, how many girls get to play in the official league championships? It'll be, like, totally cool."

"Yes, well, when you put it that way..." Hank shook the headband back into a handkerchief and wiped his face, wondering how on earth the conversation had veered into such unexpected and unnerving territory.

"Did you play football when you were a kid?" Marti asked.

"Wide receiver, high school varsity, graduating to second-string benchwarmer at UC—" He cut off the unintended revelation, taking a moment to tuck the handkerchief into his back pocket. "Let's just say that college football was a bit beyond my expertise. Or more specifically, beyond my physique. I was too skinny to compete with those meaty linebackers."

Marti's green eyes warmed with compassion. "So I guess while girls are waiting for boobs, guys are waiting for muscles, huh?"

"Something like that."

Marti considered this for a moment, then cocked her head, hoisting her pug nose in the air. "So, what did you do after?"

"After what?"

"After, you know, you got done with college and stuff."

"I joined the army." The moment the words slid out, Hank wished he could snatch them back and swallow them whole, but it was too late. Marti was already lit up like a Christmas tree.

"That is too much!" she squealed, her cheeks glowing. "My daddy was in the army, too."

Hank managed a sick smile. "Was he?"

"Uh-huh. Mom says he was the smartest, bravest soldier in the whole wide world." The sparkle faded. "Only he died."

"I know. I'm sorry."

To Hank's horror, a sheen of moisture beaded her lashes. "How did you know about my dad?" she asked. "Did Mom tell you?"

"Ah, yes." Scooping up the football, Hank walked

toward the diner, where repairs on the north wall were almost completed. He didn't have to look back to know that Marti was following. When she fell into step beside him, he tossed the football under the plywood table and nodded toward the freshly caulked windows. "You did a great job today."

"I love my new caulk gun. It's really fun to use."

Marti was such a spirited child, so bright and sassy, with her grandfather's smart mouth and her mother's soft heart. Hank was nuts about her. Because he couldn't help it, he ruffled the short, fuzzy hair that made her look a bit like Little Orphan Annie. "Somehow, I can't imagine many kids who'd give up an entire Saturday to caulk windows, and consider the job to be fun."

"There's nothing else to do around here." She slipped a sideways glance toward the street, where a flannel-clad woman with stringy gray hair toted a bulging shopping bag toward the woods. "That's Erma, the squirrel lady," she whispered, even though the woman was well out of earshot. "Chipmunks come right up and eat out of her hand. I thought that was pretty neat, only Gramps said I should stay away from her."

"Why, because she likes to feed squirrels?"

Marti shrugged. "Gramps says anybody who spends their whole danged social security check to fatten up ugly rodents can't be the brightest porch light on the block."

"What does your mom say?"

"Oh, Mom likes Erma. Says she's just a lonely lady who likes furry critters and doesn't hurt anybody." Marti glanced around, as if assuring herself that she wouldn't be overheard. "When Gramps isn't looking, sometimes I go with her and help. I like squirrels. They're real cute, and I love the way they smoosh up their noses when they're smelling stuff."

Hank reached into a small cooler, pulling out two cold cans of soda. "Sounds like you've got the lowdown on everyone in town," he said, handing one of the cans to Marti.

"You hear a lot hanging around the diner. Everybody talks about everybody." She popped the soda top, took a noisy gulp, then wiped her mouth with the back of her hand, just the way Hobie did. "Did you know that the mayor used to be a big-city lawyer?"

"Really?"

"Uh-huh. He got de-barred."

Hank smiled. "I think the word is disbarred."

"Whatever. Mom says that every time he gets in front of the town council, he acts like he's dressing the Supreme Court."

"You mean addressing."

"Uh-uh, I mean dressing." Wiping her mouth again, Marti angled a mischievous grin at him. "Martha Merryweather says the mayor likes to, you know, wear frilly girl stuff under his trousers."

Coughing up soda, Hank set down the can and stared at the child, who made no attempt to hold back a saucy, self-satisfied grin. "Now, how on earth would Martha Merryweather know what the mayor wears under his trousers?"

"Oh, you'd be real surprised what Martha knows," Marti insisted, then launched into a racy tale about clandestine affairs of the lusty, thrice-widowed motel owner, whose husbands and at least two lovers were rumored to have expired in the throes of passion, to meet their Maker wearing nothing but a satisfied smile. "If you know what I mean," the girl added with a just-between-us-kids elbow nudge.

"Yes," Hank murmured, tugging the neck of his T-shirt. "I know what you mean." He leaned against the freshly sanded clapboards, crossing his ankles. "Are you sure you're only nine?"

Marti giggled. "Mom says I'm precocious."

"Your mom is right."

Flashing a proud smile, Marti hoisted her soda can for another noisy slurp, then glanced toward the parking lot in time to see Steve Ruskin drive in. She issued a resigned sigh, but made no other comment.

Hank followed her gaze. "I thought you liked Steve."

"He's okay. I mean, he's real nice to my mom and stuff, but he's always, you know, fussing about things. He's got Mom all worried about losing the diner and going broke and living on the street like a bag lady."

The reminder of Rae's very real problems hit Hank like a cold fist. He hesitated, choosing his words carefully. "Your mother doesn't strike me as a person who'd allow someone else to tell her what to worry about. If she's concerned about the diner's future, she must have good reason to be."

Marti shrugged, unwilling to concede that. "Gramps says worrying doesn't get a body anywhere. He says that God gave us strong backs and clear minds, and if we use them right, we can have anything in the whole world as long as we want it bad enough."

Glancing away, Hank rubbed his eyelids, feeling sick. Feeling empty. Once he'd shared that childlike vision, that fairy-tale confidence. He'd viewed life as a banquet of wondrous adventures, a feast consumed by those with the guts and the spirit to partake. Hank had gorged himself at that table, turning away from a mundane, meat-and-potatoes existence to taste spicier dishes, more exotic fare.

But a repast without nourishment withers the heart and poisons the soul. That was life's true lesson, a lesson Hank had learned too late.

Rae stepped softly onto the warped planking that served as the bungalow's ratty front porch. Her knuckles paused an inch from the peeling green door, held there by a sudden frisson of apprehension. She could have sent Marti to deliver the message. Instead, she'd chosen to come herself. And she wondered why.

Chewing her lower lip, Rae squared her shoulders and rapped sharply. A split second later the door opened. She staggered back, touching her throat.

Hank Flynn stood there like a mythical god, his glossy mane wet and wild, his chest bare and shining, a white towel draped around his neck like captive prey. There was a savage quality to him; he exuded danger, excitement, the ultimate in masculine strength and grace.

The scent of soapy pine wafted from the doorway. He smelled of freshness and musk, and of maleness masked by manufactured grooming products designed to disguise but not erase the erotic aroma of his gender. He smelled of supple leather and laundromats, of shampoo and turpentine, fresh powder and sawdust, and of sweet memories.

His gaze devoured her softly, but with a thunderous power that transported her back to another time, a time of love and laughter and a happiness so bright she'd thought it would last forever. It hadn't lasted, of course. The end had come swiftly and tragically, plunging her world into darkness. Until Hank Flynn had turned on a light—

"Hello," he said, raising the towel hem to dab his damp face.

She stood there staring, vaguely aware of a peculiar ache in her chest.

"Is anything wrong?"

As Rae opened her mouth to speak, the breath she'd been holding rushed out like a sexually satisfied sigh. Horrified, she concealed her embarrassment with a feigned cough, yanking her gaze away from the doorway and focusing somewhere in the dim depth of the tiny, one-room cottage. "Everything's fine, thank you. I just, ah, came to tell you——" Her mind went blank.

He cocked his head, waiting.

"Something," she finished lamely.

With his powerful hands clutching each end of the draped towel, he smiled. Just a tiny curve of the mouth, but enough to focus attention on firm, sculpted lips beneath his dark mustache. His eyes warmed with empathy. "You look tired. Has anyone ever told you that you work too hard?"

"No, actually, no one ever has." She twisted her hands together, a nervous childhood habit that returned to haunt her when she was feeling particularly vulnerable. "I, ah, haven't had a chance to thank you yet."

"Thank me?"

"For yesterday, when you were ready to hike twenty miles to search for my wayward daughter."

Shifting, he released the towel long enough to run his fingers through his damp hair. "It was nothing."

"It wasn't nothing," Rae insisted, her gaze riveted on the roughened planes of his face. Odd, she thought, that she hadn't noticed the small scar on the side of his nose, along with a slight hump at the bridge, as if it had been badly broken and poorly healed. "When Marti didn't get off that bus, I went to pieces inside. I wasn't thinking rationally, and you were. It may not have seemed like it at the time, but your calmness, your determination to find her gave me a very real sense that—I don't know—that everything would be all right. And it was."

Hank, clearly unsettled, wiped his palms together, avoiding her gaze. "Everything would have been all right whether I'd been there or not."

"Yes, but you were there, and I'm grateful."

He shrugged, nodded, sucked in a breath and scratched the back of his neck. "I was just cleaning up for supper," he said, slanting her a glance that plainly begged a change of subject. "What's the diner's Saturday-night special?"

"Fried chicken," she replied quickly, remembering why she'd come in the first place. "Also, I wanted to let you know that the diner closes at noon on Sundays, so I hope you won't mind having supper with us at the house. We'll be back from afternoon church services by four, and we usually eat about six—" she sucked a quick breath "—unless that's too early for you...or too late? I don't want you to starve waiting. I'll, ah, pack you a lunch before we close up."

He was watching her with his mouth slightly ajar and a frown of disbelief.

Rae knew she was babbling incoherently, but for some reason, every circuit running from her brain to her tongue had misfired. If her mind had been a computer, it would have flashed a "General Protection Fault" error and crashed to a blank screen, which would have been a massive relief, because silence was a blessing compared to the mad utterings of an idiot.

"Sunday is Hobie's day in the kitchen," Rae was saying, with a grin that felt as if it had been thumbtacked in place. "The diner kitchen, that is, because heaven knows I'd never let him in *my* kitchen—not that he can't cook, of course, because if he couldn't cook, I wouldn't let him near the diner, either, but I do because the regular cook doesn't work on Sunday and it's such a busy morning, what with people wanting breakfast either before church or after, depending on whether they prefer early services or late. Which do you prefer? Or do you even go to church? Not that there's anything wrong if you don't. I mean, some very nice people don't go to church regularly, and that doesn't necessarily mean that they're going to hell or anything—"

Dear Lord, please strike me mute.

"Although according to our pastor, anyone who's ever

had a sinful thought is going to hell, which means just about everyone on earth, and certainly the entire population of Gold River, because I don't think there's a single person here who hasn't had at least one sinful thought—"

Please, please, tear out my tongue!

"Except maybe the children, very young ones, like, under the age of three, because I don't know about anyone else's children, but mine started having sinful thoughts as soon as she was old enough to figure out how to pick a lock on the candy drawer, then lie about the chocolate spread all over her face—"

Forget mute. Just strike me dead.

"But that's not really a sin-type thing, is it? I mean, all little kids lie because they don't know any better. They're still works-in-progress, after all. Oh, gracious, look at the time." She ripped her gaze away from his blank eyes and stared at her naked wrist, hoping he wouldn't notice she wasn't wearing a watch.

"Well," she chirped as her traitorous eyes shifted toward a tantalizing arrow of dark hair pointing from his muscular abdomen toward the gaping snap at the waistband of his jeans. Talk about sinful thoughts... "Gotta go. See you."

Spinning on her sneakers, she practically sprinted through the woods, a mad dash that didn't slow until she'd rushed into the safety of her own living room. She slammed the front door, then sagged against it, panting. "All right," she murmured, raising her eyes toward heaven. "You've had your fun. You can wake me up now."

The wind howled with laughter.

"Sit by me!" Marti squeaked, patting a vacant stool.

Hank dodged his way through the crush of customers to join the child, who was attacking a sticky stack of pancakes with gleeful enthusiasm. He sat down, taken aback by the flurry of activity. Rae hadn't been exaggerating when she said Sunday mornings were busy. He glanced around, finally spotting Rae behind the cash register, where she was madly ringing up order slips while a milling line of churchly-dressed folks awaited their turn to pay.

"If you want breakfast, it'll take a while, on account of Gramps isn't too fast." Marti took a gulp of milk and started to wipe her mouth with her hand when, having apparently realized where she was, she skimmed a wary glance at her preoccupied mother and snatched up a paper napkin instead. She rotated the stool until she was facing Hank. "Want me to take your order? Mom lets me help out on Sundays."

Before Hank could reply, a familiar—and clearly irritated—voice echoed from the kitchen. "When I say 'pick up,' I mean sometime this year, dang it."

"I'll be right there," Rae called over her shoulder.

"Them poor hens been working their feathers off," Hobie grumbled from his invisible post behind the passthrough counter. "It's only respectful to serve up their eggs while they's still spitting steam."

Issuing a tense smile to the next customer in line, Rae excused herself, balanced several breakfast plates on her arm and whisked the meals to a family in booth five. A moment later she was back at the cash register.

"Well, whaddaya want?"

"Hmm?" Hank glanced over to see a pair of bright green eyes peering across the counter. After Marti hoisted herself up, presumably on a small step stool, Hank saw that she was holding an order pad. "Aren't there child labor laws against this kind of thing?"

Marti giggled. "Does that mean I don't hafta do dishes or even clean my room?"

"I don't think the laws go quite that far." He propped

a forearm on the counter, slipping a concerned glance at the child's frazzled mother. "How about a cup of coffee?"

"Don't you want anything else? Gramps isn't *that* bad a cook." Shielding her mouth with her hand, she whispered, "I'd stay away from the soft-boiled eggs, though. He makes them kinda gooey."

"Coffee's fine."

With a lackadaisical shrug, Marti scurried behind the counter, snagged a half-full coffee carafe and a fat ceramic mug and served up the steamy brew like a pro. "Mom said we should make you a lunch, too. What kind of sandwich do you want?"

"You don't have to do that. I doubt I'll starve in one day."

"I dunno. You're kinda skinny for a guy."

"Thanks."

"Oh, don't get all bent. You're still a babe."

Fortunately, Hank hadn't gotten the coffee mug to his mouth yet. He peered over the rim. "A what?"

"A babe," Marti explained patiently. "That's a really cute guy. I heard some old ladies talking. They think you're a real hunk."

"Old ladies?"

"Uh-huh." The girl nodded toward the corner booth. "Those over there."

Hank followed her gaze and saw two attractive women in their mid-thirties eyeing him with blatant appreciation. He turned away, feeling an embarrassed flush crawl up his throat. "At least Madeline Rochester isn't one of them."

"Madeline Rochester wouldn't give you the time of day," Marti replied with just a hint of indignation. "Everyone knows she's got the hots for Gramps. Is ham and cheese okay?"

"Ham and cheese?" Glancing across the counter,

Hank saw that the insistent child had already laid out two pieces of white bread.

"You don't want tuna, do you?" Marti rolled her eyes. "Honestly, I get so sick of tuna. Sometimes I think Mom forgets there's anything else a person can make a sandwich out of. It's a wonder I haven't grown gills." She blinked, leaning across the counter. "So, what'll it be?"

"Ham and cheese is fine."

"Good choice."

As Marti slathered out a generous scoop of mayonnaise, Hank's attention refocused on Rae, who was laughing happily, apparently amused by a customer's joke. She laid several bills in the man's palm, closing the register drawer with her flat tummy. Along with her usual work uniform—a white blouse, black slacks and the ever-present, pocketed apron—she wore a droopy pink sweater, which she'd probably donned to ward off the predawn chill. Now, however, the crush of customer body heat had warmed the place almost beyond comfort, although Rae seemed too busy to notice.

But nothing about Rae Hooper escaped Hank's notice. Every inch of her slender frame was fascinating, but it was her lovely face that drew his most rapt attention. There was something ethereal about her expression. He couldn't tear his gaze away, and was mesmerized by the tiny lines bracketing her full mouth, and by the way her thickly lashed eyes squinted when she smiled. Despite smudges of obvious fatigue, there was genuine joy in her eyes. She loved her work. She loved the diner.

And she was in danger of losing both.

"What kind of chips?"

Hank focused back on Marti, who was quizzically eyeing a carousel of cellophane bags. His gaze settled on a particularly colorful one. "How about cheese puffs?"

"Sure." Marti tucked the requested item in the bag and set it on the counter in front of Hank. "I'm really glad you're coming to dinner tonight. We're gonna have so much fun—'' Her smile flattened as she gazed past his shoulder.

Turning around, Hank looked straight into Steve Ruskin's angry eyes. Ruskin stared at Hank as if seeing a roach in his soup, then stalked across the diner, found an empty stool and sat there, brooding.

"Well, maybe not *that* much fun," Marti murmured with a pained sigh. "He's gonna be there, too."

Hank, having been shooed away from his construction project because Rae wouldn't allow him to work on Sunday, paced his tiny bungalow and watched out the window, waiting. By the time Hobie's old pickup truck shuddered out to the street, Hank's boot heels were in the starting block. The truck turned left, heading up the hill toward church.

Hank waited until it disappeared from sight, then took off for the Hooper house, filled with nervous determination.

Rae's old car sat in the driveway, sad and rejected. Hank patted the oxidized hood. "Keep your chin up," he mumbled as he scanned through the windshield. "You'll be humming down the road in no time."

Opening the unlocked driver door, he peered inside. There was an empty lunch bag on the floor, along with a couple of wadded-up pages out of a coloring book. No water pump, though. The thought crossed his mind that Hobie might have been stretching the truth about having procured a replacement pump. It wouldn't have been the first time the old geezer had embellished intent into action.

There was always a chance that Hank could coax the old pump back to life, but installing was considerably faster than rebuilding. On a hunch, he used his pocketknife to pop the trunk. There, between a rusted jack arm and a pile of crumpled blankets, was Hobie's junkyard water pump.

Relieved, Hank studied the pump, which thankfully included a rubber dust seal that was in fairly good condition. Palming it, Hank closed the trunk and went around to hoist the hood. He gave the air cleaner an affectionate rub, thinking that they just didn't make cars like this anymore—sturdy, roomy, easy to work on without having to pull the whole damned engine. With any luck, he should be long gone before the family returned. Assuming, of course, he could find the tools he needed.

Using his trusty pocketknife again, he jimmied the garage door, then headed straight for a corner piled with cardboard boxes so thick with dust that they'd probably been there since the 1930s. Beside the stack of boxes, almost totally obscured by a cockeyed tire propped against the stud wall, was a small tool box.

Hank grabbed it, headed back to the driveway and went to work.

Two hours later, as he'd just finished hot-wiring the ignition to test the newly installed pump for leaks, Hobie's truck rumbled up the driveway.

Rae emerged from her father's truck cab, clearly stunned. "What are you doing?"

Clearing his throat, Hank wiped his hands on a rag. "I, ah, put in your new water pump."

"New—?" She shook her head, smoothing the lace bodice of her demure but sinfully flattering church dress. "I don't understand."

At this point, Hobie, looking Sunday spiffy in a Western-style cowboy shirt and brown Dockers, emerged to hobble around his truck. His rheumy gaze bounced from the exposed engine, which was humming happily, to the cluttered tool chest lying beside the right front tire. The old man then studied the open garage door before focusing on Hank, who was growing more apprehensive by the moment.

"Hobie picked up a new pump last week," Hank told Rae, although he never took his eyes off the old man's face. "He asked me to take a look at it."

Rae spun toward her father. "You did that?"

Hooking his thumbs in his empty belt loops, Hobie rocked back on his boots, regarding Hank thoughtfully. "Guess maybe I did."

Rae massaged her forehead, looking as unnerved as Hank felt. "I'm so sorry," she said finally, spreading her hands in a pleading gesture. "You must think us awful, the way we keep taking advantage of you. Naturally, I'll pay you for your trouble."

"It wasn't any trouble." Reaching inside the open driver door, Hank plucked the twisted wires apart, and the engine shuddered into silence. "I adjusted the idle, and tweaked the plugs a bit. It's running pretty good now, but keep an eye on the engine temperature. If it starts to creep up, let me know. We may have to change the thermostat." As he spoke, Hank followed Hobie's gaze back to the open garage door. "I took a chance that you'd keep tools in the garage," he said quickly. "Most people do."

For once, Hobie had nothing to say.

Hank wasn't particularly reassured, and was relieved when Rae's efforts to get Marti out of the truck suddenly took center stage.

"Come out of there," Rae said, her patience waning. "You can change as soon as you get into the house."

"Make Hank go away," came the whiny reply. "Then I'll come out."

Startled, Hank met Rae's resigned gaze with one of surprise. "Is Marti angry with me?"

"No." Heaving a parental sigh, she bit her lower lip,

as if trying to stave off a smile. "She's just a little, well, embarrassed."

"Why?"

The smile Rae had been struggling with broke free. She turned quickly, concealing it behind a loose fist. A moment later Marti climbed out of the pickup, scowling and furious, garbed in a frilly, bibbed thing that looked for all the world like a ruffled, grape-and-lemon fruit salad. She flopped against the fender, arms folded, glaring at the ground.

Hank swallowed, at a loss.

The child skewed him with a look. "Don't even think about saying how 'cute' I look."

"The thought hadn't occurred to me," he replied honestly.

"Good, because then I would have to kill you, and the diner would never get painted." With that, she flung herself away from the pickup truck and stomped into the house.

When the front door slammed shut, Rae lowered her hands to reveal a lush mouth twisted by suppressed laughter. She tried to speak, swallowed a giggle, then tried again. "Marti, ah, isn't fond of ruffles."

"I can see why."

"Yes, well, it was a gift." She coughed into her hand, then tilted her head, eyeing him thoughtfully. "Thank you for fixing my car. I can't tell you what a relief it is to have reliable transportation again."

He shrugged, uncomfortably aware that Hobie was still staring with unnerving acuity. "No problem. I'll, uh, just finish cleaning up here."

Rae nodded, twisting her fingers together. She took a step toward the house, then paused, slanting a glance toward Hank. "I hope you like pot roast."

"Yes, ma'am."

Her smile sent a ray of sunshine into the center of his chest. "Good. I'll call you when it's ready."

Hank watched, mesmerized, until Rae had disappeared into the house and the swinging screen door broke the spell. Tucking the grease rag into his pocket, he knelt, and as he tossed tools back into the metal carrying case, a pair of scuffed boots settled in his line of sight. He glanced up to see Hobie standing over him, scratching his Sunday-shaved chin.

The old man eyed the toolbox, then perused the inside of the engine. "Hot-wired her, didya?"

Hank placed a rachet in the tool case and snapped the lid. "I couldn't check out the pump unless the engine was running."

"Makes sense," Hobie said agreeably.

Standing slowly, Hank hoisted the closed carrying case in his left hand. "I hope you don't mind that I borrowed your tools."

"Dang things ain't mine." Turning his face, Hobie spat on a rock. "Someone left 'em here, long time ago. I don't guess he'd mind seeing 'em get some use now and again." The old man ambled toward the house, pausing at the porch. "You might as well put them tools away," he said with a crafty gleam in his eye. "Seeing as how you already know where they belong."

Chapter Six

"I don't see why you had to invite him," Steve grumbled. "He's a bad influence on Marti."

Rae glanced up from the carrots she was peeling. "Why on earth would you say that? Hank's been wonderful with Marti. She adores him."

Apparently that wasn't what Steve wanted to hear. His comma-shaped brows dipped into a frowning furrow between guppy blue eyes. "Which is exactly my point," he argued. "The man is a vagabond, a drifter. What kind of role model is that for an impressionable young girl?"

"He's not trying to be a role model, Steve. He's trying to be a friend, and for my money, he's doing a fine job of it. Would you hand me that knife? Thanks."

As Rae sliced the carrots into fat chunks, Steve hovered in the kitchen like a worried honeybee. "A child like Marti does not need a scraggly hitchhiker as a friend. She needs children her own age."

"She has lots of friends her own age."

"I mean female friends, little girls who nurture baby dolls, and have tea parties and play dress-up with their mommy's clothes. Little girls who are developing a sense of their own style and femininity."

There seemed no sense in reminding him that when it came to style, Marti was in a class by herself. Steve steadfastly refused to recognize that notion, let alone accept its validity. It was a divisive chasm in their relationship, this frantic insistence Steve had to imprint his values onto Marti's impressionable little mind.

Not that his values were bad; they were, in fact, quite universal—hearth, home, two-parent family, with each member firmly ensconced in his or her carefully constructed place. A strong, responsible father figure; a nurturing, loving mom; children who are cherished, guided and unquestionably loved.

It was, after all, the family Rae had always dreamed about, complete with the emotional and financial security that seemed destined to bless other families, but never her own. It was what she wanted for Marti. It was not, however, what Marti wanted for herself.

Muffled screeches vibrated through the wall separating the kitchen from Hobie's living area. "Roll me o-over, in the clo-over...aww-rk! Cruncho Flakes are fun to chew!" *Squawk.* "Gimme a beer dear, Louie's a good bird, cheese puffs!" *Squawk.*

Annoyed, Steve stared at the wall. "What on earth is wrong with that animal?"

"Hmm? Oh, I don't know. Louie's been kind of agitated this afternoon. Maybe Hobie forgot his Sunday sunflower seeds or something."

"Birds are disgusting creatures," Steve mumbled, smoothing his conservative navy suit coat. "I don't know how you can live with all that noise."

"Louie's part of the family. As for noise—" She

jerked her thumb toward the living room just as a raucous cheer sent Steve marching to the kitchen doorway.

"Good grief," he muttered, clearly distressed. "They're watching hockey. *Hockey!*"

"Marti loves hockey," Rae replied, dumping the carrot chunks into the bubbling broth. "In fact, Marti loves all sports."

Steve waved that away as irrelevant. "Yes, yes, but hockey isn't even a real sport. It's a bloodbath on skates. Grown men pounding each other with sticks, tripping, punching, maiming. My God, it's positively barbaric." He glanced back just as Rae dumped the last of the vegetables into the pot. "Be careful not to cook the carrots too long, or all the nutrients will be boiled out."

"I know how you like your carrots, Steve."

He crossed the room to peer over her shoulder. "Potatoes can be mushy, of course, but other vegetables are ruined if they don't require a bit of tooth— Are those onions?"

She covered the pot, obscuring his view. "Pearl onions."

"I despise onions."

"They're just to add a little interest. You can pick them out."

"Of course." His disappointment, punctuated by a brave-but-tortured smile, pricked her conscience.

"I made homemade biscuits."

He brightened. "For me?"

Among others, she thought, but said only, "Yes."

Plainly delighted by that, Steve took hold of her shoulders, turning her to face him. His eyes glowed with childlike pleasure. "You are so very thoughtful, Rae, and so very kind."

"It's just a batch of biscuits, Steve."

"But you made them for me. Don't you see how special that is?"

Rae tensed, knowing from experience where the conversation was heading. Avoiding his gaze, she studied the fingernail she'd just torn while opening the knife drawer, and hoped he'd deduce from her body language that this was a discussion she'd prefer to postpone.

Reading body language, however, was not Steve's forte. "That's what I love about you, Rae, your kindness and compassion. I need that in my life." His grip tightened. "I need you in my life."

"Steve—"

"Marry me, Rae. Now, today. We can drive to Tahoe in less than an hour."

She licked her lips. "How very, uh, spontaneous. You surprise me."

"I can be spontaneous," he insisted, his bulgy eyes wide and imploring. "I can be anything you want me to be. I love you, Rae."

"We've discussed this before," she said carefully. "You know how much I care about you, and what a fine, fine man I think you are. I'm honored that you want to marry me, but—"

"But you don't love me."

"Not yet, not in the way you deserve to be loved."

"That will come, and if it doesn't, there are more important criteria in selecting a life partner. Respect, for example, compatibility, matching goals and similar values. You need stability in your life, Rae, and so does Marti. She requires guidance, a strong hand, a father figure to provide a firm male model in her life."

"She has Hobie," Rae countered, realizing even as she spoke how ludicrous that was. Before she could modify the pronouncement, another jeer rose up from the living-room hockey watchers.

"Ooh!" Marti squealed. "Did you see how hard he fell? Ooh, ooh, *ooh!* Wow! He really got smacked that time."

"Penalty," Hank agreed. "While they're playing a man down, we have a chance to score."

Hobie's raspy voice joined the fray. "Reminds me of the winter of '74, when Dungaree Dugan was a-fighting the Sandusky boys over an ice fishing hole up on the summit. Whapped 'em with his rod, he did. Well, sir, that there was the bloodiest row ever seen in them parts..."

The rest of Hobie's story was drowned out by crowd screams from the television.

Steve spread his hands. "I rest my case."

"I know," Rae mumbled, frustrated and feeling trapped. "My father is basically a good person, and he absolutely adores Marti, but Hobie will always be, well, Hobie. We have to accept people, warts and all, I suppose."

"Your father lives in a fantasy world of illusion, false hope and foolish dreams. Is that what you want for your daughter?"

Rae turned away, unwilling to answer. Of course she didn't want Marti to emulate those idealistic fantasies, but she didn't want to be put in the position of criticizing the man who had, despite his faults, done the best that he could for his family. If it hadn't always seemed good enough, well, perhaps Rae's expectations were too high.

That had always been a problem for her, after all—expecting too much from people, expecting too much from life. She'd wanted her father to throw away his dreams and take on hers instead. That had been unfair, just as it had been unfair to expect that Martin would instantly evolve from the adventurous thrill-seeker with whom she'd fallen in love into a stable banker-type in a three-piece suit.

Rae had equally unfair expectations of herself, the most blatant of which was the condition that marriage required the same heart-pounding, pulse-stopping, dizzying sense of romantic love that she'd felt for Martin. Intellectually, she knew that would never happen, just as she knew that Steve Ruskin would make the perfect husband and father. He was everything she'd ever wanted in a man.

Heaven help her, Rae truly wanted to love Steve. All these months she'd waited patiently, hoping against hope that elusive sparks would ignite into the flame of love and eventually lead to physical intimacy. So far, that hadn't happened. The kisses she and Steve shared had yet to elicit even a tingle and seemed, in fact, more like the chaste expression of sibling affection than true passion between lovers.

As much as Rae had hoped that would change, she secretly knew that it wouldn't. Martin had been her one true love. Deep down, she realized that no man would or could usurp his place in her heart. Since his death ten years ago, she'd never so much as looked at a man with longing.

At least, not until Hank Flynn came along.

Rae acknowledged a visceral attraction to the handsome stranger, although she was deeply perplexed by it. Hank Flynn was the polar opposite of all that she wanted in her life, and all that she needed. He was dangerous, reckless, unpredictable, a man for whom the road was a lover, for whom the uncharted adventure beckoned with erotic allure. He was heartbreak in blue jeans, mysterious, aloof, secretive, the last person on earth any reasonable woman would allow into her life.

He was also the most exciting man she'd met in years.

"Louie!" Hobie hollered from his easy chair in front of the television set. "Gol-dang it, bird, shut your beak." Shifting his bony rump, the old man shook his head, muttering. "Dadgummed parrot makes such a ruckus, a body can't hear hisself think."

Louie's muffled shrieks continued to vibrate down the hall, rivaled only by crowd noise from the hockey game on TV. A moment later Hobie's attention was riveted on the screen as the home team skated madly toward the goal. Marti, sitting cross-legged on the floor, pumped her fists, bouncing and cheering loudly enough that the bird's plaintive wail was swallowed up by her excited squeals.

Hank stretched his legs, shifting sideways on the sofa. A glance toward the kitchen confirmed that Rae and Ruskin were still inside, apparently engrossed in serious conversation. Hank had been furtively watching them for the past hour, wishing he could read lips.

He knew the conversation was none of his business, but he'd have sawed his arm off with a steak knife for the opportunity to hear what was being said.

"Aw-rrk! Louie's a good bird, cheese puffs!"

The scratchy scream from the hallway propelled Hank into action. With both Hobie and Marti completely mesmerized by the exciting climax of the game, Hank figured he could slip away without much notice.

He figured wrong.

"Whatcha doing?" Hobie asked just as Hank reached the doorway leading into the bedroom wing of the house.

Pausing, Hank tossed a casual glance over his shoulder. "Bathroom."

Hobie eyed him a moment. "End of the hall, on your left."

"Thanks." He followed directions, past the doorway leading to a mess of crumpled clothes and clutter that he presumed to be Marti's room, then past Rae's bedroom, which was as neat and tidy as he'd expected.

Louie's scratchy bird-babble emanated from behind a closed door across the corridor from Rae's room.

Finding the bathroom, Hank went inside long enough to turn on the light, then stepped back into the hall and pulled the bathroom door shut so that anyone looking down the hall would assume the room to be occupied. He angled a quick glance through the corridor to make certain he couldn't be seen from the living area, then went directly to Hobie's room and slipped inside.

Louie greeted him with a stubby wing flap and a shriek of pure delight. "Whaddaya know, Joe? Cheese puffs!"

"Hush," Hank whispered, digging into his jeans pockets to pull out three slightly squashed cheese puffs. The bird went wild. "If I give you these, will you settle down and be quiet?"

Louie bobbed his head. "Louie's a good bird."

"Yeah, yeah." Hank laid the treats on the dresser beside the parrot's perch.

Instantly the animal leapt from the perch and flappity-hopped over to snag one of the lumpy orange-yellow tubes in his claw. "Roll me over," Louie croaked happily between bites. "In the clover. Gimme beer, dear."

"Don't press your luck."

"Aw-rrk."

"You're a royal pain in the tail," he told the munching bird. "I kept my part of the bargain. You keep yours."

"Fast, fast, fa-ast relief!" *Crunch*.

Beating a stealthy retreat, Hank peeked into the hallway and, finding it empty, slipped out, closing Hobie's door behind him. He sneaked back into the bathroom, flushed the commode, counted to five, then headed back to the living room, where Marti was glaring at the television as if wishing it dead.

"We lost," she grumbled. "What a rip."

Hank settled back onto the sofa. "We'll take them next time."

"Next time I'm gonna bet on the other guys."

"Bet?" Hank glanced at Hobie, who was grinning broadly. "Tell me you aren't actually going to take a little girl's money."

"'Course not," Hobie replied with appropriate indignation. "I don't go a-betting hard cash with young'uns. What kind of grampa do you think I am? We just had us a little chore wager to make things int'resting."

He studied Marti's irritated face, noting that the bridge of her nose puckered the same way Rae's did. "A chore wager?"

Marti gave a glum nod. "Taking out trash is supposed to be Gramps's job, but now I'll have to do it for a whole week."

"What if you'd won?"

The girl's eyes lit with a crafty gleam. "Then Gramps would have had to write my book report for me."

Hank flinched at the thought. "Somehow, I think you're better off having lost."

"Hey, now, I can read and write, don'tcha know. I done right good in school, too."

Rae appeared in the doorway, arms crossed, lips pursed with disapproval. "Probably because you coasted through by scamming some poor schlock into doing your homework, the same way Marti was trying to scam you."

Hobie shrank into his easy chair as if trying to disappear. Marti, however, responded with wide-eyed innocence that was as transparent as cellophane. "Why, we were just fooling around, Mom. I wouldn't have really let Gramps do my book report, just like he's not *really* going to make me do his chores."

"Huh?" Hobie reared out of his chair.

Marti batted her eyes at him. "Well, you're not, *are* you?"

Hobie swallowed hard, shifting his beady eyes from Rae to Marti and back again. "Well, 'course not. We was, uh, just joshing."

"I see." The knowing sparkle in Rae's eyes clearly indicated that she wasn't fooled by either her father's denial of the wager or the wily way her daughter had weaseled out of fulfilling its terms. "Dinner's almost ready," she told Marti. "Will you please set the table?"

"Okay."

"Need help?" Hank asked as the girl scampered to a huge antique buffet in the dining room.

The offer seemed to please her. "Sure. You can do the silverware and stuff."

Hank tossed down the magazine he'd been about to peruse, and went into the dining room, where Marti had just removed five dinner plates from the buffet's upper shelves. "We're using good china," she told Hank. "On account of it being Sunday and all."

"Gee, and here I thought it was because of me." With a wink at the giggling child, he reached into the center drawer of the buffet and began counting out place settings of Sunday silver. He scooped up the flatware and set them around the plates the way he'd been taught as a child. "Sharp knives or dull?"

Marti glanced up, then over at the open drawer. "How'd you know where the silverware was?"

"Hmm? Oh, lucky guess. Most people keep their good silver in the same place as the good china. Say, where are the glasses?"

"I'll get them." Marti retrieved the crystal water glasses from the buffet's lower cupboard and handed them up to Hank, who situated them carefully around the table.

He looked up to see Marti eyeing him strangely. "What's the matter, do I have crumbs on my chin?"

"Uh-uh. I was just wondering... I mean, you really like it here, don't you, Hank?"

A cautious tingle eased across his nape. "Yes."

"So maybe you could stay around for a while, you know, after you're done with the diner and stuff. I mean, there's lots of work around here. Almost every building in town is being fixed up, and you could help." She peeked up from beneath a thick fringe of stubby, red-blond lashes. "Couldn't you?"

Steve Ruskin, who'd apparently been eavesdropping just beyond view in the kitchen, now stuck his head through the doorway, visibly shaken. "Marti, please come into the kitchen. Your mother needs help." Before she could protest, Ruskin plucked the glasses out of her hand. "I'll finish up here."

Marti eyed him for a moment as if deciding whether or not to comply, then heaved a sigh, angled Hank a see-what-I-put-up-with eye roll and trudged into the kitchen.

When the child was gone, Ruskin set the glasses in place. "So, Rae tells me you're from Atlanta."

"I spent some time there."

"That's not where you're from? Originally, that is."

Hank studied the table. "Napkins," he murmured, slipping Ruskin a pleasant smile. "Do you know where Rae keeps them?"

"Ah, in the buffet. First drawer."

Hank already had his hand on the knob. "Thanks."

After removing five neatly folded linen squares, Hank made a production of arranging them above each china plate, hoping Ruskin would drop the inquisition about his past.

"Actually, I've never understood why folks use linen napkins," Hank announced, initiating a verbal spurt considerably more loquacious than the terse replies that had been his custom. "Me, I'm a paper man myself. I mean, why do all that extra washing and ironing if you can just wad the darn thing up when you're through and toss it away, right? Then again, there are always environmental concerns. Like, when does a tree's right to live outweigh a human's God-given need for a clean face? A moral dilemma, wouldn't you say?"

Ruskin stared at him. "Did you move frequently as a

child, or has your traveling life-style been a more recent acquisition?''

So much for distraction, Hank thought. The man had the tenacity of a prosecutorial pit bull.

Marti's fortuitous reappearance with a fragrant bowl of fresh biscuits provided the distraction Hank had been seeking. Hobie, who'd been watching the interchange between Hank and Steve with amused interest, now hobbled to the table, sniffing the air like a starved grizzly. "Umm, if that don't put a man's mouth to watering. Where's the gravy?''

"Coming up.'' Rae floated from the kitchen to set a steaming boat of dark gravy on the table, thanking Hank when he yanked open the middle buffet drawer to retrieve the gravy ladle. "Would you get the carving knife, too? Oh, and we'll need serving spoons.''

"How many?''

"Three should do it.''

Ruskin, having been eased into a corner by the flurry of activity, tried to regain Hank's attention. "I believe we were discussing—''

"Coming through.'' Marti ducked under Ruskin's arm to plop a heaped bowl of mashed potatoes on the table.

Ruskin pressed against the wall, his head swiveling, his bulgy eyes blinking madly.

"Serving spoon,'' Marti called to Hank, who whipped one out of the drawer, and faked left.

"Go deep!''

She danced around the table edge, holding out her hands. "I'm clear, lemme have it!''

Hobie sat down, smacked his lips and snagged a biscuit.

"Fourth and goal,'' Hank said, miming a spiral pass with the spoon as he leaned over and plopped it into the girl's outstretched hand.

"Where's the butter?" Hobie asked of no one in particular.

Marti's arm arched in front of her oblivious grandfather's nose as she jammed the serving spoon into the bowl of potatoes. "Touchdown!"

Ruskin was horrified. "Martina, really—"

"Biscuits ain't no good without butter," Hobie whined.

"Watch out." Zipping out of the kitchen, Rae hoisted the roast platter over Marti, who was doing a wiggle-butt victory dance at the end of the table. "Marti, would you please bring in the peas?"

"Sure."

Hobie looked up. "And the butter."

"Okay, Gramps."

"Wow," Hank murmured as Rae set down a platter of melting tender meat surrounded by a colorful array of steamed vegetables. "Onions."

She flushed prettily. "Ah, Steve, would you like to carve the roast?"

If Ruskin's dark expression was any clue, he'd have rather used the knife on Hank's throat, but all he said was, "Certainly."

As the befuddled fellow set about his task with grim determination, Marti dashed in carrying a bowl of peas, along with a tub of butter that was intercepted by her grandfather. The bowl, however, was circled around the table in an awkward imitation of Hank's serving-spoon spiral pass.

"And the rush is on," Marti chirped, holding the serving dish in midair. "The defense shifts, but wait! The kicker fakes...pitchout, roll left..." She slid the bowl between the salt and pepper shakers, plopping it down with enough force to vibrate a half-dozen peas onto the tablecloth. "Two points!"

The carving knife clattered onto the platter. "That's

enough," Ruskin said, clearly annoyed by the perfor-
mance. "This is Sunday dinner, Martina. Your behavior
is quite inappropriate."

Rae, who'd been hiding a smile behind her hand,
cleared her throat and avoided her daughter's inquiring
gaze. "Steve is right," she said without much conviction.
"Please sit down, sweetie, so we can offer the blessing."

Subdued and embarrassed, Marti flopped into her
chair, clasped her hands at the table edge and glared
down at her empty plate.

"It's my fault," Hank said quickly. "I'm afraid I
started this."

Ruskin gave him a withering look. "Yes, you did."
With that, the man closed his eyes, waiting for silence
before intoning heavenly thanks while Hank, pricked by
guilt at having initiated the behavior for which poor Marti
had been reprimanded, watched from beneath solemnly
lowered lids.

He wanted to resent Ruskin. Instead, he secretly ad-
mired him. Throughout the evening he'd watched the
man consistently treat Rae with affection and respect,
while guiding little Marti with quiet parental direction.
Ruskin was a natural father figure, authoritative and firm,
everything that Hank wanted to be, but wasn't. Rae and
Marti would be okay with a man like Steve Ruskin looking out for them. That was a relief to Hank. Oddly
enough, it was also a major disappointment.

After dinner Rae relaxed in the living room, sipping
coffee and feeling deliciously pampered. Hank and Marti,
having praised her culinary prowess to embarrassing
heights, had insisted on cleaning up the kitchen, a process
punctuated by delightful childish giggles and masculine
laughter that warmed her heart.

It occurred to Rae that with his furtive shell breached,
Hank Flynn had a whimsical sense of humor that was

almost as silly as Martin's. If Steve didn't appreciate Hank's anecdotal absurdities, well, Marti certainly did. Rae had never seen her daughter happier.

"Right odd," Hobie mumbled, shuffling out of the hallway.

Rae glanced past Steve, who was seated beside her on the sofa, scowling at air. "What's odd?"

"Louie's a-sitting on his perch, grinning like he'd just skinned hisself a cat."

"Birds don't grin," Rae observed. "But at least he's finally quieted down. I was about ready to tape his beak shut."

"Yep, he's quiet, all right. Too quiet." Hobie settled into his easy chair, frowning at the television. "What's a porky-pine doing in the middle of my basketball game?"

Steve glanced up. "Martina has seen enough sports for one day. Nature programs are more educational."

"What's educational about a dang porky-pine? She can walk out the back door and see all she wants."

Hobie's protest dissipated as Marti suddenly darted out of the kitchen and dashed down the hallway. A moment later Hank Flynn appeared, looking strangely unnerved. He gazed toward the front door, as if considering a quick retreat, only to be cut off as Marti reappeared carrying a silver picture frame that Rae recognized as containing the portrait of Martin that the child kept by her bed.

Flushed and clearly excited, Marti thrust the photograph into Hank's hands. "This is my daddy," she told him proudly, grinning down at the image of the young soldier with bright eyes and buzzed hair. "He was the bravest man in the whole entire world."

Rae could have sworn Hank flinched.

"Doesn't he look handsome in his uniform?" After posing the breathless question, the girl didn't wait for an answer. "Mom says that the army had to send my daddy to Europe—do you know where that is? Anyway, a whole bunch of people were fighting, so my daddy went to keep them from hurting each other, and then they got mad at my daddy, on account of him being so brave and all." Her voice quivered slightly, slicing an arrow of pain straight into her mother's heart. "Mom says my daddy was a hero, that he died trying to protect his whole entire platoon from the mad people who were shooting at them. Isn't that the bravest thing you ever heard?"

"Yes," Hank whispered, looking positively ill. "Very brave."

"After my daddy died, the army gave him a whole bunch of medals. Mom keeps them in a box in her closet." Marti brightened. "Want to see them?"

"Another time." Handing back the photograph, Hank edged toward the front door. "It's late. I should be going."

"So soon?" Rae stood. "There's pie for dessert."

Marti seconded that with a furious nod, adding, "I thought you were going to teach me how to play cribbage."

He smiled then, touching the child's flushed cheek with the tip of his finger. "Can I take a rain check on that? The truth is, I'm kind of tired."

Plainly disappointed, Marti issued a limp shrug while Hank politely thanked Rae for the meal, then made a beeline for the door.

Outside, he hesitated only long enough to gulp a breath of bracing, frigid air before descending the porch steps and heading down a winding path he knew would lead to the river. The wind lifted his hair, whipping it into his face and blocking his vision. He wiped it away angrily, taking out his fury and his frustration on the hapless strands.

The image of Martin Manning burned into his brain, along with the memory of how Marti's eyes had sparkled with pride when speaking of the father she clearly adored. If she ever learned that her beloved daddy wasn't the courageous icon she thought, her little heart would be broken.

But that wouldn't happen. Marti would never learn the bitter truth about her father. It was a secret Hank would take to his grave.

Chapter Seven

The moon was waning that night, but there was enough illumination to forgo a flashlight, particularly since Rae was heading down a familiar pathway to the creek behind her house. As a child, she'd skipped over the crisp carpet of pine needles, excited simply to be alive. As a teenager, she'd trudged moodily through the thick woods, fighting hormones and hopelessness.

And as a young woman, she'd swooned down the path hand in hand with the only man she'd ever loved.

She'd shared this place with Martin, offering it as a special gift, a piece of herself that was sacred. They'd spent hours there, talking, laughing, making plans for a life together. It had been a shrine to their love.

Then Martin had ruined it.

Now she retreated here to be alone, to relive sweet memories and revile the bad ones, to let the soothing babble of a rushing creek calm her troubled mind.

The pathway ended abruptly at a large boulder. Beyond the massive rock was the creek. She could hear it, feel it, sense the icy flow of purity rushing from its Sierra womb to its warm ocean home. There was a comforting permanence to the creek's travels, a cyclical rebirth that offered a sense of peace, and made the future seem less foreboding.

Rae picked her way around the boulder, following the creek sounds down a gentle embankment. She emerged on a pebbled beach, and almost tripped over him.

Alerted by her startled gasp, he stood quickly, a looming silhouette in the moonlight. The silhouette leaned forward. "Rae?"

She pressed a palm over her pounding heart. "Dear Lord," she whispered between ragged breaths. "You scared me half to death. Again."

Since she'd stepped away from his extended hand, he tucked it into his jeans pocket. "I'm sorry. I didn't expect anyone else to be here."

"Neither did I." She managed a nervous smile. "I suppose we should stop meeting like this. People will talk."

"Yeah, I suppose." He moved from beneath the concealing tree boughs to lean against the trunk, fidgeting with something between his fingers. A moment later he tossed what appeared to be a broken twig into the lapping waters at the edge of the creek.

A strained silence stretched between them. Hank shifted, turning his head so that silver light bounced off the sharp planes of his face. "It's nearly eleven."

"I know." Calmer now, Rae peeled away from the tree against which her back had been pressed. "I couldn't sleep."

"Again?"

She could tell by his voice that he was smiling. She smiled back, although she doubted he could see her clearly enough through the shadows to notice. She stepped out from beneath the tree, emerging into the rocky clearing. "It seems that we're both prone to alleviate insomnia by prowling the woods. How did you find this place?"

He shrugged, turning toward a ribbon of moonlight quivering over the surface of the water. "Just wandering."

"Oh."

She absently rubbed her upper arms, wishing she'd worn a jacket instead of her droopy work sweater. Hank, however, was wearing the same clothes he'd worn to dinner earlier that evening, a thin black cotton T-shirt, blue jeans and boots. He wasn't even wearing the sleeveless denim jacket. "Aren't you cold?"

"Not particularly." He regarded her for a moment, then glanced back up the path. "You'll be all right here? By yourself, I mean."

"You needn't leave."

"I don't want to intrude."

"Actually, I'm the one who's intruding. You were here first, remember?" Oddly enough, Rae was buoyed by Hank's presence. She crossed the small clearing and sat on the flat rock where Martin had first mentioned the overseas assignment from which he'd never returned. The memory was a bitter one, because Martin had told Rae something else that night, something that she'd never revealed to another soul. Something that had broken her heart.

The crunch of pebbles caught her attention. Hank had moved to the edge of the creek, and now squatted down, sitting on his heels as he fingered one of the smooth river rocks blanketing the small beach. "Dinner was great. Thanks again for inviting me."

"You're welcome." Rae wrapped the sweater around her chest, watching him. He moved with such stealth, a graceful fluidity that reminded her of a jungle cat. "Marti was disappointed that you left so early."

He flicked a pebble into the creek, then stood, brushing his palms together. "Marti is a great kid."

"Yes, she is. A bit of a smart aleck at times, but she comes by that honestly, I suppose."

The shadow of his mouth curved. "I'll bet her first words were 'rotten claim jumper.'"

"No, those were Louie's first words. Marti just said 'mama.' Boring, but predictable. After that, though, all bets were off. By the time she was two, her vocabulary was so colorful that she was nearly expelled from preschool."

"Thanks to Hobie, no doubt."

"No doubt at all." Rae scooted over, making room for Hank on the flat bench rock.

He accepted the invitation, sitting so close that she could see the excitement in his shadowed eyes. "Has Marti always been so athletic?"

"Yes, as a matter of fact, she has. From the time she could walk, she wanted to be outside. At three she asked Santa for a baseball and a fielder's mitt." Rae laughed softly. "I made the mistake of getting her a baby doll instead."

"What happened?" Hank asked with surprising eagerness.

"She commandeered a gardening glove, decapitated the poor doll and played ball with its head."

Hank's chuckle rolled into a deep, rollicking belly laugh that did peculiar things to Rae's pulse. After a moment he leaned against a tree that split the bedrock bench and wiped his eyes "That must have been a sight."

"Oh, yes. Hobie was amused. I wasn't."

He regarded her thoughtfully. "So what did you do?"

"I bought her a ball and a mitt, of course, which was exactly what she'd expected me to do."

"That seems a bit calculated for a three-year-old."

"Marti was not your average, run-of-the-mill three-year-old. Don't let those innocent eyes fool you. She's a born bunko artist who can coerce just about anyone into providing what she wants and still manage to convince them that it was all their idea. You wouldn't believe some of the pranks she's pulled over the years."

Hank leaned forward, propping an elbow on his bent knee. "Tell me."

Rae hesitated, momentarily mesmerized by the sudden intensity of his gaze. She moistened her lips, forcing herself to look away. "It's just kid stuff," she finally murmured. "I'm sure you wouldn't be interested."

"I'm interested. Please, tell me everything."

There was something hypnotic about him, something that pierced her very soul. She heard her own voice, soft, hesitant at first, yet quivering with the excitement of sharing all those special moments that mothers love to talk about.

And talk she did, for hours, relaying everything she could remember about Marti's childhood, from the night she was born to her first step, first tooth, first day of school and beyond. Hank was an avid audience, absorbing every detail, every nuance with abject fascination. He laughed when Rae described how Marti took vigilante justice in kindergarten by pasting the class bully's hair to an easel. He looked appropriately shattered during the story about repeated episodes of strep throat that doctors feared might evolve into scarlet fever.

He actually became misty-eyed when told how seven-year-old Marti had stayed up all night nursing a sick kitten, and how the child had sobbed when the tiny animal had died despite her tender ministrations. "Poor little tyke," he murmured, shaking his head. "Children shouldn't have to deal with sickness and death. It isn't right."

"It's the way things are." Twisting the bent twig she'd retrieved from a nearby bush, Rae stared into her lap and shrugged. "If motherhood has taught me anything, it's that life isn't fair. What children should have and what they actually receive are sometimes very different."

She gazed over the creek, remembering that night ten years ago, when Martin had sat where Hank now was. His voice had been quiet, like Hank's, but less mellow, sharper, quivering with youth as he'd uttered the words that had changed the entire course of her life, and that of their unborn child.

"You're thinking about him, aren't you?" Hank asked.

Her gaze snapped around. "Him?"

"Marti's father."

Something cold and tight squeezed her breath away. A lump of pure misery wedged in her throat. Rae looked away, fighting a sudden surge of tears. She didn't respond, because she couldn't.

Hank leaned forward until he was so close she could feel the heat from his body. "Martin's gone," he whispered. "He can't hurt you anymore."

It took a moment for that extraordinary statement to sink in. When it did, she looked up, stunned. "Martin was a wonderful man. He never did anything to hurt me."

"Then why are you crying?"

Rae wiped her eyes. "Because I miss him."

"You miss him because he wasn't there when you needed him." The bitterness in Hank's voice took her by surprise. "He's never been there for you, he's never been there for your child. There's no excuse for that."

Twisting sideways on the rock, Rae stared up and was struck by the hard fury in Hank's eyes. Her voice sounded odd to her own ears, hollow and tinny. "Martin was a soldier. He died for his country."

"Did he?"

"Of course." Angry now, Rae pulled back, turning away from the man who'd committed heresy by verbalizing the pain that had been secretly, silently locked away in her heart. "Martin didn't ask to die. How dare you imply otherwise?"

Below the mustache, Hank's mouth had flattened into a grim line. "I'm sorry. I had no right—"

"You're damn right you didn't." Standing, Rae twisted her fingers together, trying to stop the rush of angry words that flew from her tongue without permission. "Martin loved me. He wanted to marry me, and he would have if he hadn't been ordered overseas. Neither of us knew then that I was pregnant. If he'd known…if he'd known…" She flailed her hands up helplessly. Words failed. Memories crushed down with the weight of utter despair.

Pivoting away, she stumbled to the edge of the creek, pressing her palms to her temples. She didn't want to think, didn't want to remember. It hurt too much.

Behind her, Rae heard the crunch of pebbles and felt Hank's presence a moment before his palms wrapped her shoulders with gentle strength. "If he'd known," he whispered behind her ear, "no power on earth could have kept him away."

Her anger drained as quickly as it had erupted. She turned slowly, and was lost in the depth of his compassion. "How can you possibly know that?"

"I know you," Hank said quietly. "No man, no real man, would ever turn his back on a woman like you, or a child like Marti. If Martin Manning could have come back to you, Rae, he would have."

That was precisely what Rae needed to hear because she was so desperate to believe it. Grateful tears slid down her cheeks, leaving warm trails on her chilled skin. Intellectually, she knew perfectly well that Hank Flynn had no way of knowing what Martin would or wouldn't have done. It didn't matter. She wanted to believe that somehow he *did* know and, most important, that he was right.

"Thank you," she whispered, and was instantly aware that something else was happening, something warm and wonderful.

Hank framed her face with his hands, stroking the callused pad of his thumb across the moistened path of her tears. "The time for tears is over," he murmured. "You're so sweet, so beautiful. You're every man's dream, Rae Hooper. It's time for you to love again, to go on with your life."

"I can't," she whispered, yet was acutely aware that beneath her fingertips his chest muscles vibrated with a power belied by the softness of his gaze. She was hypnotized, completely entranced by his masculinity. By him.

"You can." His mouth was so close she could feel the gentle warmth of his breath against her lips. "You must."

Rae knew Hank would kiss her. Her ankles went limp in anticipation, yet even if she could have moved away, she wouldn't have. She wanted to taste him, to be held and cherished and to feel like a woman again, if only for this moment.

A voice echoed at the edge of her mind. *Really, Rae, this is most inappropriate.* It was Steve Ruskin's voice, tinged with reproach, heavy with disapproval and, as always, impeccably correct.

Rae tuned the voice out, pushed it away, closed her eyes and gave in to the deliciously unfamiliar thrill of doing exactly what she wanted, no matter the consequence.

But she had no way of knowing how intense the consequence would be.

The lightest brush of his lips sent an electrical charge through her entire body. She heard the startled gasp, and knew it had come from her. He might have withdrawn then had her fingers not gone into spasm, clutching and twisting the fabric of his shirt as she pulled him closer, and closer still.

After the merest hesitation he lowered his mouth with excruciating care. She felt the silky stroke of his mustache, and was as surprised by its softness as she was by the erotic thrill of its touch. She'd never thought much about male facial hair one way or the other, but the masculine tickle at the corner of her mouth was the most exquisite sensation she'd ever experienced.

Hank kissed one edge of her lips and then the other before thrusting his fingers deep into her hair and molding his mouth to hers in a kiss so deep, so incredibly hot that Rae felt as if she was melting in his hands. It was fiery, it was passion, it was the ignition of carnal hunger that she'd been waiting for, praying for. It had been inside her all along, dormant and inert, just waiting to burst forth with molten sensuality that left her breathless.

Just waiting, she realized with wonder, for the right man to unlock the hidden passion and set it free.

The emotional explosion ended as quickly as it had begun. Hank suddenly ended the kiss and stepped back, clearly shaken, while Rae swayed forward, clinging to his shirt as the world swirled in vivid hues of fuchsia and violet.

"I—" Hank's voice cracked. He stood there, looking shocked and shattered. "Forgive me."

The red world dissipated slowly, returning to the familiar silver of night. "It's all right," Rae said in a froggy croak that made her cringe inside. "It was...just a kiss."

His shuttered gaze penetrated the lie. It was so much more than that. And they both knew it.

* * *

Hank waited until Rae had waved good-night and slipped into the darkened house, then he shoved his hands into his pockets and walked—no, he bounced through the woods toward his bungalow. He paused at the peeling porch, afraid to enter, afraid he'd view his own body lying in bed and realize that this beautiful evening had been nothing but a dream.

Leaning against the porch pole, Hank crossed his ankles and pulled the tattered photo from his pocket. He gazed at it in wonder, contemplating the indefinable force that had drawn him to Gold River. After reading the article about the town's economic demise, he hadn't expected that Rae Hooper would still be here—and he certainly hadn't expected that she'd have a child.

And never in his wildest dreams could he have anticipated what had happened tonight. The chemistry between him and Rae had been hot enough to melt rock. She had dissolved into his arms, her eyes glowing, so radiant and beautiful that he'd nearly wept from pure joy. She'd actually wanted him. *Him,* Hank Flynn, not that sniveling coward who'd wreaked havoc on her life. Thank God, Rae was finally over Martin Manning. After all the years and all the tears, she was finally strong enough to let someone else into her heart.

The possibility that Hank had an opportunity to become that person made him happier than he'd ever have thought possible. For the first time in more years than he cared to remember, Hank Flynn felt truly alive.

"It looks wonderful," Rae said, tilting her head to study the diner's new soft beige exterior. "You've done a terrific job."

Hank issued a shy shrug, and used a shop rag to wipe paint smears from his fingers. "I'll start the trim tomorrow, after the clapboards are dry. By summer the whole town is going to be beige and white. But it looks okay, I guess.''

"I love it." Rae tossed a sassy smile over her shoulder. "What's really fun is that my place is the first one finished. It's great to be all dressed up for the prom when everyone else is still in their underwear."

"They'll be dressed soon enough," Hank said, amused by her excitement. "I've been talking to the contractor who's fixing up the museum down the street. He plans to be finished by the end of the month."

"Hmm." Still smiling, Rae backed up several feet to shade her eyes and study the freshly painted building from a new perspective. Her obvious excitement warmed Hank to the bone. "That's good. We were hoping to have the entire town completed by summer."

"So I hear." Shifting his stance, Hank dropped the rag on the ground, angling a glance at the rolled paper tucked in the tool case. "I was wondering if you'd be willing to let me use the bungalow for a while longer." Noting her perplexed frown, Hank deliberately focused his gaze down the street, nodding toward the flurry of construction activity that was about a half block away. "From what I was told, the state grant money is being used to buy materials and supplies, and the town is providing matching funds with the use of volunteer labor."

She cocked her head, giving him a quizzical look that was downright unnerving. "Yes, that's right. Why?"

He cleared his throat. "I, ah, drew up some plans." Bending, Hank grabbed the rolled paper on which he'd sketched out his ideas. "It's still pretty rough."

She hesitated, then took the sheet and unrolled it on the plywood table.

Hank moved to her side, pointing out various dimensions and architectural highlights of the random sketches. "The way I figured, we could spruce up the bungalows, then construct a visitor center with a panning trough here." He pointed to a dimensional blueprint roughed out in the corner of the paper. "You could charge a buck a head for folks to try their hand at gold panning."

"Gold panning? Why on earth would anyone want to do that?"

"Tourists would love it. I mean, they call this Gold Country, after all, and can you imagine how thrilled a Wisconsin family would be to return home from vacation with a vial of gold flakes that they panned themselves?"

Frowning, Rae shook her head, and Hank's hopes plummeted. "We'd have to salt the pans to make sure everyone saw a little color. Even so, nobody is going to pay a dollar for a nickel's worth of flakes."

"The value doesn't matter, Rae, it's the fun of doing it."

She angled him a wry look. "Speaking as one who had a gold pan shoved in her hands before she was out of diapers, I can seriously say that there are few things on earth as physically demanding as gold mining. It is not—read my lips here—*not* fun."

"Look, I'm not suggesting we have tourists hauling pay dirt out of Hobie's hardrock mine. We'd bucket the gravel up here and let them pan it out, that's all. I saw a similar attraction down in Southern California once, and people were lined up for hours just to spend ten minutes at the trough. Hungry people," Hank added quickly. "People who've just spent half a day panning will work up one heck of an appetite." He gestured toward the diner. "Convenient, huh?"

For the first time since his sales pitch had begun, he saw genuine interest in Rae's eyes, and could practically hear the gears turning in her head. He pressed the advantage. "There's other recreational activities, too. The creek's just a short walk down the hill. Folks can rent a cottage for a couple days of swimming and fishing and—" he nodded toward the café "—eating out."

Rae's eyes widened. A smile twitched its way along her lush mouth and a moment later her head swiveled around to study the sketches with renewed interest.

Hank held his breath, waiting for her response. Three days had passed since they'd kissed on the pebbled beach, three days of yearning looks and dizzy smiles, yet neither of them had so much as mentioned what had happened between them that night. And what was continuing to happen, at least to him.

Even now, standing so close that he could see the fine blond hairs whisper at her nape, Hank's heart pounded with percussive intensity. Her fragrance wafted around him, overwhelming the pungent scent of fresh paint and turpentine. He was so very aware of her, of every nuance in expression, of the gentle sweep of her hand as she laughed, and the adorable way she tangled her fingers, childlike, when she was nervous.

But she wasn't nervous now. At the moment, she was bent across the plywood table, holding the curled edges of Hank's sketch down with her elbows so her hands were free to point out areas of interest. "These funny squiggles here...what do they mean?"

Hank leaned over her shoulder, his cheek close enough for her hair to brush his skin. A frisson of pure heat shot through his groin. His hands were suddenly clammy, trembling. He felt like a schoolboy in the throes of his first crush.

"Those are wiring diagrams." His voice sounded like the squeak of a startled mouse. He stepped away, clearing his throat. "I checked the cottages over, and most of them are in pretty good shape. The porches need a little renovation, but otherwise they're structurally sound. We'll want to check out the electrical systems carefully, though, to make sure that rodents haven't chewed through the wires."

Other than a curt nod, Rae made no other response,

but continued to scrutinize the plans with an expression Hank interpreted as, well, hopeful.

"So," he said finally. "What do you think?"

She pursed her lips, straightened and made a production of rerolling the plans. "I think," she said, with the merest twinkle in her eye, "that it's an absolutely brilliant idea."

A wave of relief nearly knocked him over. Initially he'd come up with the plan as a way to ease Rae's financial burden by increasing her revenues. Deep down, however, he had a less altruistic motive. Work on the project would take several weeks, weeks he'd be able to spend with Rae and Marti.

"I'll have to check with Steve," Rae said suddenly. "But I'm sure he'll agree that this is worth a shot. Certainly, it's better than tearing everything down and putting the lot up for sale. May I keep the plans for a while?"

"Ah, sure." A jealous surge took Hank by surprise. He shuffled a few tools across the plywood, avoiding her gaze. "Out of curiosity, why do you have to check with Ruskin about what to do with your own property?"

From the corner of his eye Hank noticed the thoughtful furrow of her brow as she tucked the rolled plans under her arm. "Steve is the official liaison between the town and the state controller's office. He has to approve everyone's renovation plans for conformity and compliance with the terms of the grant."

"Oh." Hank smiled, feeling silly. "That makes sense."

Her eyes twinkled. "I know you and Steve aren't exactly cut from the same cloth, but I can assure you that he's not the type to abuse the power of his position. He's not going to dismiss an idea that would be good for the town simply because he doesn't care for your hair."

"Ruskin doesn't like my hair?"

"Well..."

"What's wrong with it?"

"I think it's just a little long for his taste." Rae laughed as Hank made a production of smoothing a few flyaway strands that had escaped the neat ponytail at the base of his neck. "Don't worry about it. Personally, I think men with long hair are very sexy." The moment the words left her mouth she turned beet red. Coughing lightly into her hand, she shifted sideways, casting a glance toward the street. "Well."

"Well," Hank agreed, folding his arms. He desperately wanted to revisit her statement about long-haired men being sexy, but was unwilling to add to her obvious discomfort.

Rae cleared her throat again. "Since you have to let everything dry before painting the trim, I guess that means you're done for the day."

"Yeah, guess it does."

She issued an awkward nod. "Marti won't be home for a couple of hours. What are you going to do with yourself?"

"Hobie's been harping on me to see his mine. I thought maybe I'd drop by and watch someone else work for a while."

Cocking her head, she looked back over her shoulder. "It's a little tricky to find. The creek splits upstream. Follow the left fork until you pass a boarded-up cave."

"Hobie gave me directions. I'll find it."

"Okay." Rae hesitated a moment, then flashed a nervous smile. "I guess I should get back to work. Thanks again for this." She patted the paper roll under her arm, then turned and went into the diner.

Hank took a deep breath of the sweetest air he'd ever tasted, then spun on his heels and fairly floated down the path toward the creek. He followed the rocky bank absently, without paying much attention to the various landmarks along the way. His mind was replaying memories of Rae, of how the sun had bounced through the wild mane of curls atop her head, and how the tiny character lines around her eyes crinkled with her smile. She was without doubt God's most perfect creation.

Little Marti ran a close second.

Glancing up, Hank realized that he'd reached the creek's fork, and used a low-hanging branch to hoist himself up the embankment, to a path that was easier to follow. A few minutes later he saw the boarded-up cave, which was actually the remnants of an old mine shaft that had petered out decades ago. Hobie's newest digs were just around the bend.

Hank emerged from the woods to see Hobie sitting on a rock with a beer can in his hand. "Working hard, I see."

Hobie spun around, grinning broadly. "Well, I'll be danged. How'n hell did you find the place?"

"Rae gave me directions," Hank said, picking his way across a shallow rock bridge to join Hobie on the rock. "She just said to take the left fork and keep going past the dynamite cave."

"Did she, now?" Hobie took a deep swallow, then wiped his mouth with his hand and squinted at Hank. "That's mighty strange, her saying that."

A prickle of apprehension straightened Hank's spine. "Why is it strange?"

"Well, sir, it's strange on account of her not knowing that I used to keep dyno-mite in that there cave. Come to think of it, weren't nobody ever knew that." Hobie took another swallow of beer, smacked his lips and gazed across the creek. "Take that back. There was one." Hank started to retreat, but it was too late. The old man had already grabbed hold of his wrist. "Sit yourself down, Martin. We've got us a lot to talk about."

Chapter Eight

"To tell you the truth, Madeline, I'm not sure how Hobie's back is feeling. Better, I think." Shifting the telephone, Rae glanced through the front window just as Steve's car drove up. "I'll tell him you called, though.... Yes, I'll remind him that acupuncture is the most widely used therapy in the world. Uh-huh. Right. Bye, now." She hung up just as the front door opened. "Steve, what a nice surprise."

He sat at the counter, laying his briefcase on a vacant stool. "I had business in Auburn this morning, so I thought I'd stop by for a late lunch. Is there any soup left?"

"Always." She headed to the kitchen tureen, ladled out a steaming bowl of the diner's trademark hearty vegetable beef, then hurried back to serve the dish. "This must be serendipity," she said, arranging several cracker packages around the soup plate's rim. "I was just thinking about you."

Steve brightened, holding his raised spoon in midair. "Were you?"

Reaching under the counter, Rae retrieved the rolled plans Hank had drawn. She turned the sheet so it faced Steve, then spread it on the counter, holding the curled edges in place with squeeze bottles of ketchup and mustard. "Look, isn't this wonderful?"

Steve laid down his spoon, clearly perplexed. "Isn't what wonderful?"

"Why, Hank's plans."

"Flynn drew these?" The question was issued softly, expressing surprise tempered with annoyance. "For what purpose?"

Normally Rae was attuned to the nuances of Steve's voice, but on this day excitement overshadowed caution and she blurted out everything Hank had told her about his idea to renovate the cottages into recreational rentals.

Steve listened carefully, studying the plans as Rae spoke, and had yet to look up as she completed her exuberant sales pitch.

"The panning trough would be visible from the street, so curious tourists would have easy access. Once they're parked, they'll see the bungalows, and we'll have a visitor center here—" she pointed to a small sketch at the top left of the plans "—and a bunch of free brochures— with lovely color photos of the creek—that highlight fishing, swimming, hiking…and mining, of course, for those who actually enjoy swirling dirt in a pan for hours on end."

Finally, her breath expended, Rae straightened, pushing an obstinate strand of hair from her flushed face. As Steve continued to study the plans without comment, her optimism faded.

Rae added a final hopeful plea. "With so many people around, the diner's business is bound to increase, don't you think?"

For several long seconds Steve said nothing. Then, when Rae felt the last shred of hope slipping away, he turned away from the plans and looked up. "It's a fine idea."

Rae pressed a palm against her chest, certain she'd misheard. "It is?"

"Yes, actually." He angled another glance at the plans. "Simple, minimal capital requirement, well within the parameters of the grant terms. Quite viable, really. I wish I'd thought of it myself."

Her breath rushed out in a relieved hiss. She steadied herself on the counter, thrilled yet not quite believing that the fiscally conservative Steve Ruskin actually favored Hank's plan.

Clearly, he did. "I'll prepare the documentation to release grant funds for materials," he was saying. "Then I'll speak with the museum contractor to see when he'll be free to start the project."

"Oh, Hank will do it."

Steve stiffened as if his blood had turned to concrete. "Excuse me?"

This time Rae saw the warning in his eyes and reacted to it. A nervous twitch worked its way along her jawline. "I, ah, kind of agreed to let him do the work and continue our original agreement."

"I see." Steve removed the napkin from his lap, dabbing the corners of his mouth more out of habit than need, since he'd yet to even taste his lunch. "I don't think that's wise, Rae. The man is clearly taking advantage of you."

"That's unfair, Steve, and not true. Hank has done a wonderful job on the diner. He knows construction and—" she gestured at the plans "—he obviously has more than a passing familiarity with the details of architectural design. If you calculate the economics of our arrangement, Hank has worked his heart out for the price of a few meals, which probably averages out to less than a dollar an hour. That hardly sounds like the M.O. of a scam artist.''

''Rae—''

''And besides, Hank Flynn is quiet and unassuming, he's wonderful with Marti and has the patience of Job with Hobie's tall tales. He's a very, very nice man, and I like him.''

Steve gazed at her for a moment, then laid his crumpled napkin beside the untouched bowl of soup. ''Yes,'' he murmured. ''I can see that.''

He picked up his briefcase and left.

Hobie tossed the crushed beer can into a bucket. ''Yessir, almost had me fooled, with that fat mop of hair and the fuzz under your nose. 'Course, I was a-wondering why a man supposed to be scared spitless of birds would be a-feeding wild jays, but then I figured out you was only scared of Louie 'cause he knew who you was.''

''You're mistaken,'' Hank said quietly.

Ignoring that, Hobie squinted at him. ''Look a bit beat-up, too, like your face got squished in a rock crusher. But it's you, all right.''

''My name is Hank Flynn. I was born in Ogden, Utah. I went to college in Salt Lake City, and—''

''Thing I want to know is, why you run off the way you done.''

Sighing, Hank rubbed his face. ''Listen, Hobie, I am not the man you think I am. Martin Manning is dead.''

An angry flash in the old man's bloodshot eyes was the only indication he'd heard. Hobie spat on a rock, then reached into the cooler for another beer. He offered one to Hank, who refused without comment.

''I don't want to be playing these games,'' Hobie said finally. ''You was the one got Louie hooked on cheese puffs. After you left, he wouldn't take 'em from no one else. Hadn't asked for 'em in ten years, until he saw you again.''

He paused long enough to pop the top on his beer can. "I figured maybe that were co-incidence, y'know? And maybe it were co-incidence that you knew where Martin kept his tool case, and where Rae kept her good silver. Maybe it were just co-incidence that you got the same mechanical know-how as Martin, and that after Louie stopped his hollering last Sunday, I found cheese puff crumbs on my dresser. Yessir, that could all be purely co-incidence.''

Hobie took a deep swallow of beer, then balanced the can on his knee. "But weren't no one knew about keeping dyno-mite in that cave, no one but me and Martin.'' He gave Hank a fishy-eyed stare. "You're Martin, all right, and I got me a heap of questions 'bout where you been all these years.''

Hank, who was still standing, jammed a fist on his hip, blew out a breath and gazed down at the foam licking at rocks at the edge of the rushing creek. "Have you said anything to Rae about this?''

"Nope.''

Hank closed his eyes. "Good.''

In the darkness of his mind there was silence for a moment. Hobie broke it with a terse question. "Why'n hell didn't you come back?''

A spasm tightened his throat. "I couldn't.''

"That don't do it for me,'' Hobie snapped, sounding angrier than Hank had ever heard him. "Rae and your daughter, they needed you. You left 'em alone, just ran off like a yeller-dog coward and left 'em to fend for themselves. That ain't right, Martin, ain't right at all.''

Suddenly exhausted, Hank sat on his heels, propping his limp arms on his knees. "I didn't know about Marti.''

"That ain't no excuse.''

"No, it isn't.'' Feeling empty inside, Hank absently

traced circles in the embankment's gravel skin. "Martin Manning can't come back. He doesn't exist anymore."

Hobie emitted a disgusted snort. "What kinda cockamamie double-talk is that?"

"You want the truth, and I'm willing to tell it, but only on one condition. Rae and Marti must never know."

Squinting irritably, Hobie eyed Hank with blatant suspicion. "They gotta right to know."

"When you hear what I've got to say, you may think otherwise."

"I ain't heard much of anything yet."

Hank turned away, shaken to the bone. He licked his lips, forcing his mind back ten years, to the horror that would destroy his life forever. Then, speaking in a voice that quivered with emotion, he told Hobie how his unit had been sent on a top-secret mission to aid Central American rebels. After two weeks in the jungle, there'd been an ambush. Three men had been captured; the rest had been killed.

"I was in command," Hank said quietly. "If I hadn't made the decision to split the troop, those men might be alive today."

"Most likely you'd all be dead," Hobie said.

Hank only shrugged. "All I know for certain is that I took my two best soldiers out on patrol. When we returned to camp, there was nothing left but carnage, and a jungle full of government troops waiting to swoop in on us. They took the three of us captive, gave us a phony trial, then sentenced us to life in prison as enemies of the state. We were hauled off to a hellhole somewhere in the bowels of the city. I was put in a windowless room the size of a closet. They took my men away. I never saw them again."

Hobie shuffled beside him. Neither man spoke for several minutes, and they listened to the sounds of the forest.

It was Hobie who broke the silence. "How long was you in there?"

"Four years." Hank flicked a pebble into the creek. "The guards showed up one day, but instead of shoving a bowl of slop into the cell, they dragged me out. It seems there was some kind of prisoner exchange, only the State Department had expected someone else, and wasn't particularly pleased to end up with me."

"How come?"

"It took a while for me to sort through the bureaucratic bungling, but I finally found out that someone in the military brass had tried to conceal my unit's botched mission by declaring that we'd all been killed rendering humanitarian aid in Europe. They covered their butts by declaring us heroes, and showering our loved ones with condolences and posthumous medals. Obviously, my unexpected survival tossed a monkey wrench in their story." Hank sat back, brushing his palms together. "According to the powers that be, our nation's security was at stake. They wanted Martin Manning to stay dead, and they were quite persuasive."

Hobie cocked a mean eye. "Threatened you, did they?"

It would be so easy to lie, Hank thought, so simple to say that he'd been coerced and forced into taking on a new identity. But the lies were over now. It was time to face the truth. "Once they explained the situation, I realized that full revelation of our military involvement would have far-reaching consequences. They offered to set me up with a new life. I took it."

"Just like that?" Hobie snapped his fingers, scowling.

"Yes, just like that."

The old man glowered for a moment, then muttered an epithet. "None of this makes a lick of sense. You coulda come back, told Rae what happened. You didn't hafta slink into the woodwork like a crawly-legged bug."

Hank managed not to flinch. Hobie was right, of course, but he still didn't know everything. He didn't know that Rae wouldn't have taken Martin back, and he didn't know why. There was no reason to tell him, because reasons wouldn't change the facts. Hank was every bit the coward Hobie thought him to be. He'd deserted the woman who'd loved him, he'd allowed good men to die, then he'd avoided responsibility by giving up his own identity rather than face what he'd done and risk military retribution.

And there'd been other reasons, too.

After learning that his beloved mother had died during his captivity, Hank had gone into a state of emotional collapse. She'd been his only family, the center of his universe. He'd grieved himself hollow, taking comfort only in the knowledge that at least she'd believed her son to be a man of courage. Rae had believed that, too, and would have been shattered by the ugly truth.

It had seemed so much simpler to leave Martin Manning buried in a hero's grave to honor his mother and instill proud memories in the only woman that Martin had ever loved. Besides, in every way that mattered, Martin Manning had never come out of that jungle. He'd died with his men, leaving a directionless drifter named Hank Flynn in his place.

Now it was time for the drifter to move on.

Marti shot through the diner like a fuzzy-headed bullet. "Mom, Mom! Where's Hank?" She skidded to the counter, flung down her book bag and leaned over, panting. "The diner's all painted and Hank's gone. He didn't leave, did he, Mom? He wouldn't go away without saying goodbye."

"Shh." Rae issued a reproachful frown, nodding her head toward the startled customers at the cash register. Marti bit her lower lip, dancing from foot to foot while her mother completed the transaction. Finally, Rae closed the register. "Have a nice day," she told the smiling couple, then turned to her frantic daughter. "So, how was school?"

"Mom!" Marti wailed.

Rae chuckled, feeling slightly guilty for teasing the child, who was obviously distraught by the possibility of having been deserted by the man who'd become her best buddy. "Calm down, sweetie. Hank just went to see Sadie. He'll be back in a little while."

Relief poured into her little eyes. "Oh, wow." She sat heavily on a stool, wiping her forehead, but still looked oddly glum.

"What's wrong, Marti? I thought you'd be pleased that Hank's still around."

She shrugged. "After he's done working on the diner, I'm still afraid he's gonna go away."

The child's bleak expression touched Rae, and worried her. "Honey, you have to realize that Hank doesn't live here. Sooner or later, he'll probably want to go home to his friends and family."

"He doesn't have any family," Marti said, fidgeting with a napkin holder. "He's all alone."

"How do you know that?"

"He told me."

"Really?" Odd, Rae thought, that he'd apparently answered Marti's inquisitive questions at the same time he'd been patently evasive with everyone else's. "What else did he tell you?"

"Oh, lots of stuff." She brightened, relaying the information with great pride. "Hank's done all kinds of neat things. He's traveled all over the whole entire world, and he even speaks two languages! Not real good, of course, but enough to get by. *Buenos días, señorita. ¿Donde está el hotel?* Know what that means?"

"Ah, no, actually, I don't."

"It means 'Good morning, young lady. Where is the hotel?' Isn't that neat?"

"Yes," Rae murmured. "Neat."

"He worked on a shrimp boat once. Did you know that?"

"No, honey, I didn't know that, either."

"He said it smelled real bad, and he got kinda seasick, so he went to Texas and worked on a cattle ranch. A cattle ranch! Did you ever hear anything so fun? He says cows are really neat, and kinda friendly, if you're nice to them. He says the babies are the cutest things in the whole wide word."

"Well." Folding her arms, Rae propped a hip against the counter, shaking her head. "I'm amazed that you know so much about the mysterious Mr. Flynn while the rest of us know so little."

"You just gotta know how to ask the right questions," Marti observed. "He kinda clams up when he thinks people are being, you know, snoopy or something."

"I'll keep that in mind."

Marti heaved a sigh. "I told my diary that Hank is my very best friend in the whole world, and I wish he'd stay here forever and ever."

The heartfelt hope mirrored Rae's deepest feelings, feelings that until that moment she'd never acknowledged even to herself. The truth was that Hank Flynn's presence had evoked deep changes in the way both Rae and Marti felt about life, the future and even themselves. Marti, who'd been emotionally beaten down by Steve's well-intentioned attempts to change her, was now filled with enthusiasm and pride in her accomplishments.

Rae, too, was different. Before Hank had entered her life, she'd felt dead inside, frigid, unloving and unlovable. Now she was alive again, filled with that jittery anticipation of youth that she'd thought lost forever.

Those feelings had been recaptured with Hank. He

made her feel beautiful, and cherished. He made her feel
worthy of love.

Sometimes at night she'd close her eyes and dream
about the way his eyes glowed when he looked at her.
She'd relive the soaring pleasure of his touch, the electric
excitement of his kiss.

"Mom?"

"Hmm?"

"You all right? Your face is all pink and you look
kinda fainty."

"I, ah—" Rae coughed lightly, avoiding her daughter's crafty little eyes. "I'm fine, sweetie. As for Hank,
I think I can safely say that he'll be hanging around a
while longer."

She retrieved the rolled plans from under the counter,
spread them out and couldn't contain her excitement as
she shared Hank's idea for a future tourist attraction right
next to the diner.

Marti was beside herself. "That's gonna take weeks,
months, even!"

"It certainly could."

"Do you think Hank will let me help?"

Rae rerolled the plans, laughing. "I'd be willing to bet
on it."

"Yay!" Grabbing her book bag, Marti shot toward the
front door, turning expectantly when her mother called
her name.

"If you're thinking about going down to the mine,
forget it." The child's crushed expression indicated that
was exactly what she'd been thinking. Rae added a gentle
reminder. "You have chores and homework."

"Sure, I know that."

Because she recognized the shrewd gleam in her
daughter's eye, Rae was considering a more explicit

warning when Marti suddenly blurted, "I knew Hank wouldn't leave. He loves us, Mom. He's gonna stay here forever."

"I'll leave tonight," Hank said. "The only thing I ask is that you not repeat anything I've told you to Rae or Marti."

Hobie stood slowly, rubbing the small of his back. He straightened, rotating his upper torso as if working out kinks. "So, where'll you be running to this time?"

"I don't know."

"Don't seem much like a life."

"It's what I have."

Wiping a grimy forearm across his forehead, the old man gazed across the creek. "Seems to me it's what you want. Otherwise, you'd hike up your shorts and do the right thing."

Hank stood, feeling sick and empty. "Steve Ruskin is a fine man. He'll make a good husband for Rae, and he'll be the kind of father to Marti that I could never be. They need someone like him in their lives."

"Horse pucky." Hobie spat on the ground, then kicked a rock into the creek. "Rae don't love Steve. Never has, never could. He ain't right for her and she knows it. As for Marti, hell, poor child is gonna pop a vein trying to please that man. She's always been a free spirit, kinda reckless, maybe, but still full of life and craving adventure. Ruskin don't understand that. He's trying to break that poor child and it ain't right."

An icy fist closed around Hank's heart. "Ruskin means well."

"Y'know what the road to hell is paved with, don'tcha?"

Hank sighed. "Good intentions."

"There you go."

"Ruskin will come around," Hank insisted. "He cares

about Marti. I can see it in his eyes, in the way he offers guidance and—''

''Ruskin don't guide folks, he pushes 'em, shoves 'em right up to a cliff, then kicks their fannies over the edge. He's been a-courting Rae for so long, he's near got her wore down. She thinks Marti needs a daddy, and by God, she's gonna get her one. Trouble is, Ruskin's the only one in line for the job.''

The image of Rae with Ruskin, or any other man, made Hank's head spin. He sucked in a breath, and steadied himself on a nearby sapling. ''Rae has a right to go on with her life, and Marti has the right to a father who can instill good, decent values.''

Hobie clamped his scruffy jaw. ''Your blood flows in that child's veins. Outside, she looks like her momma but inside, she's got her daddy's heart and soul. She's you, Martin, and you're the only one who can raise her to 'preciate that.''

Shading his face, Hank bowed his head, swallowing a lump that threatened to cut off his breath. He tried to speak, couldn't, took another breath and tried again. ''You saw her eyes glisten when she talked about her father, how proud she was that he'd been so brave, that he'd been a hero. Do you want to take that away from her?''

''Ain't wanting to take nothing away. The child deserves her daddy, her real daddy.''

''She deserves a father she can be proud of, and at the moment, that's exactly what she has.'' With some effort Hank stood, willing shaky legs to support his weight. ''I'm leaving, Hobie. Trust me, it's better for everyone.''

Hobie's droopy eyelids tightened in anger. ''You ain't going anywhere. If'n you try, I'll tell the sheriff you done assaulted me and stole my gold stash. Folks 'round here don't take kindly to that.''

Hank smiled sadly, shaking his head. ''Do what you

have to do, Hobie. I've seen the inside of a jail cell before."

"Reckon you have." The old man's eyes softened. "Did they beat you, son, is that what happened to your face?"

The question evoked harsh memories. For a moment Hank relived the sound of breaking bones, the smell of his own blood. He turned away, shaking his mind clear. "Goodbye, Hobie."

Hank hadn't gotten ten feet when the old man said, "I wouldn't do that if I were you, unless you want your child to know that her daddy's a live coward instead of a dead hero."

Hank froze, looking over his shoulder in fear and disbelief. "You wouldn't."

"Yessir, I would. Be a shame, though, seeing how much she worships her daddy's memory." Hooking his thumbs behind his suspenders, Hobie hobbled forward. "Now, if you was to stay around for a while, I might think twice about telling. Up to you, son."

"You son of a—"

Hobie shrugged. "Just looking out for my own. More'n you ever done for 'em."

Hank couldn't dispute that, but was furious that the blackmailing coot would actually sell out his own granddaughter. "If you tell Marti, you'll destroy her," Hank growled, balling his fists at his sides.

"If you desert that child to the likes of Steve Ruskin, there won't be nothing left to destroy." Hobie ambled closer, then rocked back on his heels. "So what's it going to be, son, you gonna hang around for a while, or am I gonna have a little talk with my grandchild?"

But Hank wasn't listening to Hobie. He stared past the old man's shoulder, right into Marti's guileless green eyes.

Chapter Nine

Hank froze, staring at the bewildered child who was standing less than fifty feet down the path. He wanted to speak, to ask how long she'd been there and—most important—what she had heard, but his mouth was so dry he couldn't pry his tongue off his teeth.

Following Hank's gaze, Hobie bounced a curious gaze over his own shoulder. "Well, whaddaya know, we got company. Does your mama know you're down here?"

Marti's eyes shifted. "Not exactly."

Cocking his head, Hobie scratched his stubbled chin, but unlike Hank, who'd been shocked into silence, the old man kept his cool. "Didn't think so. Rae doesn't much cotton to visiting Sadie on school days, what with homework and such."

"I don't have homework," the child blurted, twisting her fingers into a nervous tangle. "Teacher got called to the phone just before the bell rang and, well, he kinda forgot to give us any."

With a spasm, Hank's paralyzed lungs refilled. He licked his lips, returned Hobie's wary glance and offered the girl the most sincere forced smile he could muster. Judging by her obvious apprehension, it wasn't particularly effective. "So," he said jovially. "You've probably been standing there wondering why your grampa and I were arguing with each other."

She responded with a limp shrug. "You did look kinda mad."

Hank was only slightly relieved by the assumption that if she'd heard details of the discussion, she would have mentioned it. Still, he wasn't ready to leave anything to chance. "Well, you know what we were talking about, don't you?"

Eyes wide, she shook her head.

His smile loosened, but only a little. "The fact is, we're low on beer, and neither one of us wants to go all the way back to the diner for more. Isn't that right, Hobie?"

"Huh? Oh, yessir, right as rain. 'Course, hard as I've been a-working, it don't seem fair, me having to do it." Heaving an exaggerated sigh, the rusty old miner made a production of dabbing his forehead with the back of his bony hand. "All the chores I got around here, it's a wonder I ain't dropped dead already."

"Chores!" Marti straightened, blinking madly. "That's why I came, Gramps, because Mom wanted me to make sure all the chores got done, so I figured I'd better remind you to take the garbage out, on account of tomorrow being trash day and all. So I'm not disobeying Mom or anything, honest, I just came to remind you about chores."

The plea in Marti's young eyes spoke volumes. Clearly, she *had* disobeyed her mother and was not only trying to justify that fact, she was also trying to coerce Hank and Hobie into going along with it.

Realizing that her nervousness was caused by a guilty conscience rather than anything she'd overheard, Hank had to fight a bark of relieved laughter. He went limp inside, and wiped his face with his palms.

When he peered over his fingertips, Hobie was eyeing him with a crafty grin. "Trash, huh? Thing is, that ain't my chore anymore," he told the startled child.

Marti cocked her head, plainly perplexed. "How come?"

"Well, sir—" The old man slapped a hand on Hank's shoulder "Hank, here, he done volunteered to take it over."

"Now wait just a darn minute—"

"Right nice of him, weren't it?" Grinning smugly, Hobie retrieved his hand, tucked a thumb around his elastic suspenders and rolled back on his boot heels. "What's more, Hank is gonna paint ol' Madeline Rochester's house—"

Hank's head snapped up.

"On account of him being so worried about my bad back and all."

"Gee," Marti said, clearly impressed. "That's real nice of you, Hank."

He managed a sick smile before turning his head to whisper through clamped teeth. "Your days are numbered, old man."

Ignoring that, Hobie slipped Hank a happy smirk and continued speaking to his granddaughter. "Yep. Fact is, I wouldn't be surprised if he didn't decide to do all my chores, including Sunday KP at the diner," he intoned, ignoring Hank's choked gurgle. "On account of him being so helpful and all. Ain't that right, son?"

Since the conniving coot was clearly solidifying his extortive hold, Hank could do little more than stare furiously. "Perhaps," he said tightly, "we should discuss the details of our arrangement later. In private."

"Why, we ain't got no secrets." The rheumy eyes gave an innocent blink. "Do we?"

For Marti's benefit Hank pasted on a pleasant smile as he turned to whisper in Hobie's ear. "Be careful, you blackmailing old coot. Not a court in the land would convict me."

Chuckling, the old man slapped his shoulder. "Good to have you back, boy. Sure'n hell is good."

Rae picked her way through dusky shadows, shifting the load of fresh linens in her arms. As she passed the north bungalows, she saw light spilling from the open door of Hank's cottage, and noted that the small porch lamp was on, as well. He was clearly visible, sitting on the postage-stamp stoop fiddling with a thin, reedy pole of some kind.

Despite her stealthy approach, he suddenly laid the pole in his lap and stared into the shadowed woods. "Nice evening."

Rae moved farther down the path, into the scant illumination cast by the final remnants of sunset. "Yes, it's lovely. A pleasant reminder that spring is just around the corner." She was almost at the porch now, close enough to see that Hank was holding an open pocketknife in his right hand.

As he stood, he snapped the blade closed and dropped the knife on the wooden planks. "Thanks," he said, reaching for the stack of folded sheets and towels.

She stepped aside, maintaining her hold on the linens as she stepped onto the porch. "I'll just make up the room for you."

"You don't have to do that."

"I don't mind. That way, I don't have to make another trip for the soiled things."

Hank shifted his weight, seeming unsure of what to do with his hands. He finally used one to rub the back of his neck and propped the other one on his hip. "I could bring the used linens up to the house, so you don't have to come all the way out here."

"It's only a few hundred feet. Honestly, I really don't mind." Her gaze fell on a thin, peeled branch that was lying on the porch. "What's that?"

"Hmm? Oh." He glanced down with an endearingly sheepish smile. "I noticed a nifty trout pool not far from Hobie's claim. Marti mentioned that her fishing pole was broken, so I told her I'd have a look at it." He nodded toward the open door, where Rae saw both pieces of the snapped rod on a table inside the cottage. "I'd hoped I could fix it, but it's pretty much shot, so I'm making a new one."

"You're actually carving a fishing rod out of a tree limb?"

He shrugged. "It's no big deal. I'll use the line loops from her old pole, and the reel is still good. As long as she doesn't hook a twenty-pound monster, it should work out pretty well for her."

"That's so nice of you," Rae murmured, touched that he'd spend so much time pleasing a child he barely knew. "Marti will be thrilled to pieces."

Clearing his throat, Hank dragged his gaze from the peeled limb to the toes of his boots. "Like I said, it's no big deal. Every kid needs a fishing pole."

"Not everyone would agree with that." The sharp reply was out of her mouth before she realized it was even in her mind. She turned away, feeling a warm flush prickle her cheeks, and unsure if it was caused by embarrassment or anger. "I'll, ah, start changing linens now, if it's all right with you."

Hank frowned, unwilling to let the intemperate statement pass. "Marti gave me the impression that her pole was broken by accident, and that it would be all right with you for her to have another one."

"It is all right with me. I mean, I certainly don't have any qualms about girls learning how to fish, or... or...whatever," she finished lamely, and flinched at the knowing glint in Hank's eyes.

"But Ruskin doesn't approve."

It was a statement, not a question. Rae hurried inside the cottage, hoping to forestall a response. She laid the fresh linens on the table beside the broken pole and immediately busied herself pulling sheets off Hank's neatly made bed.

She didn't have to look to know that Hank had also entered the room. His presence was as tangible as a touch and just as arousing. A subtle warmth radiated deep inside her, a soothing comfort that she knew from experience would escalate into a throbbing, unsated need. Only Hank Flynn evoked these stirrings inside her. Only him.

That frightened Rae. It also excited her beyond reason.

She gave the coverlet a mighty yank, concealing her discomfort with cheery chatter. "Marti told me you were in the army. Of course, anyone could see that. You could actually bounce a nickel on this bed, and the corners are so tight they have to be pried off. Not that I'm complaining. I'm just surprised. Most people don't even bother to make the beds. I guess they figure that's the maid's job. It's not their fault that we've never been able to afford a maid."

Rae knew she was babbling, and wished to heaven that she would shut up. For some reason, her tongue was completely out of control around this man, and she chattered in a squeaky voice that made her sound like a chirpy little chickadee. "Then again, that doesn't much matter anymore, since we haven't rented these cottages out in years. But of course, that's going to change, thanks to you. Did I tell you that Steve loved your idea?"

She ripped off the lower sheet, wrapping it with the upper covering, and proceeded to prattle on as she peeled off the pillowcases. "He dropped by earlier this evening to pick up your plans. They have to be approved by the state, of course, and then the county has to issue permits, but Steve's going to take care of that. He's really wonderful, don't you think? I mean, it's not like he's getting paid for his effort. He's just doing it because he cares so much about the town. And the people, of course."

As she shook out a clean sheet, Hank flanked the bed to tuck the fresh linens into the other side of the mattress. At the same moment, a cease-and-desist order finally made its way from Rae's frantic brain to her jabbering mouth, which instantly clamped itself shut and was thankfully silent.

They worked quietly, tucking bedclothes and smoothing the coverlet. Rae avoided Hank's gaze until the hot flush of humiliation had subsided, and she'd garnered some semblance of control over her faculties. Finally she straightened and flashed a pleasant smile. "Well, that wasn't so bad. Thanks for the help."

Hank regarded her thoughtfully. "Did Ruskin break Marti's pole?"

Her heart sank like a rock. "Not intentionally. I mean, yes, I suppose that he meant to do it, but he was upset at the time, and he had a good reason."

Hank stood there, waiting.

Tossing up her hands, Rae gave in. "Marti was supposed to be working on a school project that was due the next day, but she sneaked off to go fishing."

"So he hunted her down and broke her pole."

"It wasn't the first time Marti had disobeyed him, er, us." Rae turned away, feeling hurt and miserable. "Steve acted on impulse. He regretted it later."

"If he regretted it so much, why didn't he buy her another pole?"

"He was planning to, this summer." Rae chanced a look over her shoulder. "When the school year is over."

Hank nodded, although the grim line of his mouth revealed that he considered such compensation as inadequate and untimely. Unfortunately, Rae agreed. The only reason Steve had consented to replace the pole in the first place was that Rae had been so furious with him. They'd gotten into a terrible argument.

Actually, it hadn't exactly been an argument; more like an angry monologue. Rae had yelled and flailed her arms like a wild woman, while Steve had regarded her with the cautious pity one bestows on a rabid skunk. In the end, Rae had wound up feeling like a failure as a mother, not only because she hadn't been able to control her child, but also because she hadn't been able to protect her from the heartbreak of losing something that she dearly loved.

The worst part was that in a weird, distorted kind of way, Steve's logic had been flawless. Consequences, he'd said, are the natural result of behavior. Marti had to learn that lesson, and to respect it.

Rae didn't dispute the rationale. She just didn't believe that a deliberate act of destruction was an effective teaching tool. Apparently Hank didn't, either.

He was, however, too gracious to say so. "You have every right to raise your daughter as you see fit."

Returning to the porch, Hank tucked the knife back in his pocket and scooped up the partially carved rod.

"What are you doing?" Rae asked as he stepped into the darkness. She ran outside in time to see him heading toward the street, where a neat line of garbage cans awaited morning pickup. "Wait a minute. You're not going to throw it away."

He stopped, angling a perplexed glance over his shoulder. "It's just a hunk of wood."

"But you've already put so much work into it, and..." Rae sighed. "I'd like you to finish it for her."

He turned to face her, clearly mystified. "But if she's being punished—"

"She's not. I mean, she was, but it's over now." Actually, Rae didn't have a clue what she meant. "All right, the truth is that I never approved of the punishment in the first place. I'm Marti's mother, and I'll decide whether or not my daughter deserves a new fishing pole."

A twitch at the corner of his mouth suggested that he was holding back a smile. "So does she? Deserve a new pole, that is."

"Yes, she definitely does."

His smile broke free. "Then I guess I'd better get back to work."

"Hank went *where?*" Rae gaped at her father, certain that Hobie must be playing another of his nefarious pranks.

His shifty eyes said otherwise, and the nervous bounce of his stubbled Adam's apple made her heart sink. "Hank, uh, went to Madeline's house."

Crossing her arms, Rae fixed the fidgety man with a suspicious stare. "And why, pray tell, would he do that?"

Marti, who'd been watching the interchange with wide-eyed interest, instantly sprang to her grampa's defense. "Hank's going to paint Ms. Rochester's house for her. Isn't that nice?"

It took a moment for Rae to digest that startling bit of news. She shook her head, completely befuddled. "That doesn't make any sense at all. Madeline was quite insistent that she wanted Hobie to do that. Besides, Hank already has more work stacked up than a half-dozen men could handle. Why on earth would he volunteer for more?"

Rae spun around just as Hobie was sidling backward,

presumably planning to slip behind the nearest cottage and flee into the woods. She marched forward, wagging a finger in his face. "You're behind this, Hobie Hooper. I don't know how, and I certainly don't know why, but this whole idiotic situation has your name written all over it."

Dipping his scruffy head, Hobie scratched his scalp, shuffled his feet and launched into whining mode. "It's my back, don'tcha know. Hank didn't want me a-climbing ladders and such, on account of my back's been a-paining me." He peeked up to judge his progress, apparently didn't like what he saw and refocused on the ground, clearing his throat. "Tried to stop him, I did, but he's a stubborn man. Said he was gonna do ol' Madeline's house, and that's all there was to it."

"Right. Next you'll be trying to sell me a bridge."

"It's the truth, Mom. Hank is gonna do all of Gramps's work until his back gets better. I heard him say so."

Rae would have argued the point had a familiar figure not caught her eye. She looked up just as Hank sauntered through the thick stand of pines that separated the bungalows from the sidewalk.

He emerged into the clearing looking immensely pleased with himself. "Good afternoon, all. Great day, isn't it?"

"Hank, Hank, are we going to start building the panning trough?" Marti, having just gotten home from school, bounced around him like a fuzzy-headed ball. "I can help, can't I? Mom says it's okay with her. Will you teach me how to read blueprints? I'm going to be a carpenter when I grow up."

"Whoa, squirt." Grinning, Hank squatted down to the child's level. "And the answers are yes, yes and yes."

"Yay!" She spun like a top, then sprinted away, hollering, "I'll get the tools."

"Marti, homework first!" Rae sighed as the child dashed out of range. She turned her attention to Hobie, who was issuing a series of frantic hand signals to Hank.

When Rae cleared her throat, the old man heaved a sickly sigh. "Was just kinda wondering when ol' Hank here was gonna get around to doing Madeline's place."

"Right away," ol' Hank said with peculiar enthusiasm. "I'm looking forward to it."

Hobie's jaw dropped. "Y'are?"

"Sure. Madeline's a fascinating woman."

Hobie poked a finger in his ear as if clearing debris, then slapped the side of his head a couple of times and gave Hank a surly stare. "Come again?"

"Fascinating lady," Hank repeated, grinning like the proverbial cat. "Reads all the time, great conversationalist—did you know she has a degree in geology?"

"Geo-what?"

"Study of rocks, alluvial formations—" Hank slipped Rae a conspiratorial wink "—mineral deposits."

That got Hobie's attention. "Y'don't say."

"Knows her stuff, too." Digging in to his pocket, Hank retrieved a two-ounce placer nugget shaped like a fishtailed teardrop. "This is a down payment on my wages."

Hobie's eyes nearly shot out of his head. "Where'n hell did you get that?"

"From Madeline. She's got jars of them."

"Get outta here," Hobie mumbled, looking faint. "Where'd a weird ol' duck like her find that kinda gold?"

"On her claim." Hank tucked the nugget back into his pocket just as Hobie made a move to touch it. "Actually, it was her husband's, but it's hers now. She says anyone who paints her house can work the claim all he wants and keep whatever he finds."

"Is that a fact?" The old man's eyes lit like neon. "So, where exactly is this claim o' hers?"

"Oh, well, I won't know that until her house is done, but from what I saw, shelves of mayonnaise jars and coffee cans loaded with—"

Hobie's head snapped up. "Coffee cans?"

"The big three-pound cans," Hank said, barely able to suppress a grin. "Filled to the brim, and so heavy a man would need a forklift just to get one off the ground." He let that sink in for a moment, then slapped the old man's bony shoulder. "Just think, if it wasn't for that bad back of yours, you'd be the one getting rich instead of me. I sure do thank you."

Rae stood there completely confused, looking from Hank to Hobie and back again. She didn't have a clue what was going on, but strongly suspected that her devious dad was finally getting a taste of his own medicine. That thought alone was enough to keep her watching the interaction with rapt fascination.

After a moment Hobie cleared his throat. "That, uh, nugget of yours. Could I mebbe, y'know, hold it for a spell?"

"Hmm? Oh, sure." Hank dug the requested item from his pocket and dropped it into the old man's outstretched palm. "It's a beauty, isn't it?"

"Sure is," Hobie agreed, studying the metallic luster with a steady eye. He tested the weight in his palm, scratched the surface with his fingernail and finally shook his head, clucking. "It's the real thing, all right." He squinted at Hank. "And you're a-saying there's more where this come from?"

"Lots more."

"Well, whaddaya know." Hobie bounced the nugget in his palm. "Maybe I oughta drop in on Madeline, y'know, just to explain 'bout my back and all."

"She'd appreciate that."

"Thing is, my back's been feeling a mite better lately."

Hank merely feigned surprise. "Has it?"

"Yep. In fact, I might even be able to, y'know, take over that job myself, seeing as how you're gonna be so busy around here anyway."

Sighing, Hank shook his head. "I don't know, Hobie. I was really looking forward to working that claim."

But Hobie wasn't listening. He'd already tucked the nugget into his own pocket and was hobbling toward the street.

When he was out of earshot, Rae burst into laughter. She tried to talk, couldn't, and ended up chuckling so hard she could barely breathe. Hank watched, amused, until she finally sucked in a breath and wiped her wet eyes.

"That," Rae told him, "was the meanest trick anyone has ever pulled on Hobie."

Hank smiled. "I certainly hope so."

She regarded him with new respect. "There isn't any gold claim, is there?"

"Actually, that part was true."

"And the coffee cans filled with nuggets?"

He shrugged, his eyes gleaming. "A slight exaggeration."

Rae laughed again, shifted her stance and tried to imagine her father's indignant sputterings when he learned he'd been bamboozled into painting Madeline Rochester's house. "I never would have believed you to be this devious, Hank Flynn. Madeline, yes. She set her cap for Hobie years ago, and would do just about anything to have her way with him...but you?" She shook her head, tsking. "I'm shocked, Hank, shocked and dismayed."

"You're just jealous because you didn't think of it."

"That's absolutely true." Rae glanced over her shoulder as Marti struggled up the path toting a tool case.

The girl puffed her way to where the adults were standing, then plopped the heavy toolbox in the dirt and wiped her forehead. "I got everything we're gonna need," she informed Hank proudly. "Hammers and screwdrivers and measuring tapes and that little bubbly level-thing you showed me how to use, and—" she paused to gulp air "—and even our caulking guns and stuff."

"Whoa. I'm impressed." He sat on his heels to flip the case open. "Actually, all we're going to do this afternoon is lay out the panning trough and visitor center with stakes and string. I'll see about getting a few bags of concrete delivered so we can set the foundations tomorrow."

"And I can help, right?"

He stroked her cheek with his fingertip. "I won't be able to do it without you."

Marti's little chest puffed until she looked ready to pop with pride.

Rae watched as Hank and her daughter rooted through the tools, retrieving some and leaving others, while engaged in animated discussion of the best way to attack the project. Both were clearly excited, with Marti's green eyes and Hank's dark ones reflecting identical exuberance. Marti brought out a sense of joy in Hank, who was otherwise quite quiet and withdrawn. Around Marti, Hank was more outgoing, cheerful and optimistic.

The changes Rae saw in her daughter were even more startling. Marti, who'd grown increasingly resentful of Steve's feminization efforts, had blossomed under Hank's supportive attention, exhibiting a pride and confidence that warmed her doting mother to the core. Hank was constantly encouraging the girl's inquisitive nature, praising her ingenuity and showing a parental-type pride in her accomplishments. What child wouldn't flourish in that kind of nurturing atmosphere? Marti was absolutely nuts about Hank.

And she wasn't the only one. The sexual tension between Hank and Rae had an electric quality, a crackling sensuality that made her feel more alive than she'd felt since those exquisite days with Martin. Rae had long ago accepted the sad fact that breathless desire and heart-melting hunger were part of her past, a fond memory that could never be recaptured. Now, with her heart racing and her pulse pounding hot in her veins, Rae realized that the fire inside still burned, awaiting just the right moment—just the right person—to burst into a blaze of passion.

Hank had reignited those flames, but Rae had learned hard lessons in her life, the most important of which had taught her that love and passion are not the same. Passion is fleeting; love is forever. Once, she'd confused the two, but never again. The last thing on earth she wanted was to fall in love with another dreamer, another adventurous risk-taker who, like Martin and even Hobie, would eventually succumb to the call of the wild.

So Rae was determined to resist the whispers of a heart she could no longer trust. It had deceived her before. She wouldn't allow it to deceive her again. Not for Hank Flynn. Not for anybody.

Chapter Ten

The sun was shining, the sky was blue and distant peaks gleamed white against the crystal-clear horizon. Surely this was the most glorious day ever created.

Walking briskly, Rae rounded the diner carrying two bagged lunches for the toiling duo that had been hard at work since sunrise. She was so in tune with her own buoyant mood that she'd nearly wound her way past the bungalows before she noticed a peculiar sound.

Silence.

No hammering. No grunts of effort or joking giggles. Nothing.

The staked layouts had been completed late last evening, and since a dozen bags of cement had been delivered early this morning, compliments of the government construction grant, Rae expected Hank and Marti to be busy mixing and pouring the foundations for the two small structures that held the key, she hoped, to the family's financial future.

As she eased into the construction clearing, she saw a pile of rumpled cement bags. They were empty, and a pair of plastic mixing troughs, rinsed clean, were lying beside a garden hose that snaked from a nearby spigot. Wooden stakes at the load points of the buildings had been replaced by fat cardboard canisters filled with fresh cement studded with I-beam braces and anchor bolts.

She glanced around, noting the pile of lumber that had been unloaded earlier in the day along with roofing materials, boxes of nails and other building supplies. The only thing missing was the construction crew.

A scuffling sound caught her attention. She glanced up to see Hobie sauntering over, heading in from the general direction of the main-street sidewalk.

He eyed the bags in her hand. "Lunchtime, is it?"

Rae nodded, shading her eyes as she scanned the surrounding woods. "Unfortunately, there doesn't seem to be anyone around to eat it." She angled a glance at him. "Are you hungry?"

"Me? Nope. Madeline done fixed me up with a pot o' chili that'll still be sticking to my ribs come Christmas." Rubbing his stomach to emphasize that, Hobie blinked benignly, alternately licking his lips and pursing them to indicate that he was indeed satisfied.

"Have you started painting Madeline's house yet?"

"Hmm? Oh, well, that's a big job, don'tcha know. Gotta set things out, make plans—" he avoided her gaze "—kinda slip into it, real gentle like."

Responding with a sage nod, Rae shifted the lunch bags to her left hand. "So what have you and Madeline been up to all morning?"

The old man's eyes gleamed. "Maps."

"Maps?"

"Yep. Topos of a spot not too far from here, where a half-dozen feeder creeks hit the river." Hobie's eyes shifted, as if he feared being overheard by squirrels. "I'd bet me a bucket o' paydirt that the old gal's mine is somewhere 'round them creeks.''

"Is that what she told you?''

A snort of disgust indicated that he thought that a stupid question. "'Course not, child. Don't you know nothing about mining? A person don't just come out and say where the good stuff is. They just, y'know, hint around, make you figure it out for your own self.''

"Ah.''

"That Madeline, she's sharp as a whip. Ain't never noticed that before." He scratched his chin, which was freshly dewhiskered despite the fact that his Sunday-go-to-meeting shave wasn't scheduled until tomorrow. "Yep, she's a right smart woman. Knows the difference between old placer and fresh just by looking, and ain't fooled by dry gravels at the river bar. Whaddaya think of that?''

"Smart,'' Rae assured him. "Very smart.''

She chose not to point out that Madeline's mining acumen appeared to be a somewhat recent acquisition. Even though the smitten woman had been unsuccessfully pursuing Hobie for years, it seemed a peculiar coincidence that she'd never once mentioned sharing such a notable common bond with the object of her affection, nor did it escape Rae's notice that Madeline's sudden interest in mining had come to light within mere hours of Hank Flynn's visit.

"Which reminds me,'' she murmured, glancing around the deserted site. "I wonder where Hank and Marti are.''

"Hmm? Oh, prob'ly went to see Sadie.''

Rae widened her eyes. "Why?''

Hobie made a production of clearing his throat. "Well, y'see, Hank was gonna clear a little rock for me, maybe 'barrow a few loads of gravel—'' he swallowed hard and tugged his droopy earlobe "—just to help an old man out, don'tcha know.''

"No, I don't know. First he takes over your house chores, then he volunteers to paint Madeline's house for you, and now he's down working your mine?" She skewered him with a look. "Exactly what is going on between you and Hank?"

"Why, nothing, child. The man's just a helpful sort, that's all."

Ordinarily Rae wouldn't believe a word her father said unless it was written down and notarized, but this time there was an odd ring of truth to his explanation. She thought of the fishing rod Hank had carved for Marti, and how he'd fixed Rae's car without expecting so much as a thank-you in return. If anyone could be described as the 'helpful sort,' it would certainly be Hank Flynn.

Somewhat mollified, she fell into step behind her father, who was hobbling down the path toward the creek.

They'd barely reached the mine path when the sound of childish giggles floated from around the next bend. "Look, Hank, they're all sniffing my worm."

"Fish don't actually 'sniff,'" came the amused reply. "But I'd say they're definitely checking it out. Be real quiet now. They can feel vibrations."

Rae quickened her pace, picking her way along the path to where several boulders extended into the creek to form a deep pool inside its rocky cradle. Hank was crouched beside Marti, who was kneeling on a boulder with her new fishing pole clasped in one hand while the other pointed frantically down at the water.

"He's gonna bite," Marti squeaked, bouncing on her knees. "He's gonna bite!"

"Easy, squirt. If you don't stop hollering— Oops."

Marti gasped, staring miserably over the edge of the boulder. "Aw, man. They all ran away."

"Hmm, just slipped on their little fin-Nikes and sprinted off." Chuckling, Hank slipped the pole out of the disgruntled girl's hand. "They just got spooked," he said, reeling in the line. "They'll be back."

"Yeah, but I want to catch one *now*." Scooting backward, Marti spun around and instantly brightened. "Hi, Mom! Hank made me a brand-new fishing pole and I almost caught me a fish!" Her happy gaze settled on the white bags Rae was carrying. "Did you bring us something to eat? I'm so empty I could fit in a door crack."

Before Rae could respond, the child scrambled to her bare feet, bolting across the slippery rocks like a sure-footed mule deer. She snatched one of the bags and peeked inside. "What kind of sandwiches did you bring?"

"One guess," Rae murmured, her gaze locked on Hank, who was watching her with eyes that smoldered with sensual longing. Her heart skipped a beat, and blood rushed past her ears with such force that she barely heard her daughter's disgusted moan.

"Oh, cripes, not tuna again." Heaving a resigned shrug, she nabbed the second bag and wiggled it over her head. "Hey, Hank! Mom brought food."

He laid the fishing rod down on the rocks, and spoke to Rae. "That was very thoughtful of you."

Rae moistened her lips and tangled her empty fingers together. "I just thought you might be a little hungry."

"I am." Their eyes met, their gazes locked in mesmerizing intensity. Hank was hungry, all right, but not for food.

The thought made Rae shiver. "I'm glad."

Marti's perplexed gaze wandered from Hank to her mother, and settled on her grampa, who'd finally hobbled into view. She jerked a thumb toward the mooning adults, and rolled her shoulders. "Hank must really like tuna."

Hobie chuckled. "Reckon he does, child, reckon he does."

* * *

"Thanks again," Hank said, tucking wadded-up lunch bags into a bucket beside Marti's can of beloved worms. "That really hit the spot."

"I'm glad you enjoyed it."

He drained the last of his soda before dropping the empty can into the bucket, as well. With a contented sigh, he pulled up one leg and propped an elbow on his thigh. "Other than Sunday afternoons, I think this is the first time I've ever seen you get farther than a few feet from the diner in the middle of the day."

"Arlene works every other Saturday. She needs the money and I need the rest."

"Arlene." Hank frowned thoughtfully. "She's the night-shift waitress, right? Nice lady. Every time I take a sip of coffee she refills the cup, and no matter how full I tell her I am, she insists on shoving a massive piece of pie in front of me."

"Arlene thinks men should be pampered."

"That's why I like her." He fiddled with a twig, slanting a mischievous glance at Rae, who was adjusting her position on the rock outcropping. "Arlene said you gave strict instructions that I was to have a hot meal every evening, and she wasn't to be stingy with the portions."

"That was your fault."

"My fault?"

"Since you insisted on ordering the cheapest cold sandwich on the menu, I had to look after my investment. Even a skinny man needs nourishment to put in a proper day's work."

He straightened his spine. "You think I'm skinny?"

"Lean," she amended, smiling at his worried frown. "Attractively lean."

"Attractive, huh." He shrugged. "I can live with that."

Rae sighed, wondering if *she* could live with it. Attractive was an understatement. The man was drop-dead gorgeous. Oddly enough, he didn't seem to realize that, which only added to his appeal. Hugging her knees, she forced her gaze across the creek where Hobie and Marti were perusing cracks in exposed bedrock for glints of trapped gold. Out of the corner of her eye she noticed Hank toss the twig into the stream and shift his bent leg until the crotch of his jeans stretched indecently.

Gulping, Rae returned her focus across the creek. "I, ah, went to the construction site. It looks like you got the foundations poured without any problem."

Beside her, he shifted again, seeming nonplussed by her comment. "The cement has to cure overnight before we can start framing. Marti has been such a good little helper, I thought she deserved a treat, that's all. Fishing was my idea, not hers."

Rae faced him curiously. "I wasn't criticizing. I think it's wonderful that you took Marti fishing."

His eyes warmed. "You do?"

"Of course." Her gaze flickered to the lovely hand-carved pole lying behind them on the rock. "I just wish I'd been there to see the expression on her face when you presented her with a gorgeous, hand-carved fishing rod. She must have been ecstatic."

"She seemed pleased."

"Which means she jumped in place, flailed her hands in the air and shrieked at the top of her lungs."

"That about describes it," Hank confessed, chuckling. "The child does get excited." After a moment his eyes clouded with peculiar nostalgia. "Marti is a beautiful girl, Rae, happy and loving and so filled with life. You've done a magnificent job raising her."

His earnest expression startled her. "You give me too much credit. Marti may look like me, but that's where the resemblance ends. Despite a chatterbug streak, I've always been rather shy, but my daughter was hell on wheels from the day she was born. I like to think she inherited that part of her personality from her father.''

Hank's gaze flickered away. "All that Marti is now and all that she will ever become is because of you, Rae. You've been everything to her, sacrificing your own needs, your own happiness to give your child the best life possible. I don't know how you managed, but you did. I understand…that is, Marti understands how difficult it's been for you, how much you've given up. She understands, and she loves you all the more for it.''

As he spoke, so softly at times that Rae could barely hear over the quiet rush of water, a cautious tingle radiated from within, cooling her skin. His whispered words were hallowed, almost devout yet oddly reticent, as if a sacred prayer had been uttered by one unworthy of such honor. There was wonder in his eyes, and sadness—a deep, profound sadness that touched Rae to the very core of her being. She wanted to heal him. She wanted to take away the pain. She wanted—

"Hank!" Across the creek Marti was waving her hands over her head. "I found a nugget! Can I borrow your pocketknife?''

It took a moment for Hank to shake his distant mood. He blinked at the beaming child, then turned to Rae. "Is she allowed to use a penknife?''

"As long as there's an adult to supervise." Rae slid a resigned look at Hobie, who was squatting beside his granddaughter, idly gazing into air and scratching himself. "Or at least, a reasonable facsimile of one.''

They shared a knowing smile. Reclining until his shoulders were mere inches above the rock, Hank dug the requested item out of his jeans pocket. He feinted a couple of tosses. "Go deep," he called, then flipped the closed knife across the water and right into Marti's waiting hands.

"Thanks!" Grinning happily, she dropped to her

knees, flipped out the blade and pried into a bedrock crevice just above the lapping water. A moment later she popped to her feet with something tiny pinched between her thumb and index finger. "It's a beauty," she squealed. "Big as a match head!"

Hobie peered over her shoulder. "Ain't never seen a match that teensy."

Refusing to acknowledge her grandfather's lack of enthusiasm, the thrilled girl promptly plopped her find in a small tube, screwed on the top and stuck the vial in the front pocket of her cutoffs. "I want to show Hank," she said, crawling along the embankment to a fallen log they'd used as a bridge.

Hobie leaned against a tree. "Y'know," he whined, "there'd be a heap more gold to see if Hank was to start hauling out Sadie's gravel like he promised."

Apparently pained by the reminder, Hank shot the old man a flinty stare, but made no other comment. Rae, who was already more than a little curious about the peculiar goings-on between Hank and her father, would have taken the opportunity to pose a pointed question except that little Marti was suddenly screeching along the rocky outcropping at a full sprint.

"Hank, Hank, want to see my nugget?"

Hank straightened. "Watch out, squirt, the rocks are—"

As Marti's foot shot out from under her, she let out a shriek and lurched into the trout pool.

"Slippery," Hank finished lamely.

A mass of soggy curls bobbed to the surface, then Marti stood in chest-high water, sputtering and stunned. She stared up, her eyes huge, with rivulets streaming down to drip off her quivering chin.

Rae scrambled to her knees, leaning over the edge. "Oh, sweetie, are you okay?"

"I'm all wet," she wailed, flapping her arms.

Rae bit her lip to keep from smiling. "Yes," she finally murmured, struggling with the laughter that was bubbling up her throat. "You certainly are."

"Mom, it's not funny!"

"No, of course not." Turning away before her grin broke loose, Rae shielded her face with her hand and concealed a chuckle with a cough. Her smile faded when she saw Hank yanking off his boots. "What on earth are you doing?"

"Taking Marti's suggestion."

"What suggestion— Oh, you're not."

He left his jeans on but slipped out of his T-shirt, then stood with his bare toes wiggling over the edge of the rock, pinching his nostrils shut. "Geronimo!" he bellowed, and leapt into the deep part of the pool.

Swamped by Hank's wake, Marti came up sputtering again, but this time she was also grinning. "Now you're all wet, too."

"That's the idea," Hank said cheerfully. "No self-respecting trout is going to be heading back this way until things quiet down, so I don't think they'd mind if we used their pool for a while."

"Maybe they'll come play with us."

"I doubt it. Trout are pretty bashful."

Hobie looked up. "Hell, trout ain't bashful. If you ask me, they's downright aggravating. Why, I remember once in '68, when me and ol'—" A blast of icy water drowned out the rest of the story. Hobie leapt to his feet, cussing and wiping his wet face. He glared at the two grinning creatures who bobbed in the creek, flat hands hovering over the surface in a silent dare. Hobie snorted. "If'n you don't wanna hear no stories, all you hafta do is say so."

"We don't wanna hear no stories," came the simultaneous reply.

Sniffing, Hobie probed his ear with a fingertip, then spat on a rock and ambled toward his mine, mumbling.

"Think I'll go have me a chat with Sadie. Now, there's a gal can 'preciate a good tale now'n again."

Giggling madly, Marti dug in to her pocket and handed the precious vial to Rae. "Hold it for me, okay?"

"Okay." Rae laid the glass tube in the bucket, beside the worm can. "There. Nice and safe."

Satisfied, the girl flopped on her belly and wiggled like a dolphin toward the deepest part of the pool. She surfaced, treading water, frowning as she glanced around. "Where's Ha— Eee!" Her startled gasp turned into delighted giggles as Hank popped up beside her. "What are you doing?"

"Just checking the depth," he said, gliding onto his back. "See that branch?" As Marti looked up, so did Rae. Both focused on the huge oak limb protruding over the deepest part of the pool. "Looks like a great place for a rope swing, doesn't it?"

Marti's eyes sprang wide open. "Where would we get the rope?"

"Hobie has rope down at the mine."

"Think he'd let us use some?"

"We could ask." While Marti whooped with excitement, Hank rolled lazily, floating on his side. He gestured up at the branch and called out to Rae. "Is it okay with you?"

Her smiling nod created a whirlpool of activity as they raced each other to the bank and dashed down the path. Moments later they returned with a huge coil of orange-and-black rope draped like a bandolier around Hank's bare chest. The sight nearly stopped Rae's heart. She puffed her cheeks, breathing in quick, shallow gasps as if she was in labor. In a sense, she was.

Shirtless, Hank Flynn was just about the most entrancing human Rae had ever seen in her life. His attractively lean muscles rippled in the afternoon sunshine, drawing her hungry gaze the way nectar draws bees. The sexy

mane of wet hair clung to his shoulders, evoking an enigmatic, almost mystical appearance. That alluring mustache added intensity to his gaze, making him seem even
more gothic, more mysterious. More thrilling.

At that moment it would not have seemed out of character for him to whip out a jeweled saber and proceed to
slay any dragons foolish enough to emerge from the quiet
waters.

Rae was entranced, mesmerized, completely lost in the
flood of emotions evoked by a fantasy that was far too
vivid for sheer imagination. The rush of blood past her
ears was no dream; the painful pounding of her heart was
as real as the rock beneath her; and the dizzying twist of
time and space, the sensation of yesterdays and tomor-
rows all tangled up in her mind—that also seemed real
despite the tiny voice of reason whispering in her ear.

With great resolve Rae closed her eyes, concentrating
on the here and now, the place where a man she hardly
knew and the daughter she adored were enjoying a mild
spring day splashing in the creek. That was reality, and
Rae's mind closed around it like a fist.

From a distance she heard Marti's shouts of encouragement, Hank's teasing replies. Taking a deep breath,
Rae opened her eyes just as Hank climbed the tree and
shimmied across the low-hanging branch. Standing below, Marti watched, shading her eyes while he knotted
the rope around the branch, then fashioned a foot loop at
the end of the newly created swing. That completed, he
called Marti over, and in less than a heartbeat two Tarzan
wanna-bes were swinging over the creek, yelling, laughing, splashing into the icy pool and generally having so
much fun that Rae was absolutely mesmerized by their
joy.

There was something so familiar about the scene,
something she couldn't quite put her finger on—

Of course. The thought hit like a body blow. Everything fell into place. Hank, she realized, related to Marti the same way Martin would have. He would have encouraged his daughter's inquisitive nature, taken pride in her rebel spirit and nourished her wonderful zest for life, just as Hank was doing now. And as he'd done since the day he'd thumbed his way into their lives.

Rae was stunned by the revelation, and might have carried it through to its logical conclusion had a furious voice not startled her.

"My God," Steven roared, marching down the path like an avenging angel in a gray flannel suit. "Have you all taken leave of your minds?"

Rae stood. "Hello, Steven. How did you know where we were?"

"The entire town knows where you are," he replied tightly. "I've never heard so much hollering in my entire life."

At that point Marti yelled, "Watch me, Mom!" Then she stuck her foot in the rope loop, swung out over the pool, shrieking, and dropped into the water, swamping Hank. A moment later both heads popped to the surface, grinning madly. Marti waved. "That was good, huh?"

"Very good, sweetie." Rae waved back, then turned toward Steve, who was white as a glacier.

He clenched his fists, glaring at the two swimmers. "Martina, get out of there at once."

Marti's grin faded. "How come?"

"I expect obedience, not questions. Come here, young lady." He pointed to a spot directly in front of him. "Now!"

Shocked silence gave way to instant anger. Rae held up her hand, indicating that Marti should stay where she was, then fixed Steve with a furious stare. "How dare you speak to my child in that tone?"

"Excuse me?"

"You heard what I said."

Clearly he had indeed heard her, and wasn't the least bit pleased. "You saw what she just did. Don't tell me that you actually approve?"

"I'm right here, watching. If I didn't approve, don't you think I would have made that clear by now?"

The man's jaw slackened, his eyes clouded by confusion. "Good Lord, Rae, can't you see how dangerous that is? If she misses the center of that small pool, she could either land on that bedrock—" he pointed to an embankment of solid granite a few feet from where Hank and Marti were bobbing "—or hit the shallows. Either way, she could break her neck."

Although Hank spun around, frowning, to follow Steve's gestures, Rae had already considered both possibilities, and found them to be remote. A flick of her hand relayed that to Steve. "There's an element of danger in everything, Steve. The proper precautions have been taken, and my daughter has a right to play like any other child. I'm not going to put her in a bottle simply because you're paranoid."

"Paranoid?" The hurt in his eyes pricked her. She regretted her thoughtless words, but before she could amend them, Steve spoke again. Quietly this time, and with great sadness. "I don't understand, Rae. You are deliberately questioning my authority in front of Martina. We have discussed this before. If I am to become her father, she must respect my—"

Rae laid a hand on his arm, stopping him. "Steve, please. Let's not talk about it now."

His eyes widened, then narrowed in comprehension. "You've decided not to marry me, haven't you?"

Rae looked away, wishing the ground would swallow her whole. "The truth is that I never made that decision in the first place, Steve. You know that. I promised only to consider it and, well..." She paused to moisten her lips. "I just don't think it would work. I'm very sorry."

The silence was deafening. It took a moment for Rae to muster enough courage to meet Steve's gaze, and when she did, she nearly broke into tears. The man was clearly shattered.

All he said was, "I see."

"I don't think you do," she said gently. "Not really."

He frowned at the sleeve of his wool suit coat, and brushed away imaginary lint with his fingertips. "It's Flynn, isn't it? You're…attracted to him."

Rae couldn't deny it, but wasn't ready to admit it aloud, either. If she did, she'd have to explain her feelings. How could she possibly explain something she didn't understand?

"All I know for certain is that marriage between you and I would be a terrible, terrible mistake. We're too different, Steve. We'd make each other miserable."

A sheen of moisture brightened his eyes. "You could never make me miserable, Rae."

She lowered her gaze, trying desperately to swallow the lump wedged in her throat. She couldn't cry; refused to cry.

A tear slid down her cheek. Steve tenderly wiped it away. "You're right, of course. Marriage is a lifetime commitment, not to be taken lightly. In the face of such awesome responsibility, a certain amount of anxiety is to be expected. I understand your distress."

She simply shook her bowed head without comment. He didn't understand. He couldn't, but she was too drained to enlighten him.

Steve lowered his hand, clicking his heels together the way he did when a decision had been reached. "So, it's settled, then."

Rae's head snapped up. "What's settled?"

"We'll not speak of marriage again until you're ready."

"Steve—"

"Until then, things will remain as they are. Shall I bring anything for dinner tomorrow evening?"

"I, uh—"

"Wine, perhaps?" His eyes pleaded with her.

Rae's shoulders lowered. "Yes, that would be lovely."

"Very well, then."

As he turned to leave, Rae touched his sleeve. "I don't understand, Steve. After what I've just told you..." Words failed. Her hand fell helplessly to her side. "Why?"

Steve's gaze slid past her shoulder, to settle on Hank, who'd emerged from the pool and was leaning against the rope tree, watching them from across the creek. "He will leave someday," Steve said quietly. "Men like that always do."

With that chilling pronouncement, Steve spun on his polished heel and disappeared into the woods.

Rae stood there, staring at nothing, with the frightening words circling her mind. *He will leave someday.*

Men like that—

"Mom, tell him it's okay."

Always do.

"Please, Mom?"

Taking a ragged breath, Rae turned in time to see Hank shimmy along the drooping branch to remove the rope swing. At the base of the tree, Marti was hopping from foot to foot, plainly distressed.

Rae called out to Hank. "You don't have to take it down. Maybe if it was shortened a bit..."

But Hank was already coiling the loose rope around his bent arm. "Ruskin is right," he said. "The rocks across the creek are much too dangerous. I wasn't thinking."

"Mom!" Marti stamped her bare foot so hard she flinched.

"Hey, squirt," Hank said, climbing down. "There are lots of safer ways to have fun."

The girl folded her arms, glowering up at him. "Name one."

"Well, let's see." He laid the rope coil on the ground, pretending to consider that. "Instead of naming one, how about if I demonstrate?" With that, he hoisted the startled child over his shoulder as if she were a sack of grain, then charged into the creek. A moment after he'd dumped the squealing girl into the deep pool, he dived below the surface, pulling her down. They both came up sputtering and laughing.

Marti pushed a mop of wet hair out of her face. "Come swimming with us, Mom. It's real fun."

"No, I—"

"Afraid to get your hair wet?" Hank taunted. "Or maybe know that as trout pool divers go, you'd be way out of your league?"

She skewered him with a look. "Don't even go there, Hank. I'm a better swimmer than both of you put together."

"Talk's cheap." He shrugged. "That's okay, Marti, if your mom is scared of a little water, we shouldn't make fun of her."

Rae yanked off her shoes. "I hope you can breathe with a trout stuffed up your nose."

She dived in and shot smoothly to the bottom of the pool. A moment later she surfaced, but not before she'd stuffed a smooth river rock into Hank's jeans. He flailed his hands, feigning panic, and sank out of sight. Temporarily. Before Rae could swim out of his way, he'd grasped her around the waist and was dragging her below the surface.

Hank kissed her there, beneath the cool water. And Rae responded, with more heat and passion than she'd have believed possible. Then they surfaced, laughing, and spent the rest of the afternoon trying to drown each other between stolen underwater kisses.

Rae had never been happier in her life. The afternoon would have been absolutely perfect except for the warning that continued to circle her mind. *He will leave someday. He will leave. He will.*

Men like that always do.

Chapter Eleven

Sunday mornings were the worst. The predawn pall seemed even darker, the tiresome trudge from house to diner even more sluggish and bleak. People should sleep in on Sundays to awake vital, refreshed and ready for quality time with God and family.

Rae yawned, stumbled on a shadowed rock, then heaved a weary sigh. What she wouldn't give for the funds to hire a Sunday breakfast crew. Someday, perhaps.

But not today.

From the corner of her eye she noticed an oddity that provided distraction from her gloomy thoughts. She focused her bleary gaze, hurried her gait and realized that the parking lot was illuminated by a shaft of light emanating from the front windows of the diner. Either Arlene had forgotten to turn the lights off last night—which wasn't likely—or someone was inside.

She rounded the corner, peering through the glass door. She saw no one, and vaguely wondered if Hobie had come in early to start his kitchen chores. If so, it would be the first time in living memory. The grumbling old geezer usually ambled in at two minutes of six, cranky as a stomped snake. On a good day he'd acknowledge his daughter's presence with a gruff snort; usually, however, he'd ignore her until his KP shift was over, at which time he'd fling off his apron and sprint home as if his butt was on fire. Occasionally it was, since Hobie wasn't the world's most efficient chef. There was the time he'd backed into a blazing burner—

A clunking sound startled her.

She listened, and heard it again, a metallic clatter coming from the kitchen. Stealthily opening the front door, she reached up to silence the cowbell before it could announce her entrance. Tiptoeing through the diner, she started to call her father's name when a loud crash was followed by a string of angry oaths.

Recognizing the voice, Rae swiveled around the tables, ducked under the counter bridge and skidded to the kitchen doorway just as Hank bent to recover a dropped frying pan. He straightened, frowning, and shook the pan in her direction. "Don't even think about laughing."

If Rae hadn't been so numbed by shock, she would have already been in stitches. The poor man was wrapped in a full-bib apron and wearing a floppy white chef's hat, beneath which his lovely hair had been tied and tucked into an unflattering net. He looked like an unhappy cross between Spiderman and Chef Boyardee.

It took a moment before her stunned brain could convince her tongue to move. When it did, a peculiar squeak came out. "What are…you doing…*here?*"

"Plotting revenge," Hank muttered, clanging the frying pan onto a burner.

Rae followed the motion with her gaze, and saw several frying pans had already been placed on the stove, along with a large griddle that was used exclusively for pancakes, to leave the built-in unit free for greasier fare like hash browns and bacon.

A huge stainless steel bowl piled with fresh eggs was on the counter beside the cooktop, along with the hand-written recipe cards. That seemed rather odd, since the cards were rarely used, even by Hobie.

It was almost as if...as if...

Her eyes widened in horror. "Oh, no. Tell me it's not true."

His glum gaze confirmed the worst. "Hobie has, ah, plans this morning."

"Plans?" Rae jammed her fists on her hips, leaning forward in utter dismay. *"Plans?"*

Hank issued a miserable shrug. "He and Madeline are driving up to her claim. They'll be back for church, though."

"They'll be back for church," Rae repeated with a distinctly Louie-like rasp. "Well, I'm so relieved." She tapped her foot while a familiar throb worked its way across the top of her skull. "So you volunteered. Again."

Hank hung his head, glaring down at the neat row of recipe cards as if wishing them dead. "Yeah," he said through gritted teeth. "I volunteered."

Spinning around, Rae sagged against the doorjamb, rubbing her forehead. "I'm going to kill him."

"Not if I see him first," came the dour reply.

She tossed an anxious glance over her shoulder. "I suppose it's a little late to ask, but can you actually cook?"

He puffed his cheeks, eyeing the arranged utensils as if they were the enemy. "Let's put it this way. If it's scrambled, I can manage. If it comes out of a toaster, I can manage. Anything else is iffy."

"Wonderful." She gave a dry snort and glanced at the clock. "Well, we have fifty-five minutes to turn you into a short-order chef. Lesson one—'' she gestured toward the stove ''—your griddle is upside down.''

Rae's pencil hovered over the order pad without making contact. ''To tell you the truth, Mrs. Zyack, I don't recommend the Denver omelet this morning. The, ah, green peppers that arrived yesterday didn't look fresh, so I sent them back. How about some nice scrambled eggs and toast?''

The woman frowned, gazing back down at the menu. ''Well, dear, if you think that's best.''

''I do.'' Rae snatched the menu away, and forced a cheery smile at the man beside her. ''The same for you, sir?''

The elderly man blinked up. ''Actually—''

Rae cut him off. ''Wonderful,'' she mumbled, scribbling out the order. ''I'll be right back with your coffee.''

She hurried toward the kitchen pass-through, ripped off the order slip and hooked it on the carousel. ''Two scrambled with toast,'' she called to the harried man behind the stove.

''Yeah, yeah,'' Hank muttered, swinging a spatula like a sword. ''How long is it supposed to take hash browns to brown?''

Hoisting on tiptoes, she leaned through the opening until she could see the stove. ''Forever, unless you turn on the heat.''

Hank scowled down at the forlorn frozen potato patties on the built-in griddle. ''You can't see the fire under this thing. How do you know it's on?''

''It gets hot,'' she snapped, more angry with her father than his beleaguered stand-in. ''Flip that center knob to the left—''

''Miss, may I have more coffee?''

Swallowing a sigh, she tossed a smile at the man holding up his cup. ''Right away, sir.'' A quick glance back

into the kitchen confirmed that Hank was fiddling with
the proper knob, so Rae snatched up two coffee carafes
and charged around the diner chirping, "Regular or de-
caf?" until Marti came flying through the door, flushed
with excitement.

"Mom, Mom, can I go with Gramps and Madeline,
please, please, please?"

Stiffening, Rae shot a killing look through the front
window. "Is your grandfather perchance in the parking
lot?"

"Uh-huh."

Rae narrowed her eyes into mean little slits. "Have
him come inside, please. I'd like a word with him."

Marti's shoulders slumped. "He said you might." She
watched her mother fill two more cups, then followed her
back to the coffee station. "Gramps won't come in,
Mom. He says they hafta go right away. Can I go,
too...please?"

"I don't think so—"

A frantic hand gripped her wrist. "*Please*, Mom!"

With a massive sigh, Rae shook off her daughter's
hand long enough to replace the carafes on the heating
element. Under the circumstances, she knew perfectly
well that Hobie wasn't about to set foot in the diner. He
valued his life too much, which was why he'd sent Marti
instead.

In truth, Rae could really have used Marti's help in
serving and taking orders. But then there'd be three miserable people instead of two. Besides, the least Hobie
could do was to keep his granddaughter entertained while
Rae tried to deal with the crisis that he'd created.

She sighed. "Oh, all right, you can go."

"Thank you, Mommy, thank you." Marti dashed past
the counter, then paused. "Oh, and I'm supposed to tell
you that we'll be home for dinner."

"Dinner...but what about church? Marti—" When

Rae spun around, the cowbell was still jingling and her daughter was gone.

And a man in booth two was waving at her. "Excuse me, but we have to leave soon. Will it be much longer?"

"I'm sure it won't," Rae told him, not sure at all. She hurried to the pass-through. "Where's the French toast?"

"Huh? Oh, yeah, I've got it right here...." He forked two withered sausages beside a piece of soggy, slightly singed bread, then squinted down at the recipe card. "Powdered sugar," he muttered, scowling around the room. "Where the hell do you keep powdered sugar?"

"It's in that big shaker over there," Rae whispered, slanting a glance over her shoulder as the cowbell jingled. Oh, God. A family of six. Would it never end? She refocused into the kitchen just as Hank swung the shaker around. "No! That's the wrong—"

Hank gasped as salt poured out.

Rae slapped her forehead. "Oh, good Lord."

Without missing a beat Hank snatched up the singed bread, shook it over the sink, then flung it back on the plate and doused it with fluffy powdered sugar. "One French toast," he growled, thunking the plate down beside four orders of scrambled eggs. "Now go away."

"Would that I could," Rae mumbled, staring down at the awful mess. Hopefully the guy would be too hungry to notice. She grabbed a huge bottle of syrup, just in case.

Hank hadn't felt this frantic since his days in the jungle. The diner kitchen had become a miniature war zone, with the constant cacophony of sniping appliance timers, toasters popping like small arms fire, and the occasional mortarlike resonance of iron skillets crashing to the floor.

Rae's harried face appeared over the pass-through counter. "One sun-up, two scrambleds and a short stack." She snapped a green paper slip on the carousel, threw him a terrified look and disappeared back into the chaos of the bustling diner.

Heaving a sigh, Hank sagged forward, his eyes darting toward the completely disheveled recipe cards. One sun-up. What the hell was that?

Oh, yeah. A fried egg.

Okay, he could do that. He shoveled a mostly brown, shredded potato patty onto a plate beside a pile of scrambled yellow lumps and slid the plate onto the counter. He was supposed to holler "pick up" at this point, but had eliminated that process half an hour ago because the diner was so noisy that Rae couldn't hear him anyway.

He flung three more frozen potato patties onto the sizzling grease griddle, poured a couple of sloppy circles of pancake batter onto the heated portable griddle and snatched several whole eggs out of the bowl beside the stove.

After breaking one egg directly into a small frying pan, he emptied the rest into his scrambling bowl, following directions that by now were indelibly etched in his mind: a dollop of milk, whisk until fluffy, pour into heated pan and stir until hardened into fat, dry chunks.

A moment later he portioned the congealed mess between two plates, grabbed four pieces of freshly popped toast and studied the fried egg, which stared up at him through a quivering eye of goo. The edge seemed nice and crispy, though, so he figured it was done. Or at least, close enough. When he reached for a plate, however, he came up with a handful of air.

There were no more clean plates. Great, he thought miserably, that was just great. What the hell else could go wrong?

Frustrated beyond belief, Hank plopped the fried-egg pan on a trivet, dashed over to open the dishwasher and was instantly blinded by a stinging burst of steam. Staggering backward, he rubbed his eyes and reached behind him for a counter rag.

"Three short stacks," Rae called. "Two scrambled."

Hank stumbled around, eyelids burning. The pancakes. He hadn't flipped the damned things. Unable to locate the rag, he grabbed the hem of his apron, but as he bent over to wipe his eyes, he hit the egg bowl with the top of his head and knocked it off the counter. The bowl crashed to the floor, spewing cracked shells and slippery egg guts from one end of the kitchen to the other.

"Two French toast, one bagel with cream."

Hank lurched toward the stove. One minute he was upright; the next, he was flat on his back, swimming in slime.

"Sun-up with ham, corn flakes, hold the fruit and— Oh, God, Hank! Something's burning!"

He levered himself up, horrified by a curl of black smoke simultaneously wafting from charcoaled hash browns and blackened pancakes. Shifting to his knees, he scuttled forward like a drunken crab and grabbed the griddle knob. There was a sickening crack as it came off in his hands.

Rae skidded into the kitchen, turned off the fire under the smaller pancake griddle then used her fingers to frantically twist at the bare post that controlled the sizzling grease griddle. She threw a feral look over her shoulder and practically bared her teeth. "The knob, dammit, where's the *knob?*"

Hank opened his palm to display several pieces of ragged plastic. Her jaw drooped. Behind her, smoke continued to rise from the shredded black lumps.

"Pliers," Hank mumbled, using the counter to pull himself upright. "Where do you keep the tools?"

Rae stared at him as if he'd gone mad. "This is a *kitchen.*"

Cursing under his breath, he yanked open the nearest

drawer. A moment later he attacked the bare knob post with a pair of pasta tongs and the griddle flame finally flickered out.

Rae, who was fanning the last remnants of smoke away with a dish towel, looked about ready to explode. "This is the last straw. I've had it, do you hear? *Had it.*"

"Am I fired?" Hank asked hopefully.

Ignoring his question, she flung down the towel, yanked the order pad out of her pocket and thrust it into his palms. "I'll cook. You serve." She leaned forward until her nose was an inch from his own. "Write down orders. Pour coffee. And if anyone feels the need to pay for their food—which is extremely doubtful at this point—put the money in the cash register and promise to remember them in your prayers. Do you think you can handle that?"

"I'll, ah, do my best." He flinched as she snatched off his hat. "Are you sure you wouldn't rather fire me?"

She grabbed up a spatula and advanced on him. "My father will pay dearly for this, but in the meantime, you're all I have. If you try to escape, if you leave me alone with this bedlam, I'll hunt you down like a dog. Got it?"

Indicating that he did indeed get it, Hank pocketed the order pad and went into the dining room, where he spent the rest of the morning scribbling orders, pouring coffee and imagining hundreds of innovative ways for a certain grizzled old extortionist to die ugly.

After the diner finally closed at noon, Hank stayed behind to clean up the mess so Rae could return to the house for a brief rest before afternoon church services. It had taken a while to talk her into leaving him alone again, particularly after this morning's fiasco. Eventually, however, she'd succumbed to Hank's impeccable logic and her own utter exhaustion.

It hadn't taken long to scrape and mop the floor, after which he'd wiped down the stove and counters, and loaded the deadly dishwasher. Fixing the damaged griddle, however, could be a little tricky. The knob itself was shattered beyond repair.

According to Rae, a new one would have to be ordered from the manufacturer, which could take weeks. Until then the grease griddle would be useless, an unacceptable situation that Rae feared would send the diner's temperamental chef into a rage. She was scared spitless the guy would quit, and Hank realized her fears were far from groundless. Short-order cooks didn't grow on trees, and after the chaos he'd lived through earlier, Hank had acquired considerable respect for the profession.

As for the griddle, Hank had broken the damn thing, so it was up to him to fix it. He just wasn't sure how.

Squatting so the stove control panel was at eye level, Hank studied the problem. Fortunately, the metal post that actually turned the flame on and off was intact. All he needed was something that would fit tightly around the post and provide a finger grip for the user. A pair of pliers would do the job, but would be awkward, to say the least.

No, he had to install something right on the post, something that would be easy to grasp and twist. Something like a fat wing nut.

A mental schematic formed in his mind as he studied the knob post, which was flattened on one side to provide turning torque. If he could find the proper sized bolt, then file the inside diameter to fit, it just might work.

"What do you think, little fellow?" he murmured, leaning so close that his nose brushed the post tip. "I'll need your cooperation. Are you willing to help me out here?"

The post said nothing.

Hank straightened, grinning. "That's the spirit."

He gave the wounded appliance an encouraging pat, then headed out to the construction site to pillage for parts. It took a few minutes to find a wing nut large enough to comfortably fit a man's fingers, and even longer to match it up with a bolt with a center hole small enough for precision reaming. He tucked the hardware in his pocket, scrounged a small file drill from the shed, and even managed to locate a compression nut that would keep the rigged wing-knob from sliding too far down the post.

Pleased by his own cleverness, he hurried back to the diner, whistling.

After a half hour of drilling, filing and fitting parts, Hank proudly flipped the makeshift knob and heard the satisfying whoosh of flame. "There, now, doesn't that feel better?" He squinted through a thin crack beneath the griddle, watching the flames rise and fall as he adjusted the wing nut.

"Looking good," he murmured. "A little touchy, but workable."

Flipping the fire off, he gave the stove a hard stare. "I expect you to behave yourself. If you act up again, I'll tighten your screws until your gas tubes bulge, understand? Hmm, what's that?"

He leaned down, pretending to listen. "Ah, well, I can't do anything about the cook's cold hands. You'll just have to grill and *beurre* it. Get it? *Beurre* is French for butter. Grin and bear...grill and *beurre*. It's a pun."

He paused as if expecting the appliance to giggle, then heaved an exaggerated sigh. "No sense of humor, eh? Well, don't get all burned up about it." Chuckling, he nudged a cast-iron burner grate with his elbow. "Now, you've got to admit that was funny."

The stove remained stubbornly silent.

Hank's attention, however, was directed elsewhere. As he wiped his hands on a grease rag, he studied the steam-

spewing dishwasher at the far end of the oblong room.
Earlier he'd noticed standing water around the heating
element after the cleaning cycle was complete. To Hank's
handyman eyes, that indicated that either the drain tube
was misaligned or the air gap connection to the plumbing
system was clogged. There was also the possibility that
the machine itself wasn't properly leveled.

It wouldn't take long to find out.

Hank's tool hand started to twitch. Before he could
consider the consequences, he was sprawled on the floor
removing the dishwasher's access cover. He laid the
panel aside, and used a flashlight to peer into the maze
of tubes and wiring. "This won't hurt a bit," he murmured.

Then he reached for a wrench.

Rae turned over, moaning, and buried her head in the
pillow to avoid the shaft of sunlight burrowing into her
slumber. It annoyed her, because her tightly structured
world was always dark when she went to bed and dark
when she woke up. Since sunshine and sleep simply
didn't go together, she resented the untimely intrusion.

It took a moment for her fuzzy mind to connect the
paradox and flash a warning. Her eyes flew open. "Oh,
good grief." She whipped around until her feet hit the
floor. Momentarily befuddled, she wasn't certain what
time it was, or even what day of the week.

She sat on the edge of the bed, rubbing her eyes. Visions of spilled eggs and burned potatoes danced through
her mind. "Sunday," she mumbled, peering over her fingertips. It was Sunday, and unless the clock on her nightstand was playing a bad joke, the last church service of
the day was nearly over.

With a frustrated groan, she padded into the kitchen
for a glass of water. The last thing she remembered was
laying out her church clothes, then deciding to lie down

and rest her eyes for a minute. That had been nearly two hours ago. Even if God forgave her absence, she doubted the pastor would, particularly when he learned that Marti and her grandfather had found the lure of Madeline Rochester's mining claim more appealing than one of his sermons.

Rae suspected, however, that the Hoopers wouldn't be the only family playing hooky from church. It was a glorious day, warm and clear, with just the slightest hint of cotton-soft breeze. Much too beautiful, she decided, to be cooped up inside. Actually, it was the perfect afternoon for a picnic at the creek.

Of course, she should invite Hank to join her. The poor man was certainly entitled to some rest and relaxation, particularly in light of what he'd gone through this morning. They could pack a light lunch, then stroll down a path cooled by dappled shadows until they found the perfect spot to dangle their bare feet in the creek and plot revenge on Hobie.

Afterward, with the music of the bubbling water as a backdrop, maybe Hank would slip his arm around her shoulders. Maybe he'd gaze deeply into her eyes, his lips moving closer, and closer still...

A shiver of anticipation propelled her forward. She practically ran down the steps, and skipped toward Hank's bungalow like a lighthearted teenager.

Her enthusiasm was tempered when she realized that Hank wasn't there. Disappointed, she crossed through the construction site. He wasn't there, either, so her gaze shifted toward the diner. Surely he wouldn't still be inside.

Then again, she'd left him with a terrible mess to clean up. Alone.

A guilty chill dampened her happy mood. Fatigue and anger were no excuse for having shirked her share of responsibility. Hank had been tired, too, and judging by the constant twitch of his clamped jaw, he hadn't been any happier about the situation than she'd been. But he hadn't been the one who stomped off like a thwarted child.

Rae plotted a path toward the diner, determined to apologize for her unseemly behavior and, if possible, to make amends. She entered the diner quietly, silencing the cowbell with her hand, and hadn't taken three steps before she heard it.

She stopped in her tracks, listening to the percussive rhythm of something metallic, like tools drumming on a steel pot. She'd heard that sound before, years ago. A lifetime ago.

Then came the voice, cheery, frighteningly familiar. "The concert is over, bud. Now open your mouth and hold still."

Rae closed her eyes, trying to shake off the memory. *Machines enjoy music,* he'd once told her. *It relaxes them.*

"Quit wiggling. You're only going to make it worse."

Rae's eyelids snapped open. For a brief, terrifying moment she couldn't remember if the words had come out of the kitchen, or from some lost image of the past.

"So the cook's got a girlfriend, hmm? Tsk, tsk. Gossip from a dishing dishwasher...get it?" A low male chuckle rumbled from the kitchen.

The sound hit Rae like a fist, nearly doubling her over. She gasped, clutching her midsection, realizing that she hadn't awakened at all. She was still in her house, sleeping, and this was all a dream.

No, it was a nightmare, a cruel and terrible nightmare. Any minute she'd wake up.

Any minute.

But she didn't wake up. Instead, she found herself moving toward the kitchen, drawn by a force more powerful than reason. She was in the doorway now, watching the familiar figure sprawled on the floor with his hands thrust into the innards of the dismantled dishwasher.

"You have beautiful drain tubes," he whispered to the machine. "Your wires are exquisite, so smooth, so tightly wrapped, so enticingly electric."

Rae stood there, frozen in disbelief. A tiny gasp slipped from her throat.

Instantly Hank looked over his shoulder. His eyes widened. "Rae?" The color drained from his face. He withdrew his hands from the belly of the machine, dropping his tools. "Rae." As he stood, eyes wary, his unfettered hair tumbled to his shoulders. He extended his hand, a gesture of helplessness. And perhaps, of fear.

He was speaking again, but this time Rae had been swept into a time portal, a spinning vortex where past and present swirled together in such a terrifying jumble that she didn't know where one left off and the other began. All she knew for certain was that she was looking at a man, a man she knew.

A man she didn't know.

In her mind's eye, a mental metamorphosis was taking place. Rae pictured Martin Manning, tools in hand, chatting with a conglomerate of gears and wires as if it were his best chum.

But as she studied the memory of Martin's image, something strange and terrifying happened. The softness of youth dissolved into the hardened planes of masculine maturity. Lines appeared at the corners of his eyes. His nose tweaked slightly to the left, shadowing a dark mustache that disguised the shape of his mouth. His buzzed scalp sprouted a thick mane of shoulder-length hair.

Martin Manning's memory evolved into the reality of Hank Flynn.

And Rae's entire world collapsed.

Chapter Twelve

"It's not what you think," Hank said slowly, lifting a helpless hand.

Rae touched her throat, her eyes enormous in a face white as death. She swayed slightly, and Hank moved forward, fearing she was on the verge of collapse. Before he could reach her, she sagged against the doorjamb, stiffening her arm to hold him at bay.

"Don't touch me," she whispered. Her chin quivered. A sheen of sudden moisture brightened her haunted eyes. The entire gamut of emotions flickered across her face—shock and disbelief, a fleeting surge of joy that immediately dissolved into fear, and finally into shaking rage. "How...dare...you?"

Each trembling utterance sent a shaft of pure misery into Hank's heart. "I never wanted this to happen."

She stared at him with eyes hollowed by shock. "That's obvious. A new face. A new name." She closed her eyes for a moment, then opened them, focusing with

lucid clarity. "A lot of trouble just to extricate yourself
from my life."

Bowing his head, Hank clutched the back of his neck
as if the desperate gesture could prevent his rubbery legs
from giving way. He knew that Rae's anger was caused
by more than the impact of seeing him alive after having
mourned his death for over a decade. A bitter pain was
reflected in her eyes, along with transparent memories of
their last moments together, moments when Martin Manning had shattered her faith and broken her heart.

"None of this was planned, Rae." Even to his own
ears, he sounded raspy, dull. Desperate. "When I left
Gold River, I honestly thought I'd be back in six months,
a year at most. I never meant to leave you—"

"Stop." She shook her head, biting her lower lip as if
willing herself not to cry. She took a deep breath, and
met his gaze directly. "No more lies. Not from you, not
from me." Sniffing, she wiped her wet cheek with her
thumb. "All these years I've told everyone that you'd
been ordered overseas, because I couldn't bear to be pit-
ied for the truth."

Hank looked away, unable to block out the memory
of what had happened that final night. They'd walked to
the creek, to their special place. It had been a soft evening, gentle with summer scents and warm breezes. Martin Manning had taken a night made for passion and
turned it into a black world of betrayal.

Hank still flinched at the memory of his clumsiness. A
lie would have been kinder, but it had never occurred to
him. He'd never lied to Rae. Ever.

In retrospect, that may not have been a virtue, particularly when he remembered the anguish in her eyes when
he'd told her the truth. Because Martin Manning had
never been ordered overseas.

He'd volunteered.

Now Hank recalled how she'd stood there, immobilized by shock as he'd twisted the knife in her heart by yet another self-serving confession—that he'd actually requested a special assignment because he'd needed to get away for a while.

To get away from her.

He'd loved her, of course. But he hadn't been ready to settle down, hadn't been ready for marriage. There were sights he hadn't seen, experiences yet to be savored. Twenty-three was too young, he'd told her, to be permanently tethered to a future etched in stone.

Not that he hadn't wanted that future. He'd just needed a few months of freedom first.

He'd been egotistical. Childish. Arrogant.

But mostly, he'd been scared.

Marriage was an immense responsibility. Deep down, he'd been terrified that he wasn't worthy of the task, that he couldn't measure up to the expectations of the woman whose love he never doubted.

To this day, Rae's shattered expression remained etched in his mind.

"There's no excuse for what I did," Hank said miserably. "I was still a kid, full of vinegar and chomping to see the world. I wanted one last grand adventure. It was selfish. It was stupid. But it was never because I didn't love you, Rae. I figured that a few months wouldn't make any difference, that we'd get married when I came back and—"

The slap snapped his head sideways.

"You bastard," she hissed, her eyes flashing green fire. "How dare you make that choice for me? How dare you risk death rather than choose life with me, and with the precious child we'd created? It doesn't matter whether you knew I was pregnant. What matters is you made promises to *me*, promises that meant nothing. You left *me*, and when you could have come back, you didn't.

You let me think you were dead,'' she sobbed, "and as far as I'm concerned, you are.''

Rae spun and rushed through the diner, bumping tables, knocking over chairs, blinded by the hot tears she could no longer control. Her mind whirled with pain, with confusion. And with secret joy that she simply couldn't allow herself to experience. Martin was alive.

No, Hank Flynn was alive. But he *was* Martin.

Yet he wasn't the Martin she remembered. So Martin didn't exist anymore. Hank Flynn existed.

But Hank Flynn was Martin.

Oh, God. Rae couldn't think. She couldn't see. Her chest hurt. The sun's heat burned her face. She was outside, running. Running to nowhere. Blood rushed past her ears, distorting sounds, muffling the voice behind her.

"Rae, wait!''

A ragged voice. A familiar voice. So very far away.

A tree loomed in front of her. She veered, abrading her arm on its rough bark. A sob caught in her throat, choking her. Martin was alive, but he was nonetheless gone. How could it hurt so much? How could she go on now that she understood the depth of his deception, the extent of his betrayal? How could she live with that?

How could she live with herself, because God help her, she still loved him and knew that she always would.

She ran blindly, madly. Branches slapped her, scratching her face. Her foot hit a rock. She heard a cry of pain, and knew it had come from her. One minute she was stumbling forward; the next she was enveloped in strong arms, and lifted off the ground.

"Shh,'' Hank whispered, his lips brushing her ear. "It's all right, honey, it's all right.''

She fought frantically, pounding the muscular forearms wrapped around her waist, kicking against the intrusive force that held her in such loving warmth that she wanted to weep with pure ecstasy. But the pain was too great, a tearing agony of the soul that she couldn't outrun, couldn't escape.

Ignoring her feeble blows, Hank scooped Rae into his arms as if she weighed no more than a feather. She jerked and twisted, sobbing like an infant and feeling just as helpless. She was aware of being carried. Wind rushed against her skin while sunshine and shadows alternately warmed and cooled her. She was surrounded by sound— the thrum of distant traffic, the chirp of forest creatures, the rustle of foliage in the breeze and, most of all, the moist heat of Hank's breath, shallow and strained as he strode purposefully to his bungalow.

He shouldered the door open, then kicked it shut. Crossing the small room, he sat on the bed, gathered the sobbing woman in his arms and let her cry herself dry.

Drained and empty, Rae slumped on the edge of the bed staring at her knees. Across the room, water splashed from a faucet. A moment later Hank returned with a glass of water. She was vaguely aware that he'd squatted beside the bed, lifted one of her hands and was trying to curl her limp fingers around the glass.

His palm closed around hers, supporting the glass as he held it to her lips. "Drink this, honey. It will make you feel better."

She sipped the cool liquid without protest. When she'd had enough, she turned away. Hank set the glass on the nightstand, but didn't release her hand. Instead, he turned it over, studying her palm as if future secrets were etched in the creased flesh.

Rae stared at his profile, noting the angry scar at the bridge of his nose, along with other more subtle changes in his appearance. His jawline seemed more substantial, thicker and more heavily muscled. His cheekbones were more pronounced than she remembered, although the left side seemed slightly flatter than the right, as if the bone

had been damaged. She hadn't noticed that before, nor
had she noticed that just below his mustache a thin white
line extended from the edge of his mouth. Its location
and jagged appearance suggested that his lip had been
split and healed poorly.

With his head bowed, a shaft of glossy hair fell forward, concealing a portion of his face. She reached out,
hooking the silky strands with her finger, smoothing them
back.

He looked up with wary eyes. Hank's eyes. Martin's
eyes. A rush of emotion clogged her throat when she saw
the angry red imprint of her hand on his face. She
touched it gently. "I'm sorry," she whispered. "I didn't
mean to hurt you."

He tried to smile. "I deserved it."

"No. I had no right..." She moistened her lips, wishing her voice didn't sound so weepy. "I don't know what
came over me."

Hank's eyelids fluttered shut. He bowed his head
again, and lifted her palm to his lips. The silky tickle of
his mustache against her skin made her shiver.

After a long moment he spoke. "It tears me up inside,
seeing your tears and knowing that I'm the cause of them.
I never wanted to make you unhappy, or to intrude in
your life."

"Why?" she whispered. "If you didn't want us to
recognize you, why did you come back?"

Releasing her hand on her lap, he shielded his heart
with folded arms. "I'm a weak man."

Perhaps had she not been so numbed by shock, so
bewildered by his miraculous reemergence from the
grave, she might have recognized the secretive shift of
his eyes and noted his evasive response. But her focus
was unclear, and her befuddled brain was unable to sep-
arate emotion and rational thought. She simply stared at
him.

Hank looked over his shoulder. "Marti must never know."

It took a moment for Rae to grasp his meaning. When she did, she was stunned. "She's your daughter. She has a right—"

"She's Martin's daughter." Spinning around, he sat stiffly beside Rae, clasping her hands so tightly she sucked in a breath. "Listen to me, Rae. Martin Manning is gone forever. I can't bring him back, and neither can you. The father Marti is so proud of never existed in the first place. He's an illusion, the fictional creation of a protectionist military machine."

Rae stiffened. "Martin, you're scaring me."

"No!" Standing, Hank paced the small room like a caged animal. "Haven't you heard me? Don't you understand what I've been saying? Martin is dead. *Dead!*" He spun around, breathing hard, and raked his fingers through his hair. "Marti's father was a hero. He died in Europe, trying to save his men." For a moment Hank seemed too overcome to speak. He covered his face with his hand, took a shuddering breath, and when he looked up again, his eyes were dark with anguish. "I've never even been to Europe, and my men—" his voice broke "—my men didn't die in spite of me. They died because of me."

Rae couldn't have been more stunned if he'd struck her. "I don't understand."

"I know." The words were no more than a whisper. Hank was shielding his face again, but Rae saw beyond the concealing hand to the depth of his misery and shame. "I don't want you to understand." He lowered his hand, but avoided her gaze. "But I'll tell you the truth so that you'll realize why our daughter must be protected from it."

Instantly he began pacing again, pausing by the nightstand to drain Rae's glass of water, then circling the room like a man possessed. Then he jerked to a stop facing away from her and spoke in a voice devoid of emotion. "It was a secret mission in Central America," he began. "Our directive was to supply weapons to the rebels, and train them in their use. We bivouacked in the jungle, forty miles from government-held territory. I thought we were safe. I got careless."

For the next half hour Hank told of unspeakable horrors, from the carnage of his slaughtered soldiers to the years of imprisonment where isolation and loneliness added to the terrible guilt of having survived when his men had perished. Then he told of the prisoner exchange that had freed him from physical incarceration, but left him captive in the dungeon of his own mind.

And Rae wept, suffering through his torture, enduring his grief and despair as acutely as if she'd experienced it herself. In a sense, she had. She was bonded with this man—emotionally, spiritually and physically connected only with him. It had always been that way; it always would be.

"My mother was gone," Hank was saying, his back still turned to her. "Other than you, she was all I had. I didn't want to sully the memory of her heroic son."

Rae wiped her face with a tissue. "What about me, Mar— Hank? Why didn't you come back?"

"I'd been away nearly five years. I figured you'd gone on with your life, and it didn't seem fair to interfere with that." His shoulders heaved with his sigh. "Besides, how could I face you with what I'd become when I couldn't even face myself?"

"I would have understood."

"That didn't matter." He turned around so quickly a strand of hair whipped into his face. He tucked it behind his ear. "I'd already let you down once. I couldn't do it again."

That made no sense to her, and she said so.

"Martin Manning did a lot of foolish things in his life, but he always loved you, Rae, and he wanted you to be proud of him. In life he did little to deserve your respect, but in death he could be honored, even revered. He was a man you *could* be proud of." Hank looked away. "The man who came out of that prison wasn't worthy of your love, Rae."

Suddenly the few steps separating them seemed like a giant chasm. Rae couldn't bear it. She went to him, sliding her arms around his waist and pressing her cheek against the firm muscles of his back. Her tears bled into his shirt. "You can't punish yourself for what you couldn't control. You've suffered enough."

A tremor slipped down his spine. "I don't want your pity."

"Good, because you don't have it." She loosened her grasp, urging him to turn and face her. When he did, she framed his face with her hands. "What you do have is my compassion, my respect and my love. I don't care whether you call yourself Martin or Hank or Egor. Names don't matter. People matter. This man, the man inside—" she pressed her palm against his chest "—is the man I have always loved, and always will love."

"Rae, I—"

She touched his lips, silencing him. A fresh surge of moisture swelled in her eyes, blurring his image. Her fingertips traced the planes of his face, so different now, yet nonetheless familiar. So many years, so much pain. She wanted to soothe his anguish, absorb it into herself. Urging his head down, she brushed her lips across the edge of his mouth, across the tiny white scar that suddenly symbolized lost years and wasted youth.

A tear touched her lips. A single tear, dredged from despair, sliding soundlessly down a face racked with anguish. She'd never seen him cry before. She'd never seen any man cry, and the impact of his vulnerability struck with explosive force.

Emotions long dormant burst to the surface. With a tiny whimper, Rae covered his dear face with kisses, clinging to him as if her clutching fingers could erase past pain with the promise of forever. Her mouth sought his in a frenzy of need and volcanic passion. For the first time in her life she was the sexual aggressor. And it felt right. It felt perfect.

Hank responded instantly, sweeping her into a fervent embrace. A groan rumbled from his throat, increasing their fevered passion. His mouth became Rae's entire world, a world of moist heat and unrestrained desire that was all-encompassing. She could think of nothing but him, feel nothing but his sensual hunger. He was everything.

And she wanted to swallow him whole, to take him inside herself, protecting him with her body, with her life.

She tugged at his shirt. "I want to touch you," she whispered against his lips. "Your skin against mine, our hearts beating together. I need to feel that this is real, that you're real."

As she spoke, she pulled the hem of his T-shirt free and slipped her hands underneath. She closed her eyes, weakened by the sensation of bare skin beneath her palms, and the erotic way his muscles spasmed at her touch, as if her fingers were shooting tiny sparks.

Hank shuddered, then yanked the shirt off and tossed it aside. He clasped her face between his palms, kissing her with the frantic desperation of a man thrust into a living dream from which he never wants to awaken. His fingers tangled in her hair; her fingers grasped at his fly. They were both panting, gasping for air between frenzied kisses.

Rae tugged at his waistband, frustrated that it refused

to cooperate. Her finger hit metal. A button. A damned button.

Hank's mouth slid to her ear. "Rae...honey...are you sure?"

"Oh—" she clawed at the button "—yes."

His breath warmed her jaw, then he was tasting the sensitive flesh of her throat. "I've dreamed of this, I've dreamed of you for so long." He grunted as she gave the button a mighty jerk. "The guards let me keep your picture," he murmured against her skin. "To remind me of what I'd lost. They thought it would weaken me, but it made me stronger. You made me strong, Rae. You were with me."

Tears sprang to her eyes. She told herself it was relief at having finally unhooked the lousy button, but she was haunted by the image of him isolated in a filthy cell with only a photograph for company. "I'm here," she whispered. "I'll always be here."

He raised his head enough to stare into her eyes. His mouth moved, but no sound emerged. He closed his eyes, bent forward and buried his face between her breasts.

She clutched him to her, alternately kissing his hair and stroking it. When he straightened, their eyes met and held. Hank slipped out of his jeans without breaking their visual embrace, then slowly, sensually unbuttoned Rae's blouse. She shivered as his knuckles brushed her bare skin, each inadvertent touch as exciting as a deliberate caress.

By the time he finally slipped the fabric back over her shoulders, she was trembling with anticipation. He stood there, his eyes glowing as if she were the most precious thing on earth. Unhurried now, he traced the contours of her bra with his fingertip, lingering at the cleft between her breasts before continuing the sensual journey.

And just as Rae thought she couldn't bear another mo-

ment, he reached back to remove the garment, then swept
her into his arms and carried her to bed.

He bent protectively over her, nuzzling the curve of
her throat while his hands slipped her slacks over the
swell of her hips. "Rise up," he whispered as the garment bunched above her thighs.

She complied, and the obstruction was swept away.
Hank paused long enough to discard his underwear before reclining beside her. With a tiny cry of delight she
reached for him, and their passion exploded in a writhing
tangle of slickened skin and moist kisses, of exploring
fingers and deep caresses that left her gasping for more.

Their lovemaking was magic. Rae felt as if she'd been
transported to a mystical world of pure sensation. Her
body tingled; her mind swirled with the color of total joy.
Nothing existed outside this place, this time, this eternal
moment.

They communicated with their bodies, silently,
sweetly, in the language of love that only they spoke, and
only with each other. Neither of them had to ask, because
both knew without question that there had been no other
lovers in the years they'd been apart. And when the final
joining came, he filled her slowly, with aching sweetness,
and a splendor that transcended time.

As the sun dipped low in the afternoon sky, Rae
pressed her face against Hank's chest, listening to the
reassuring rhythm of his heart. Her body was tingling,
sated. Her mind was prickling with fear. She was terrified
by the sensations coursing through her body. A heart
swollen by love was exquisitely tender, and so easily
bruised. It had been so long since she'd felt such happiness, and yet she could remember the pain of its loss
as acutely as if it had happened yesterday.

With joy came vulnerability. Weakness. She could be

hurt again. That terrified her, and with the terror came a lucid clarity of mind. "Hank?"

Smiling, he glanced down, his fingers still stroking her hair. "Hmm?"

"A while ago I asked why you came back to Gold River. You never really answered."

"Didn't I?" He bent to brush a kiss across her forehead. "You're so beautiful, Rae. You'll never know how much I've missed holding you like this, seeing your lips swollen with kisses, and your breasts—" he cupped one with his palm "—soft and sated with love."

She shifted her elbow, propping herself up on his thighs. "So you came back for sex?"

His eyes widened.

She looked away. "I'm sorry. I don't know why I said that."

Tucking a thumb beneath her chin, he urged her to look at him. "Is that what you believe?"

"No." She wanted to believe that he'd come back because he loved her, and because he wanted to be with her always. Deep down, she did believe that, but for some reason she needed to hear him say it out loud, as if the words would give substance to the reality. The question was blurted before she had a chance to think twice. "Did you come back because you loved me?"

His shuttered gaze should have set off alarm bells in her head, but she was too focused to notice. "I've always loved you," he said quietly.

That was all the confirmation Rae needed. He'd come back because he loved her. Nothing else mattered. And yet, she couldn't suppress a niggling sense that he was holding something back. The notion was sobering.

He regarded her thoughtfully. "You look sad."

"Do I?"

"Not sad, exactly. Disturbed."

She shrugged. "Perhaps a little."

The confession clearly unnerved him. "Why?"

"Because I'm so happy, I suppose." Heaving a sigh, she plucked at the bedclothes. "That sounds pretty silly, doesn't it?"

He didn't answer for a moment. Finally he stared toward the window, as if gauging the time by the rotation of sunlight streaming through the glass. "I don't blame you for not trusting me."

A guilty heat crept up her throat. "I never said that."

"You didn't have to." He brushed a strand of hair from her face, then stroked her cheek so tenderly that she ached inside. "All I've ever wanted is for you to be happy, Rae. I'll do anything it takes to make that happen. Anything."

Rae looked him straight in the eye. "Will you introduce yourself to your daughter?"

His stricken expression was like a knife in her heart. "Anything but that."

She touched his face in a caress that was infinitely soft, filled with love. "I think you're wrong, Hank. I think Marti would rather have a live father than a dead hero, but I don't want to put you through any more pain. It's your decision. I'm willing to let you make it."

His features softened with relief, and he emptied his lungs all at once. "Thank you."

Although Rae was deeply touched by Hank's fear of disappointing his daughter, she couldn't help feeling a sense of impending disaster. Secrets, she'd learned, were inevitably exposed. The results were rarely pleasant. If Marti found out from another source—

Rae's head snapped up. "Oh, Lord. Hobie." She scrambled to her knees, grasping Hank's arm. "You mustn't tell him."

Hank squirmed beneath the covers. "Why not?"

"For one thing, he'd go straight to Marti. Besides, keeping a confidence is not my father's strong suit."

Moistening her lips, she made a production of smoothing the corner of a rumpled pillow. "Hobie was quite upset over your, ah, demise. I'm not certain how he'd react if he learns that you aren't quite as dead as we thought."

"He might handle it better than you think," Hank muttered.

Rae noted the wry edge on his voice, and would have wondered about it had she not been so engrossed with her own jumbled emotions. "I honestly don't know what he'd do, or how he'd feel. I just know that I don't want to deal with his reactions until I've gotten a handle on my own."

Hank pulled her close, pressing her cheek against the hollow of his throat. When he spoke, his voice was raw, ragged. "I never wanted to disrupt your life."

"But you have," she whispered against his skin. "And I couldn't be happier."

Twisting in the cradle of his arms, she reached up to touch his face again, to trace its structure, old and new, to reassure herself that this was not just another wistful dream. Beneath her seeking fingers was warm flesh pulsing with blood, pulsing with life. He was here. He was real.

Her prayers had been answered. But even as her heart rejoiced, her mind whispered a warning. *He will leave someday.*

Men like that always do.

The next days were the fulfillment of a beautiful fantasy. Rae and Hank managed to continue their normal routines without arousing suspicion, although several customers commented on Rae's unique radiance, and one curious woman asked if she'd been using a special beauty cream. Rae had replied only with a secretive smile that left the woman frowning and frustrated.

It had been nearly a week since she'd told Steve that

she wasn't prepared to marry him. Hurting him had saddened Rae deeply, because she'd always regarded Steve
Ruskin as her dearest friend. He, however, had handled
the rejection with admirable grace, and continued to stop
by the diner as he'd always done. On those occasions,
Steve was surprisingly solicitous and impeccably polite,
and their conversations, although somewhat subdued,
were affable enough to avoid attracting unwanted attention by local gossips.

Meanwhile, Hank had continued to cover her father's
chores— Rae still couldn't fathom why he was so ac-
commodating to the old coot—and Marti still dashed directly from school to the construction site as Hank's favorite little helper. As far as Hobie and his granddaughter
were concerned, nothing had changed.

For Rae and Hank, nothing would ever be the same.
Days were filled with yearning glances and knowing
smiles; and at night, while the rest of the household slept,
Rae slipped silently toward the bungalows, and into the
arms of the only man she'd ever loved. Any nagging
doubt about the wisdom of keeping such a dangerous and
cumbersome secret was pushed aside by a joy beyond
anything she'd known.

By the end of the week Rae had adjusted to their furtive love affair. There was, she'd discovered, an erotic
thrill about the covert liaison that made her feel exotic,
adventurous and, well, downright sexy. Hank had even
created secret hand signs that they could use at the diner
to exchange amorous suggestions without raising eyebrows. Rae had been game to try, but the first time he'd
given her the signal for "let's do it on the lunch
counter," she'd promptly burst into a fit of giggles and
spilled a cup of coffee into Joe's lap.

So much for secret sex signals.

Thinking about the silly incident, which had happened

only two days earlier, still made her smile, although she doubted that poor Joe recalled it fondly.

Now, however, it was Friday afternoon, and Rae found herself daydreaming about the weekend. She and Hank had planned a picnic at the creek so that Marti and her brand-new fishing pole could have a second shot at the inhabitants of the trout pool. It would be a glorious day, and would provide a wonderful opportunity for Rae to watch Hank and Marti together, an experience that never ceased to send chills down her spine.

Since the first day Hank had arrived, Rae had noted the special bond he shared with her daughter. She'd always been aware that they were emotionally attuned to each other. Now she understood why.

Her thoughts were interrupted by the jingling cowbell. As she glanced toward the front door, a smile of welcome died on her lips.

Joe rushed in, his face white as death. He started to speak, swallowed hard, then jerked around to stare out the window.

Since he was looking in the general direction of the construction site, Rae was instantly uneasy. She laid down the counter rag. "What is it, Joe?"

"You'd best get out there," he said shakily. "I'll make the call."

"Call? What call?" A prickling sensation skittered across her nape as she ducked under the counter bridge and emerged into the dining area. Through the window she saw several people run across the parking lot toward the construction area where Hank and Marti were working. Fear settled in the pit of her stomach. "What's going on?"

He pulled off his cap, pressing it to his heart. "I'm real sorry, Rae. There's...there's been an accident."

Her heart gave a leap, then seemed to stop altogether. She steadied herself on a chair. "No," she whispered.

"You'd best get out there," he repeated miserably. "It's Marti."

Chapter Thirteen

Hank was shirtless, slumped in a chair outside the hospital emergency room when Steve strode in, his jaw clenched and eyes bulging. His frantic gaze swept the area, narrowing furiously as it settled on Hank. "Where is she, Flynn?"

"In the examination room." Hank stood, nodding toward a door stenciled with a No Admittance sign. "Rae and Hobie are with her."

Sparing him a look of disdain, Ruskin pointedly eyed Hank's bare chest before heading toward the door to the examining area. It was locked, so he pounded on it with his flat hand. Behind him, a frosted glass window slid open. A uniformed nurse gave him a chilly stare. "May I help you?"

Pivoting smartly, Ruskin marched to the counter, his features taut with tension. "I must be allowed in," he announced. "My...my friend's child has been injured."

The nurse eyed him coolly. "Relatives only."

"Now see here—"

The window slid shut.

Infuriated, Ruskin whirled on Hank. "This is all your fault, Flynn. Martina never should have been allowed to associate with the likes of you. I knew something terrible would happen. I tried to warn Rae, but she wouldn't listen and now that poor child—" His voice broke. He raked his fingers through his hair, turning a perfectly groomed business cut into a series of rumpled spikes.

The man was genuinely distressed and clearly terrified. Whatever his faults—and Hank still considered him a pompous jerk—it was obvious that Ruskin truly loved Marti. That gave them something in common.

Hank laid a comforting hand on his rival's shoulder. "Marti's going to be fine. A few stitches and she'll be good as new."

"Good as new?" Ruskin threw off his hand, spearing Hank with a venomous stare. "I saw the site. There was blood everywhere. My God, man, how could you let that happen to a *child?*"

Since Hank had been asking himself the same thing for hours and still hadn't come up with an acceptable answer, all he could do was shake his head. "You're right, it was my fault. I shouldn't have asked her to bring me that box of nails. She was running back with it when she tripped on some scrap lumber. Her chin hit the stud wall and she—" the memory of the razor-sharp protrusion made him flinch "—she cut her arm on a joist hanger."

Hank looked away, feeling physically sick. If he lived a thousand years he'd never forget Marti's scream of pain, the terror in her eyes when she saw blood spurting from her tiny arm. He'd nearly fainted. He, a man who'd lived through the horrors of war, who'd comforted dying soldiers and had once carried a comrade's severed leg to the medic chopper, had *nearly fainted.*

He'd been useless, utterly useless, so panic-stricken that all he could do was use his shirt as a pressure bandage and shout for help. Thankfully, several people in the diner parking lot had responded. A moment later Rae had sprinted over to demonstrate how a real parent behaves in a crisis.

She'd been calm, comforting, and within seconds had convinced her hysterical child that everything would be all right. She'd even had the presence of mind to ask one of the onlookers to contact Hobie at Madeline Rochester's house.

From then on everything was pretty much a blur in Hank's mind. He remembered helping Rae into the ambulance a moment before the vehicle screeched away with siren wailing. He'd still been standing in the middle of the street when Hobie's truck pulled up. Hank had climbed in, and they'd headed to the hospital.

"You ought to be shot."

Blinking, Hank glanced up.

Shaking with rage, Ruskin balled his fists into knots. "From the first day you set foot in Gold River, you've caused nothing but trouble. Do you think I don't see what's going on? Do you think I'm a fool?"

"No," Hank replied truthfully. "I think you're an intelligent man who cares deeply about his friends."

"Rae and Marti are much more than mere friends." Ruskin's jaw twitched furiously. "At least, they were before you came along. You've ruined everything."

A lump of guilt wedged behind Hank's larynx. He wanted to dispute that, but couldn't. "I'm sorry."

The man's arched brows leapt toward his hairline. "Are you really?"

"Yes."

"Then prove it."

"How?"

"Leave."

Hank studied his boots without responding.

Ruskin regarded him for a moment. "Are you in love with Rae?"

The question shouldn't have startled Hank, but it did. He briefly considered lying, then discarded the notion. He couldn't deny his feelings for Rae any more than he could deny his next breath. "Yes, I love her."

Ruskin didn't appear surprised by the response, although he was plainly troubled by it. "How very touching. I suppose you've already given due consideration as to what you have to offer. Can you provide a proper education for Martina? Do you possess the financial acumen to keep Rae's business afloat? Can you give them both the stability they deserve, or will you end up like Hobie, abandoning your family for a dream that doesn't exist?"

Each angry question was spit out like a bad taste. No answers were given. None were expected. Ruskin had leaned over the well of Hank's insecurity and poured in a bucketful of doubt.

With his next words, the well overflowed. "Martina needs a father, not a buddy," Ruskin snapped. "As for Rae, she may find you amusing, but she'll soon realize that what she needs in her life is a husband, not a source of entertainment. You have nothing to offer either of them but grief and a bankrupt future of failure and pain. If you truly loved Rae, you'd get out of her life before you destroy it."

With that, Ruskin marched out of the waiting room leaving Hank shaken and deeply disturbed.

Although Hank had repeatedly told himself that all he'd ever wanted was for Rae to be happy, the sad fact was that he'd caused her nothing but heartache. Ruskin's accusations had hit a raw nerve, exposing Hank's deepest fears.

Angry rhetoric aside, Ruskin's assessment of the situation had been both accurate and troubling. Rae needed a financially and emotionally supportive husband. Marti needed a parent, not a playmate. They both deserved a man they could count on.

As much as Hank wanted to be that man, he couldn't erase the bitter memories of the soldiers he'd failed, of the faith that he'd shattered. Rae's faith.

And Rae's heart. He'd broken that years ago. Now he was back asking for another chance, another failure.

Behind Hank, the No Admittance door swung open and Hobie ambled out, tugging his earlobe. "Hospitals," he muttered. "Never could tolerate 'em."

"How's Marti?"

"Proud as a bear cub with a salmon in her mouth. Can't wait to show off her war wounds." Yawning, Hobie scratched his belly, glancing around the dimly lit room. "This place looks like a dadgummed mort'ary. Don't seem fitting, somehow."

Hank wasn't interested in Hobie's assessment of the decor. "Does the doctor think there could be any permanent nerve damage?"

"Nope. Said she'd be right as rain in no time." Hobbling toward the emergency room exit, he paused to pat Hank's bare shoulder. "Looked worse than it was, son. She's gonna be fine."

Relieved, Hank followed the old man out of the waiting room to the hospital's spacious lobby. "Is she in any pain?"

"Don't seem to be. Was right interested in watching the doc stitch up her arm. Oh—" The old man stopped so suddenly Hank nearly rear-ended him. "Dang near forgot."

"Forgot what?"

"Marti wanted to make sure you knew that what happened weren't your fault. She's all het up that you might be feeling bad or something."

Hank sagged against an upholstered wing chair in the lobby's foyer. "She's worried about *my* feelings?"

"Yep. In fact, she's madder than a wet chicken that you couldn't come inside with her. She wanted you to see all the fancy doodads them doctors was a-using on her. Got a real kick out of it, she did." Hobie angled a sly glance at Hank. "Come to think of it, Rae was kinda put out about them making you wait outside, too. When the nurse said only relatives could come in, she started to argue, then looked over at Marti and shut her mouth real quick-like. Don't suppose she was about to tell that nurse that you was the child's daddy, do you?"

Hank emptied his lungs slowly.

"She knows, don't she?"

Hank nodded.

Hobie grinned. "I figured. Rae's been brighter than a panful of nuggets for nigh onto a week now. Got that glow, y'know? The kind a woman gets when she's feeling took care of—" he nudged Hank's ribs with an elbow "—if you get my drift."

"Yeah, I get it." Hank rolled away, tucking his hands in his pockets. "Rae asked me not to tell you. It seems she had the feeling you might not be trustworthy." He slanted a hard look over his shoulder. "I wonder why she'd think that."

Hobie had the grace to look embarrassed. "A man does what he's got to do. Hell, if it weren't for me, you'da been long gone by now. Way I figure it, I done you both a favor."

"A favor?" Whirling, Hank poked an angry finger against the old man's chest. "You blackmail me into virtual slavery, and then have the gall to say you're doing *me* a favor?"

"Now, don't get your veins a-popping, son. Mebbe I did go a bit far, threatening to tell the child who you were and all, but things done worked out. Rae's happy as a pig in mud, and Marti is—''

Hank cut him off with a snarl. "Marti is lying in the damned hospital with her arm ripped open! You should have let me go, old man."

Blinking madly, Hobie stared past Hank's shoulder. "Maybe this ain't the place to be talking 'bout such things."

Pushing off Hobie's restraining hand, Hank was too agitated to heed the warning. "What happened to Marti was my fault. I don't belong here. I never belonged here. If you'd let me leave when I wanted to, none of this would have happened."

Having said his piece, Hank spun around to leave and found himself staring into Rae Hooper's horrified face. His stomach lurched once, then sank like a rock.

Rae stood there clasping her hands together, her face white as death.

After what seemed an eternity, Hobie shuffled up to his daughter, chattering brightly. "Y'know, it's been a heck of a day. How 'bout we stop by the chicken place on the way home for some supper? Don't seem right, making you cook and such. Got me a couple bucks set aside.... Ah—" he glanced through the doorway, toward the emergency waiting room "—where's Marti?"

Rae never took her eyes off Hank. "They took her for X rays."

Hobie frowned. "She didn't break no bones, did she?"

"Probably not. It's a precaution because she hit her head when she fell." She took a shaky breath and gave her father a stinging stare. "Would you please go back to the examination area and wait for her? One of us should be there when she gets back."

"Well, now, a child needs her mama at a time like this. We should both be there, don'tcha think?" Snagging his daughter's arm, Hobie tried to pull her away, but she shook him off and cowed him with a look. He cleared his throat, gave Hank a pitying glance and ambled toward the emergency room, mumbling.

Crossing her arms, Rae glanced away from Hank, as if she could no longer stand the sight of him. Her voice quivered. "I can't believe I was so gullible."

"Rae, listen—"

She brushed past him and steadied herself on one of the lobby chairs. "To think I actually bought in to that 'volunteer' spirit of yours." When she looked over her shoulder, the pain in her eyes nearly brought Hank to his knees. "My father was blackmailing you?"

"In a sense, I suppose, but it's not as sordid as it sounds."

"Really." It was a statement, not a question. "Shall I consider that this particular form of blackmail was more altruistic than the dictionary definition?" Now, that was definitely a question, and an angry one at that.

Hank took his time, answering slowly and in a voice that he hoped would be calming. "I'm not going to defend Hobie. He turned a sensitive situation to his advantage, but I allowed him to do it."

"Why, Hank?" When she faced him, he saw the effort it took for her to maintain a stoic expression. "Why did you allow it?"

"I guess I wasn't emotionally prepared to face you with the truth."

She considered that a moment. "Then why did you come back in the first place?"

Hank looked away, not wanting to lie—not even able to lie—yet knowing how deeply the truth would wound her. Every other time she'd asked that question, he'd evaded the truth by ignoring it.

This time, however, Rae wasn't going to let him escape so easily. "Answer me, Hank. If you weren't emotionally prepared to deal with—" she paused to lick her lips "—with the past, why did you come back to Gold River in the first place?"

"Rae, this isn't the time—"

"I think it is." She squared her shoulders. "You led me to believe that you returned because you still loved me."

"I do love you, Rae, more than you'll ever know."

Her eyes narrowed. "But that's not why you're here, is it?"

Defeated, his shoulders fell forward. "I thought the town was deserted."

For the first time, her demeanor cracked. She swayed slightly, then grasped the back of a chair, staring at him as if seeing him for the first time. "Are you saying that if you'd known I was still living in Gold River, you never would have come?"

"Yes, I guess that's what I'm saying." Hank stiffened his shoulders, and forced himself to meet her stunned gaze. "I was heading toward a job in Portland when I was struck by an impulse to—I don't know—relive old memories or something. I can't tell you exactly why I took that detour. All I know for sure is that I'd read that Gold River was a ghost town. I didn't expect anyone to be there, Rae, least of all you."

Every word seemed to affect her like a physical blow. Her body shuddered as if in pain, and her complexion paled until her freckles stood out like red raisins in a rice field. "I see." Tangling her fingers together, she made a stoic attempt to square her shoulders. "So when you walked into the diner that first afternoon, you must have been quite shocked. Why didn't you just turn around and leave?"

He shifted, avoiding her anguished gaze. "Seeing you again was like living a dream. You were so beautiful, you took my breath away. Then Marti came running in and—" he paused to compose his cracking voice "—I

knew she was my child. I wanted to see her, to know
her, to make sure that you were both safe and happy.
Since you hadn't recognized me even without the sunglasses, I convinced myself that you never would.'' He
pinched the bridge of his nose, took a shaky breath, then
shrugged and tried for a thin smile. ''Then I ran into
Louie and knew I was in big trouble.''

Rae didn't return his smile. She just stood there, staring at him with numb eyes. ''That's how Hobie figured
out who you were?''

''That, and my own stupidity. The particulars don't
really matter. By that time I'd already discovered that
Marti's entire identity was centered around Martin Manning's fake heroics. I knew that the truth would destroy
her, and that I had to leave before that happened.''

''But Hobie had other ideas.''

''Yes.''

''So he blackmailed you into staying by threatening to
tell Marti who you were.''

Hank issued a helpless shrug. ''Hobie has his faults,
laziness being one of them, but I'm sure that in his own
mind, he thought he was doing the right thing. You know
as well as I do that Hobie would never do anything to
hurt Marti.''

Although the words slid from his own lips, the impact
was stunning. Hobie Hooper would never have followed
through on his threat, and deep down Hank had always
known that. He'd stayed because he'd wanted to stay, yet
he'd used Hobie's threat as a crutch to avoid responsibility for a decision that had always been his own.

Just as he'd used a dangerous mission as an excuse to
avoid facing his own fears, first by volunteering and
again after his release, by convincing himself that if he
returned home, Rae would certainly reject him.

In truth, Hank had actually been paralyzed with terror
that she *wouldn't* reject him, that she'd take him back

and discover what he'd always known—that he couldn't measure up to her expectations. Not because he hadn't wanted to, but because he hadn't known how.

Hank's parents had divorced before he was born. He'd never known his father, although his mother had pointed out unfavorable comparisons between him and his absent parent whenever she was angry. Hank had grown up without a father figure to pass on elusive rites of manhood, to share the secrets of being a proper husband and parent. Since he lacked access to those masculine secrets, failure was inevitable. At least, that's what Hank—and Martin—had thought.

The discovery was startling, but it came too late.

Rae had already turned away from him, unable to hear anything beyond the cracking of her own heart. Her thoughts traveled back to the bungalow, and to the afternoon they'd made love for the first time since Marti had been conceived. It had been only a week ago. It felt like a lifetime.

Hank had never actually told her that he'd come back because he loved her. In fact, his answers had been evasive, her questions artfully dodged. She'd believed what she wanted to believe, what she needed so desperately to believe. But it had all been a lie. A lie.

Fears from the past and present tangled in her mind, the terror of abandonment that had stalked her since childhood.

He'll leave someday.

Today, tomorrow. Next week, next year. The siren call of the road would eventually beckon and Hank Flynn, a.k.a. Martin Manning, would follow it.

Men like that always do.

But the next time, there'd be two broken hearts instead of one, because Marti loved him, too. The longer Hank stayed, the deeper the anguish when he finally moved on.

Crushed and disillusioned, Rae realized that she

couldn't protect her daughter from the pain of loss. She could, however, minimize it.

"I want you to leave," she said softly. "Today. Now."

Hank's eyes darkened with shock and disbelief. "You don't mean that."

"Yes, I do."

He was clearly crushed, although to his credit, he maintained his composure. Nodding, he looked away, but not before a sheen of moisture brightened his eyes. "May I speak with Marti first?"

Rae's stomach balled like a clenched fist. She could just see the emotional scene in her mind, with poor Marti sobbing wildly, and Hank looking as if he'd been shot. No, she wouldn't subject her child to that. "I don't think that's a good idea."

"I can't just leave without saying goodbye. Please, don't ask me to do that."

"It's not a request, Hank." Rae could barely keep from averting her gaze. The pain in his eyes pierced her like a blade. "I don't want Marti to suffer the guilt of believing her accident had anything to do with this. I'll make certain that she knows that I sent you away and that you had no choice in the matter."

"Rae, please—"

"Goodbye, Hank." As she walked away, an emptiness settled deep inside her, a barren void between body and soul. Her chest felt hollow, as if her heart had been surgically removed.

She knew without looking that he was already gone.

"This ain't right, ain't right at all." Arms crossed, face grim, Hobie skulked in the bungalow doorway while Hank stuffed his meager possessions into the duffel. "Your child needs you. So does Rae, even if she is too danged stubborn to admit it."

"Rae wants me to leave, and I can't say as I blame her. You have to admit I haven't made life any easier for her." Hank walked into the tiny bath to gather his personal belongings.

Hobie followed, still muttering. "Life ain't never been easy. As for Rae, she don't know what she wants."

"Maybe not, but she seemed pretty clear on what she doesn't want. Me." Scooping up his shaving supplies and toothbrush, he brushed past Hobie, who was partially blocking the bathroom door, and dumped the loose items into the open duffel. "Steve Ruskin's a fine man. He'll give Rae and Marti a good life."

"He ain't gonna give 'em no kind of life, 'cause Rae ain't never gonna marry that man." Clearly frustrated, Hobie snagged Hank's wrist to prevent him from zipping the duffel. "Stop fussing with that. We got to talk."

"There's nothing to say."

"The hell there ain't." Hobie's grip was surprisingly firm. "Rae and Steve took Marti out for supper. They ain't gonna be back for hours, so there's no dadgummed need to be rushing around without taking time to think things through."

"There's nothing to think about, either." Straightening, he laid a firm hand on the man's bony shoulder. "Look, Hobie, I appreciate you giving me a lift, even though I know Rae probably sent you to make sure I was gone by the time they get back from the hospital." The guess was confirmed by a guilty red flush staining the old man's cheeks. "Look, Hobie, I'm not any happier about this than you are. I'm just doing what Rae wants."

Hobie's grizzled chin jutted out in challenge. "How do you know?"

If Hank hadn't been so emotionally drained, he might have smiled. The old cuss was nothing if not tenacious. "I know because she said so."

Dismissing that with a flick of his hand, Hobie issued

a derisive snort. "Hell, them's just words. Women don't talk with words, son. Ain't you figured that out yet? Why, I remember once when Rae's mama, God rest her soul, was pinching pennies for school clothes—"

Hank moaned. "Dammit, Hobie—"

"Times was tough," he intoned, releasing Hank's wrist so he could scratch his own stubbled chin. "I was driving a truck back then, barely making enough to get by. Weren't home much, neither, but Rae's mama never complained. Always said that the diner was doing fine, so we had more than most folks. It was a recession, don'tcha know."

When he paused for effect Hank zipped the duffel and hoisted the strap over his shoulder.

He would have headed for the door except that Hobie, too, had grabbed the strap, spinning him around.

The story continued. "Now, me and the missus were downtown one day when she stopped to eye a dress hanging in one of them storefront windows."

Hank tugged at the captured duffel strap. "Hobie—"

"Pretty dress, too, the color of blue rock moss after a spring rain. Had a little jacket-thing, with sleeves and such—" he demonstrated sleeve length by pointing to an area on his own skinny forearms "—and the skirt was all pleated up like a folded dredge tarp. Well, sir, I told her she oughta buy that there dress. Y'know what she said?"

Hank scowled darkly.

"She said she already had one church dress, and there weren't no good reason to have two." Hobie nodded sagely. "'Course, I didn't pay the words no mind, on account of her eyes got all glowy when she looked in the window. So I used some of our rainy-day money, and I done bought her that dress."

Touched in spite of his irritation, Hank found himself

smiling. "I suppose she threw her arms around you, crying with happiness."

"Nope." Hobie slipped his hands into his pockets and rocked back on his heels. "Threatened to gut me with a boning knife and put me out of her bed, but that ain't the point."

"Oh, for—" Hank raked his hair in frustration. "Then what in hell *is* the point?"

"The point is that she really wanted that danged dress. She was just scared about what she'd hafta give up to get it." Hobie tossed Hank the pitying look one gives lost puppies and fools, then released his grip on the duffel strap and ambled toward the door, shaking his head. "C'mon, if you've a mind to. I'll take you on down to the bus station."

"Hobie?"

The old man looked over his shoulder.

"Did your wife keep the dress?"

"Wore it every Sunday for six months."

"What happened then?"

"Then we buried her in it." Hobie looked away. "That's the thing about living for the future, son. Sometimes there ain't one."

"I hate you!"

"Marti, listen—"

"No!" Marti shouted, tears spurting from her eyes. "Hank was my very best friend, and you made him go away. I'll hate you forever. *Forever!*"

"Oh, sweetie. I know you're hurt and angry, but there are things you don't understand."

Sobbing openly, Marti collapsed on the parlor sofa, falling into her mother's embrace.

"There, there," Rae cooed, feeling the sting of tears behind her own closed lids. "Sometimes, if we really care for someone, we have to let go."

"But Hank didn't—" she hiccuped "—want to go away."

Biting her lip, Rae took a deep breath, then pasted on a maternal smile and wiped her daughter's soggy cheeks. "Do you remember when Hank first came to town?"

Marti nodded.

"Well, I'll bet you didn't know that he was on his way north because he had a job waiting for him."

Clearly, that was news to Marti. "He did?"

"Yes."

"Then how come he stayed here?"

"Because he saw that we needed his help." Pausing, Rae struggled to express what she didn't even understand. "Hank cared a great deal for you, Marti, so much that he was willing to give up everything to stay here and be your friend. But that wasn't fair to him, was it?"

"He coulda left if he wanted to. You didn't have to make him go away." Struggling upright, Marti pushed away from her mother's embrace, torn between her need for comfort and her anger. "He didn't even say goodbye."

Rae swallowed hard. "I asked him not to."

"Mom!"

"I'm sorry, sweetie. Maybe that was wrong of me, but I didn't want you to be upset."

Across the room, Hobie snorted. "Yup, that was right smart, saving the poor child from being upset and all."

His sarcasm wasn't lost on Rae, although her attempt at a withering stare faltered into bleak acceptance. Her father was right. She'd made a terrible mistake in not allowing Marti and Hank to see each other one last time. It was selfish and unfair, and Rae knew it.

"I'll admit that I used bad judgment," she told Marti, whose eyes were narrowed into wet green slits. "You had a right to say goodbye to Hank, and I shouldn't have prevented that."

Marti was only slightly mollified by the confession. "Can we go look for him?"

"Won't do no good," Hobie said. "The bus was already loading when I dropped him off. He's halfway to Oregon by now."

"He's gone forever," Marti wailed, stricken. "We're never gonna see him again."

Before Rae could respond, the child leapt up and sprinted down the hall. A moment later her bedroom door slammed.

Hobie stood. "Need me a beer."

Flopping back against the cushions, Rae tossed a limp arm over her face. She wouldn't cry, dammit. She wouldn't.

"Oh, danged near forgot. This here's for you."

Rae peeked from under her forearm. Hobie was holding out an envelope. "What is it?" When her father didn't reply, she sat up and took the sealed envelope, which bore no stamp, no postmark, no address. "Where did you get this?"

"Hank said you should have it."

Her fingers tingled; her hands began to tremble. Hank had touched this envelope. Whatever was inside, he'd touched that, too. It was a part of him.

"Are you gonna open it?"

"Hmm? Oh, yes. Sure." After a moment's struggle, she shredded the flap and stared at the contents in disbelief. "My God," she murmured. "What is this?"

Hobie leaned over. "Looks like one of them certee-fied checks."

That's exactly what it was, over ten thousand dollars drawn on an Atlanta bank. Her head was spinning. "Where on earth did Hank get this kind of money...and why would he give it to me?"

"You got a child together, don'tcha? Seems like a right fatherly thing to do." Hobie jammed his hands into his pockets. "And he didn't rob no bank, if'n that's what you're thinking. That there's back pay from the army. After he bought his mama a proper gravestone, he stuck the rest in the bank. Said he didn't have no use for it."

Rae was numb. "He didn't have to do this. I never wanted his money."

"Then what'n hell *did* you want?"

Despite her determination not to cry, a hot stream of tears coursed down her cheeks. All Rae had ever wanted from Hank was his love, but when he'd offered it, she'd turned him away. Now her father wanted to know why. It was a reasonable question, to which there was no answer. Not for her father. Not for herself.

Hobie issued a throaty growl. "Women," he muttered peevishly. "Can't never admit they want the danged dress."

Chapter Fourteen

"Hey, Flynn! Number three forklift is down. Check it out, will you?"

Hank glanced up from the clogged chipper motor he was rebuilding to acknowledge the foreman's request. He stood, wiping his hands on a grease rag, and headed toward the malfunctioning forklift.

Around him, the lumber mill was abuzz with activity, the crush to process a spring harvest of bug-damaged trees before environmentalists got wind of the project. Personally, Hank had no interest in the political ramifications of forest management. To him, a job was a job.

At least, it always had been. Now, however, he was vaguely uneasy about the vagabond life-style he'd chosen. Over the years he'd deliberately sought temporary work that eschewed forming personal friendships or establishing a serious career. A solitary life had suited him. It was penance, he supposed, for having been a disappointment to those about whom he'd cared so deeply. Or perhaps it had merely been an escape.

Things were different now. Hank was different. He had responsibilities. He was a father.

It had been two weeks since Hank had left Gold River, but Gold River had never left Hank. He suspected that it never would, and frankly, that was okay with him. A part of him would always be there, the best part of him—enduring love, undying friendship. Immortality.

He had a legacy now, a piece of himself to share with future generations. A beautiful daughter, created by his love for her mother.

God, how he missed them. Every day it became increasingly difficult for Hank to keep his promise to stay out of their lives. More precisely, he'd promised not to interfere. There was a difference, although the end result was the same. Rae didn't want him, because she didn't trust him not to hurt her again. Even worse, she didn't trust him not to hurt their child.

Hank couldn't blame her. Through selfishness and betrayal he'd destroyed the faith she'd once had in him. One way or another, he was determined to regain it. He just didn't know how.

Hobie hobbled out of the kitchen, dropping his cooking apron behind the counter. "If'n you want, I'll finish up here so you and Marti can get ready for services."

Rae looked up from the coffeemaker she was scrubbing, glancing across the dining area to the booth where her slumped daughter stared glumly out the window. The sight brought a lump to Rae's throat. Twenty years ago she'd sat in that same booth, staring out that same window and waiting for her own wayward father to return.

The only difference was that Hobie had come back. Never for long, of course, but sooner or later he always made his way home. Poor little Marti was waiting in vain for a man who would never return, and a father she'd never have the chance to know. Rae had seen to that.

Turning back to her chore, Rae attacked the splattered metal with renewed vengeance. "You and Marti go ahead," she said. "I'm not going."

Hobie blinked. "You done missed church last week, too, and the week before that."

"I have work to do."

"It's the Lord's Day," he reminded her.

"I'm sure He'll forgive me."

"True enough," Hobie agreed. "'Though I got my doubts about the pastor. He's getting a mite testy 'bout empty spaces in his pews. Don't seem much in a forgiving mood."

"Neither am I." Rae tossed down the rag, hating the bitter edge on her voice. She rubbed her forehead, forcing a softer tone. "Next week, I promise."

For a moment she feared Hobie would continue the argument. Instead, he issued a resigned shrug and ambled over to collect his granddaughter. He gave Rae a final pleading glance before ushering Marti out the front door.

Alone in the closed diner, Rae returned to her work, scouring the coffeemaker until it shone like a new dime, then turning her attention to every appliance on the counter, scrubbing and polishing until her hands were raw. Work helped. It numbed the mind like a stiff drink but without the hangover. Work was a friend, always around when you needed it.

Her mother had said that. Rae had never understood what she'd meant until now.

From the corner of her eye Rae saw Hobie's pickup cut across the parking lot toward the diner's driveway. Marti was hunched in the passenger seat. Rae caught a glimpse of the child's bleak expression before the truck swung out into the street and drove away.

She'd seen that sad expression a lot lately. On her daughter's face. On Hobie's. In the mirror.

Frustrated, Rae grabbed the counter rag, desperately looking for something to clean. The restaurant was spotless, so she tossed the rag aside and headed to the house. On her way, she glanced at the construction site. Steve had arranged for a work crew the day after Hank left. Now the panning trough and visitor center were nearly complete. They were beautiful, too. Hank would be pleased.

She mentally amended that. Hank would have been pleased. Past tense. Pulling her gaze back to the path, she hurried to the house.

Once inside, she felt a sense of protection, as if the memories had been locked out. But they hadn't. She could still see Hank sprawled on the sofa, beer in one hand, a bag of cheese puffs in the other, cheering whatever sports event happened to be on television at the time. Every score had evoked shrieks of delight, along with an enthusiastic high five between him and his squealing daughter.

Marti didn't watch sports much anymore. She hadn't been fishing in weeks. All she did was plod through her homework and disappear into her room to write in her diary and sulk. And also, Rae suspected, to grieve in private.

She could relate to that. Even now, it was all she could do to hold back her own tears.

She rushed down the hall, past the closed door beyond which Louie amused himself with some his favorite television tunes, and into the sanctity of her private bedroom. Her frenzied gaze darted from the perfectly made bed to the freshly polished furniture and perfectly fluffed, lint-free carpet. The only portion of her personal retreat that hadn't been cleaned within an inch of its life was the closet.

Twenty minutes later she sat amidst a dozen years of clutter. The floor was strewn with piles of garments she hadn't worn since Marti's birth, along with stacks of memorabilia that had been pushed onto a shelf and forgotten.

She found a water-stained shoe box that had been sealed with tape. Although Rae vaguely recalled seeing it before, she couldn't remember what was in it. As she searched for scissors to slice through the sealing tape, the parrot's plaintive song filtered from across the hall, a raspy, repetitive rhythm that set her teeth on edge.

"The millionaire and his wi-i-fe...for fast, fast, fast relief." *Squawk.* "Gimme beer, dear! Oughta be shot, oughta be shot."

"Don't tempt me," Rae muttered, grabbing a pair of cuticle scissors from the bathroom drawer.

"You'll wonder where the jock itch went." *Squawk.* "When you spray your shorts with fungi-ment, aww-wrk, roll me over in the clover, cheese puffs!"

She closed her bedroom door, which further muffled but didn't entirely eliminate the bird's irritating chatter, then settled down to inspect the contents of the mysterious shoe box, a small reservoir of family nostalgia. Among other things, it contained several of Rae's school pictures, a lopsided clay impression of her kindergarten-sized hand, and a tiny, heart-shaped box that contained a lock of her hair along with some of her baby teeth.

Rae's attention was also drawn to a tidy stack of greeting cards wrapped with a length of yarn tied into a neat bow. Closer scrutiny revealed that the cards, which covered every occasion from birthdays to Valentine's Day, were to her mother from her father. Each card had a personal inscription in Hobie's barely legible handwriting. Some of the postings were funny; some were poignant. All conveyed the profundity of his love.

And her mother had cherished each and every one of

them. Rae could still remember the woman's glowing eyes when she'd received them. Over the years Rae had forgotten those happy times. Or perhaps her anger hadn't allowed her to remember them.

As she contemplated that, she noticed a small wooden box that had been carefully tucked beneath the stack of greeting cards. She lifted the item, nesting it in her palm as she carefully lifted the small hinged lid to reveal a golf-ball-sized piece of gold-veined quartz tucked in a cloud of blue velvet.

She sucked in a sharp breath, her mind spinning back in time.

It had been her mother's birthday. Friends had thrown a surprise party at the diner, complete with balloons and a big flat cake with so many candles it looked like a prairie fire.

Although Rae hadn't thought about that night in decades, every detail was vividly etched in her mind.

Her mother had been laughing, telling jokes, having a wonderful time with her guests. But Rae, who'd been about Marti's age, hadn't been laughing. She'd been on the verge of tears because her father was supposed to be there and he hadn't come home.

Later, after everyone had gone and Mama had closed up the diner, Rae had blurted that she hated her father, and hoped he'd never come home again. Her mother had been saddened by the outburst, but hadn't seemed horrified by it. Instead, she'd taken Rae in her arms, explaining that Hobie had been delivering a load of cabbage to the Midwest when his truck had broken down. Mama had said that it wasn't Hobie's fault, but Rae hadn't believed that, because her mother always made excuses for him.

Three days later Hobie had finally showed up, exhausted and disheveled, with a special birthday gift—the exquisite, gold-veined quartz presented in a polished wooden box that he'd carved with his own hands.

Mama's eyes had been shining with love.

Now, as Rae looked back with adult objectivity, she remembered all the wonderful times her small family had shared. She'd loved her father with all her heart, and could still recall the terror of watching him drive away in that huge eighteen-wheeler or packing up for a prospecting venture, because she never knew when—or if— he'd ever return. And she remembered the anger of a child at having been abandoned.

After her mother suddenly died of pneumonia, that anger had turned to rage. Rae's mother had always been her rock, the one person in life that she could always count on. Her death was the most devastating abandonment of all. Rae had blamed Hobie, for no other reason than if she hadn't, she would have had to blame herself. And that, she couldn't have handled.

So she emotionally withdrew from her father by refusing to call him Daddy. From the day of her mother's funeral, she'd called him by his first name.

In retrospect, she realized how that must have hurt him, but he'd never said anything. A few months later he'd quit his trucking job so he could spend more time with her, but their relationship had already been inexorably strained.

But that couldn't erase the joy Hobie had brought to her early childhood, the same joy that Hank had brought to his own daughter. Rae realized that now, just as she realized that despite the hardship, the struggle, the constant concern about money, her mother had been truly happy. She'd loved her fanciful dreamer the same way that Rae loved Hank Flynn.

Only her mother hadn't sent the man she loved away, denied her child a father, or turned a crippling fear of abandonment into self-fulfilling prophecy. Rae had done that all by herself. She'd broken hearts. She'd ruined lives.

And there was nothing on earth she could do to change that.

Rae was up to her elbows in soapsuds when the doorbell rang. She called into the living room, where her father and daughter were watching television. "Will someone get that? It's probably Steve."

Cocking an ear, she heard a muttered reply, and went back to her chore, hoping that Steve hadn't arrived with yet another round of complicated grant forms to be interpreted and signed. The state bureaucracy made it so difficult to—

A shriek from the parlor shattered Rae's nerves. She spun around, knocking a dripping glass onto the floor. It, too, shattered. "Marti?" The squeals continued, along with another, more resonant sound that Rae couldn't discern over her daughter's high-pitched howls.

Grabbing a towel, Rae stepped over the glass shards and hurried across the room, drying her hands. She jerked to a stop at the doorway. The towel fluttered to the floor.

Marti, who was leaping like a frog on a griddle, spun around, beaming. "Mom, look! Hank's back! He's *back!*"

"Yes," Rae murmured. It was all she could say before her breath backed into her throat.

"I knew you'd come back," Marti squealed, throwing her arms around the rigid man. "I knew it, I knew it, I knew it."

Smiling, Hank stroked the girl's hair, then untangled her arms from his waist and angled a wary glance at Rae. "Maybe I should have waited until she was asleep."

Rae emptied her lungs all at once. She wanted desperately to run into his arms, covering his face with kisses and begging his forgiveness for having sent him away. But she dared not. There was a warning in his eyes, a warning that he'd come for a purpose. A purpose she might not like.

She forced a thin smile. "Marti would have been terribly upset if she'd missed your, ah, visit."

"Things go bad up north, did they?"

This was from Hobie, who'd finally hoisted himself out of his easy chair to eye the scene with undisguised curiosity and, Rae thought, disturbing smugness.

Hank pulled his gaze from Rae long enough to respond. "Let's just say that I decided the job wasn't a particularly good career move."

Hobie chortled. "Career, is it now? Well, sir, that's right inter'sting, ain't it, Rae?"

Perhaps it was interesting, but Rae's mind was spinning much too wildly to connect with her father's furtive meaning. Hank was watching her again, his eyes dark with a silent plea that she wanted to answer, but didn't fully understand.

Before he could speak again, Marti was yanking on his jacket sleeve. Her expression had gone from exuberant to slightly frantic. "You're going to stay here, aren't you? You're going to move back into your bungalow and never, ever go away again, right?"

Squatting down to the child's level, he spoke in a voice quivering with emotion. "I don't think I can do that, squirt." Pausing, he dabbed her cheek with his thumb. "But I'll never be more than a few minutes away. You'll always know where I am, and anytime you—" he slanted a glance at Rae "—or your mother ever need me, I'll be here before you can hang up the phone."

Her lip quivered. "Promise?"

"Cross my heart."

Marti wavered a moment, then flung her arms around his neck. "I love you, Hank. You're my very best friend in the whole entire world."

Hank hugged her fiercely, his eyes closed, his face

twisted with emotion. After a long moment he took a shuddering breath and held the child away. "I'm more than your friend," he told her quietly. "I'm—" The words stuck in his throat as he cast Rae another pleading glance.

This time she understood the question. Her eyes misted. She bit her trembling lip, and nodded her approval.

Returning his attention to the clearly bewildered child, Hank's lips tightened. He sat back on his heels, clasping her small shoulders. "Do you remember that when you found out I'd been in the army, you asked if I'd known your daddy?"

"Uh-huh."

"I did know him, Marti."

Her eyes popped open. "Really?"

Lowering his gaze, he spoke so softly that Rae could barely hear. "Some of what you were told about your father isn't quite true." His shoulders shook for a moment, then he raised his eyes and faced the child directly. "Actually, none of it is true. Your father wasn't killed, Marti, he was captured, and he spent a long, long time in prison. When he came out, he was very sad and confused. And he was different."

"How was he different?" Marti whispered, clearly frightened. "Like, was he hurt real bad or something?"

"Inside he was hurt. He wasn't the same anymore. He didn't know he had a beautiful daughter, and he didn't want to interfere in your mommy's life, so he let the army change his name and he became another person."

The child digested that for a moment. "You mean my daddy doesn't even know about me?"

"He knows now," Hank murmured. "And he loves you so much it hurts, but he also knows how proud you are of...of the man you thought him to be. He doesn't want you to be disappointed."

Marti's head snapped around as she looked to her mother for confirmation. Unable to speak, Rae managed a shaky nod.

Turning back to Hank, Marti wiped her face with the back of her hand. "Do you know where my daddy is?"

"Yes, I do." Hank swallowed hard. "He's right here, honey. I'm your daddy."

Rae held her breath, waiting for Marti's reaction. For several seconds there was none. The child simply stood there, immobile, as if she hadn't heard, or didn't understand the monumental impact of what she'd been told.

Without warning, she spun around and darted down the hall, leaving Hank looking stunned and shattered. He stood slowly, his eyes filled with incredible sadness. "I'm sorry," he told Rae. "I should have known—"

He never finished the sentence, because Marti skidded back into the living room clutching the familiar framed photograph of her father. She dashed over to Hank, squinting pointedly at his face, then down at the picture. After repeating that process twice more, she fixed him with a narrowed gaze. "Turn your head," she commanded.

Although visibly startled, Hank complied.

Marti studied his profile. "I can't see your ears."

Hank blinked. "My ears?"

"Uh-huh. Your hair is too long."

"Oh." He obligingly raked it back, and held it to one side. "Is that better?"

The child didn't reply right away. Instead, she stared at Hank's ear with unnerving acuity. "Your lobes tweak."

"They what?"

"They tweak, they're crooked." Marti pointed to the picture of the buzz-haired soldier. "His lobes tweak, too." She looked up then, her eyes bright with moisture. "So do mine."

Rae covered her mouth with her hands, silencing a sob. No one moved, not Hank, not Marti, and certainly not Rae, who was so overcome by emotion she could barely stand on her own.

It was Hobie who finally broke the strained silence by peering over his granddaughter's shoulder and emitting a low whistle. "Well, I'll be danged," he muttered, then squinted over at Hank. "Good thing you let that hair grow, son. Them ears is uglier than a hound dog's butt."

Marti laid the photograph on the coffee table, face-down, and wiped her cheek with the back of her hand. "I guess maybe you really are my daddy."

"Yes," Hank whispered. "Does that make you sad?"

She shrugged, then shook her head.

Hank angled a terrified glance at Rae, who could do nothing to help except offer an encouraging smile. Apparently it was enough, because he sucked in a determined breath and slipped an arm around the child's shoulder. "You must have a lot of questions."

She shrugged again, and this time she nodded.

"I'll do my best to answer them all."

Sniffing, Marti peeked up, her eyes clouded beneath a fringe of stubby lashes. "It might take a long time," she murmured. "Maybe even all night."

Hank smiled. "I've got all the time in the world."

A crescent moon had risen beyond the treetops when Rae and Hank wandered the path to their special carved tree. After nearly two hours of serious discussion, Marti had finally hugged her whole-again family good-night and tottered off to bed. Now it was time for the adults to make peace, and to plan for the future.

Rae had never been so scared in her life.

"Watch your step," Hank murmured, lifting a pine bough away from the path. He waited until she'd ducked beneath the obstacle, then followed her to the clearing.

Rae hung back from the tree. It was too dark to see the etched initials, but she nonetheless pictured them in her mind. Two crooked *M*s, a plus sign, then an *R* with a pointy loop and a perfectly formed *H*. From the corner of her eye she saw Hank tracing the letters with his fingertip.

She should say something. There were so many words crowding her heart, words to express her love, her pride in his courage at having faced his daughter with the truth, her regret at having sent him away, her thrill and relief that he'd returned. So many words. Each and every one of them rushed her throat together, rendering her mute.

Hank cleared his throat. "I, ah, have a job down in Rocklin. It's a pretty good job, too, with advancement opportunities, benefits, the whole nine yards." He slipped her a rueful smile. "You look surprised."

"Yes."

"I suppose I can't blame you. I'm a little surprised myself, but there I was up in Portland, earning minimum wage to rebuild a half-million dollars' worth of machinery, and I realized that I could do better. In fact, I had an obligation to do better, because I had a child to support." He glanced over his shoulder, as if expecting her to protest. When she didn't, he seemed relieved. "So I got to thinking. Martin Manning had a degree in mechanical engineering and, thanks to a faceless computer hacker in the Pentagon, so does Hank Flynn. Of course, it's from a university in Utah that I've never set foot in, but that's beside the point. It's an honest degree. I earned the credits. I can do the work." He pursed his lips. "Did I mention that this job has benefits?"

Rae nodded.

"Did I mention that you and Marti are my beneficiaries? Only on my life insurance. Marti's covered by my health plan, too, but they wouldn't let me include you because we aren't, well—'' He coughed into his hand and looked away.

Rae had to steady herself on a nearby tree trunk. All her life she'd felt forsaken by those she'd loved to the point that she'd actually tried to drive love away. In spite of that, Hank was here, and he was staying, not because he had to but because he wanted to. It was the most touching gift he could have given her.

If she could have moved, she would have hugged him tightly enough for their bodies to fuse. Instead, she simply stood there, clinging to a tree branch and fighting tears.

Apparently Hank took her silence as anger. Still studying the scarred tree trunk, he spoke in a voice heavy with disappointment. ''I probably shouldn't have shown up tonight without having called first. The truth is that I was afraid you wouldn't let me come. It's taken me weeks to screw up the courage to, well, you know.''

Rae managed a tight nod, and mouthed the word ''Yes.''

His shoulders rose and fell quickly, as if he'd taken a giant breath and exhaled all at once. ''I meant what I said in there. I'll never leave you and Marti. Never.'' Turning, he leaned back against the tree, bowing his head and tucking his thumbs in his jeans pockets. ''But that doesn't mean that I'm going to force myself into your life, Rae, or into Marti's. I just want you both to know that I'll be there when you need me.''

Rae was startled by the sound of her own voice. ''We need you now.''

Pushing away from the tree, Hank took a step forward, then hesitated. ''I'm right here. I always will be.''

''I know.'' She wiped the dampness from her eyes. ''That's what makes you so special.''

He wavered there, as if holding himself back. ''I love you, Rae.''

"I love you, too."

"I want you to be happy."

"I am happy, happier than I've ever been in my life."
She released the tree limb against which she'd been bracing herself, then took a shaky step toward him. "You promised to marry me once."

He sucked in a breath.

So did she. "What would you say if I held you to that promise?"

When he didn't immediately respond, Rae's knees buckled, and before she realized that he was on the move, he'd swept her into his arms, hugging her fiercely. "I'd say that I was the luckiest man on earth."

Rae clung to him, returning his fevered kisses between desperate breaths. They cried together, they laughed together, they exchanged whispered words of love, first with gentle reverence, then repeated with increased exhilaration and utter joy.

Much later, with the smiling moon lighting their way through the forest, they followed the path home.

Epilogue

Dear Diary,

Well, yesterday was my birthday and now I'm eleven years old. I had a real fun party at the diner last night, with lots of neat presents. Mom let me open hers after all the guests had left, and I was really glad because it was my very first bra! My boobs aren't very big yet, but Mom says they'll grow fast. I hope so. Coach really wants to win the championship.

Steve Ruskin came to my party, too. He lives in Sacramento now, but he comes back a lot to visit and stuff, because he says Mom and I will always be his very special friends. He brought a lady friend to my party. She's real nice. Mom liked her a lot. So did I, because it was on account of her that Steve finally gave me a really swell present. It was a fishing tackle box with all kinds of great lures inside.

Steve didn't look too happy about it, because he really wanted to get me a lacy bathrobe—barf!—but when his lady friend found out how much I like fishing, she talked him into the tackle box instead. Like I said, she's really nice!

But my daddy's present is the best of all. He's going to take me on a camping trip, just the two of us. I can hardly wait. We're going to go fishing and hiking and maybe even do some gold panning, only I'm not supposed to tell Gramps or else he'd want to go with us.

I don't know why, because Gramps spends most of his time at the visitor center showing tourists how to pan for gold. He says he does it because flatlanders don't know nothing about mining, but Mom says he just likes to show off. The tourists are always taking pictures of him, and he grins real big and snaps his suspenders. Daddy says that people like Gramps because he's a colorful old coot, and because they haven't heard all his stories a hundred times already. Besides, he wears folks out so much that they get hungry. Mom's diner is always busy now.

I guess it wasn't really too long ago that things were pretty bad around here, but I can hardly remember what it was like before Daddy came home. It seems like he's been here forever. Mom says that's because in one way or another, Daddy has always been with us. I guess she's right, too.

I still have the old picture of him, the one where his hair is all buzzed and he's wearing his uniform. It's right on my dresser, next to Mom and Dad's wedding picture. When I was little, I thought he was the handsomest daddy in the whole entire world, even if his ears were a little tweaked. I was so proud of him being a hero and all, but I'm even prouder of him now. He thinks about everybody else all the

time, and doesn't hardly even think about himself.
I love him so much that sometimes I could just cry
because I'm so happy.

Mom's happy, too, especially now that my little
brother is sleeping through the night. And he's only
three months old. Daddy says that baby Joshua is
going to grow up to be almost as smart as me. I
don't know about that. I'm pretty smart.

But I really love my baby brother. Mom lets me
feed him sometimes. That's lots of fun, except when
he makes gross noises and stuff. Sometimes he
doesn't smell too good, either, but he's got the cutest
little face, and all this fuzzy dark hair. He looks a
lot like Daddy, except Joshua's got real pretty ears.
Mom thinks he's going to grow up big and strong
and handsome, just like Dad.

When Joshua is old enough, I'm going to tell him
all about our wonderful daddy, how he was once a
really brave soldier and now he works real hard to
make a good life for us. Daddy says that's just what
being a dad is all about. He doesn't think he's special, but I do. He doesn't think he's a hero, either,
but he is. He's *my* hero. Someday, he'll be Joshua's
hero, too.

The way I see it, that's the most special thing of
all.

Uh-oh. Mom's calling me for dinner, so I have to
go. I'll write some more tomorrow, all about how
Louie got loose in the dining room and did a big
birdie no-no on Mom's hand-crocheted tablecloth.
Signing off for now...

Marti Hooper Flynn

*   *   *   *   *

Silhouette's newest series

YOURS TRULY

Love when you least expect it.

Where the written word plays a vital role in uniting couples—you're guaranteed a fun and exciting read every time!

Look for Marie Ferrarella's upcoming Yours Truly, *Traci on the Spot*, in March 1997.

Here's a special sneak preview....

1

Morgan Brigham slowly set down his coffee cup on the kitchen table and stared at the comic strip in the center of his paper. It was nestled in among approximately twenty others that were spread out across two pages. But this was the only one he made a point of reading faithfully each morning at breakfast.

This was the only one that mirrored *her* life.

He read each panel twice, as if he couldn't trust his own eyes. But he could. It was there, in black and white.

Morgan folded the paper slowly, thoughtfully, his mind not on his task. So Traci was getting engaged.

The realization gnawed at the lining of his stomach. He hadn't a clue as to why.

He had even less of a clue why he did what he did next.

Abandoning his coffee, now cool, and the newspaper, and ignoring the fact that this was going to make him late for the office, Morgan went to get a sheet of stationery from the den.

He didn't have much time.

Traci Richardson stared at the last frame she had just drawn. Debating, she glanced at the creature sprawled out on the kitchen floor.

"What do you think, Jeremiah? Too blunt?"

The dog, part bloodhound, part mutt, idly looked up from his rawhide bone at the sound of his name. Jeremiah gave her a look she felt free to interpret as ambivalent.

"Fine help you are. What if Daniel actually reads this and puts two and two together?"

Not that there was all that much chance that the man who had proposed to her, the very prosperous and busy Dr. Daniel Thane, would actually see the comic strip she drew for a living. Not unless the strip was taped to a bicuspid he was examining. Lately Daniel had gotten so busy he'd stopped reading anything but the morning headlines of the *Times*.

Still, you never knew. "I don't want to hurt his feelings," Traci continued, using Jeremiah as a sounding board. "It's just that Traci is overwhelmed by Donald's proposal and, see, she thinks the ring is going to swallow her up." To prove her point, Traci held up the drawing for the dog to view.

This time, he didn't even bother to lift his head.

Traci stared moodily at the small velvet box on the kitchen counter. It had sat there since Daniel had asked her to marry him last Sunday. Even if Daniel never read her comic strip, he was going to suspect something eventually. The very fact that she hadn't grabbed the ring from his hand and slid it onto her finger should have told him that she had doubts about their union.

Traci sighed. Daniel was a catch by any definition. So what was her problem? She kept waiting to be struck by that sunny ray of happiness. Daniel said he wanted to take care of her, to fulfill her every wish. And he was even willing to let her think about it before she gave him her answer.

Guilt nibbled at her. She should be dancing up and down, not wavering like a weather vane in a gale.

Pronouncing the strip completed, she scribbled her signature in the corner of the last frame and then sighed. Another week's work put to bed. She glanced at the pile of mail on the counter. She'd been bringing it in steadily from the mailbox since Monday, but the stack had gotten no farther than her kitchen. Sorting letters seemed the least heinous of all the annoying chores that faced her.

Traci paused as she noted a long envelope. Morgan Brigham. Why would Morgan be writing to her?

Curious, she tore open the envelope and quickly scanned the short note inside.

Dear Traci,

I'm putting the summerhouse up for sale. Thought you might want to come up and see it one more time before it goes up on the block. Or make a bid for it yourself. If memory serves, you once said you wanted to buy it. Either way, let me know. My number's on the card.

Take care,
Morgan

P.S. Got a kick out of *Traci on the Spot* this week.

Traci folded the letter. He read her strip. She hadn't known that. A feeling of pride silently coaxed a smile to her lips. After a beat, though, the rest of his note seeped into her consciousness. He was selling the house.

The summerhouse. A faded white building with brick trim. Suddenly, memories flooded her mind. Long, lazy afternoons that felt as if they would never end.

Morgan.

She looked at the far wall in the family room. There was a large framed photograph of her and Morgan standing before the summerhouse. Traci and Morgan. Morgan and Traci. Back then, it seemed their lives had been permanently intertwined. A bittersweet feeling of loss passed over her.

Traci quickly pulled the telephone over to her on the counter and tapped out the number on the keypad.

* * * * *

Look for TRACI ON THE SPOT
by Marie Ferrarella, coming to
Silhouette YOURS TRULY
in March 1997.

By the bestselling author of *FORBIDDEN FRUIT*

FORTUNE
ERICA SPINDLER

Be careful what you wish for...

Skye Dearborn knew exactly what to wish for. To
unlock the secrets of her past. To be reunited with her
mother. To force the man who betrayed her to pay.
To be loved.

One man could make it all happen. But will Skye's
new life prove to be all that she dreamed of...or a
nightmare she can't escape?

Be careful what you wish for...it may just come true.

Available in March 1997 at your favorite retail outlet.

This summer, the legend
continues in Jacobsville

Diana Palmer

A LONG, TALL
TEXAN SUMMER

Three **BRAND-NEW** short stories

This summer, Silhouette brings readers a special
collection for Diana Palmer's LONG, TALL TEXANS
fans. Diana has rounded up three **BRAND-NEW**
stories of love Texas-style, all set in Jacobsville,
Texas. Featuring the men you've grown to love from
this wonderful town, this collection is a must-have
for all fans!

*They grow 'em tall in the saddle in Texas—and
they've got love and marriage on their minds!*

Don't miss this collection of original Long, Tall Texans
stories...available in June at your favorite retail outlet.

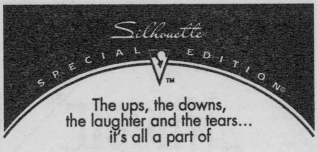

Silhouette SPECIAL EDITION

The Buchanans are back!
Don't miss
BUCHANAN'S RETURN

by Pamela Toth (Special Edition #1096, April 1997)

When she agreed to come to the Rocking Rose ranch,
Kirby Wilson was hoping only to learn a bit more about—
the Buchanan's—her "new" family. But from the moment
she laid eyes on their horse trainer, J. D. Reese, she knew
her life would never be the same....

BUCKLES & BRONCOS

The Buchanans have always ridden alone—
but love's about to change all that!

In April 1997
Bestselling Author

DALLAS SCHULZE

takes her Family Circle series to new heights with

TESSA'S CHILD

In April 1997 Dallas Schulze brings readers a
brand-new, longer, out-of-series title featuring the
characters from her popular Family Circle miniseries.

When rancher Keefe Walker found Tessa Wyndham he
knew that she needed a man's protection—she was
pregnant, alone and on the run from a heartless past.
Keefe was also hiding from a dark past...but in one
overwhelming moment he and Tessa forged a family
bond that could never be broken.

Available in April wherever books are sold.

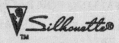

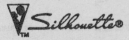